"A dysfunctional family moves into a dystopian f[...]ed by a so-called Great Leader who keeps postponing [...] It's a nightmare, but why am I laughing so hard? Rich[...]er's *It Happened Here* is the witty, resonant story we need right now."

—BETSY WEST
Codirector of *RBG* and Fred W. Friendly
Professor Emerita at Columbia Journalism School

"Oh God. It rings true."

—ROY BLOUNT JR.
Author of Twenty-Four books, Including *Save Room for Pie*,
Alphabet Juice, and *About Three Bricks Shy of a Load*

"This book is as astonishing as it is extraordinary. Richard Dresser has stared into the wounded chasm that is our political division and in it seen the intersection where reality meets fiction. He has found the heartbeat of our nightmare in the American family. With a cold eye and deep compassion, he has crafted a tale in which deep sadness gives hope and in which deep darkness brings laughter. Truly a worthy read."

—LEWIS BLACK
Actor, Comedian, Playwright, Longest-Running
Cast Member of *The Daily Show*, and *New York Times*
Best-Selling Author of *Nothing's Sacred* and *Me of Little Faith*

"Richard Dresser's *It Happened Here* is a witheringly funny, presciently wise, and deeply alarming account of a nation's corruption and a family's redemption. If you still believe a single leader can't poison a nation's soul, if you imagine the worst won't come to pass, if you presume the current assault on our

Constitution will fail, then for your own good and the good of our country, wake up and read his powerful, important novel. Dresser's fiction pulsates with truth. Don't say you weren't warned."

—**PETER QUINN**
Award-Winning Author of *Hour of the Cat, The Man Who Never Returned, Looking for Jimmy,* and *The Banished Children of Eve*

"Listen up . . . you are out of your mind if you don't read *It Happened Here* as soon as possible. It's more than a prescient prediction of our dystopian political future, more than a helter-skelter tumble down the rabbit hole of life . . . it's a heartbreaking, hilarious tale of a dysfunctional American family just as screwed up as yours. I don't know who this Richard Dresser guy is, but I'd like to shake hands with him."

—**JAY TARSES**
Writer, *The Days and Nights of Molly Dodd* and *The Slap Maxwell Story*, and Producer, *The Carol Burnett Show* and *The Bob Newhart Show*

"*It Happened Here*, as its title would suggest, is equal parts thriller, jeremiad, and comic demolition of who we are no matter where we're headed, as it tracks an extended family's disintegration that's simultaneous with its country's. It's affecting in its assertion that taking care of a community begins with taking care of one another, and it's harrowing and funny and persuasive in its claim that as a nation—and a species—we probably should have sought professional help somewhere along the way."

—**JIM SHEPARD**
Award-Winning Novelist and Author of *The World to Come* and *The Book of Aron*

it happened here

it happened here

Richard Dresser

BROWN BOOKS
PUBLISHING GROUP

It Happened Here

Brown Books Publishing Group
Dallas, TX/New York, NY
www.BrownBooks.com
(972) 381-0009

A New Era in Publishing®

Publisher's Cataloging-In-Publication Data

Names: Dresser, Richard, author.
Title: It happened here / Richard Dresser.
Description: Dallas, TX ; New York, NY : Brown Books Publishing Group, [2020]
Identifiers: ISBN 9781612544649
Subjects: LCSH: Presidents–United States–21st century–Fiction. | United States–Politics and government–21st century–Fiction. | Dictators–United States–21st century–Fiction. | Families–21st century–Fiction. | LCGFT: Political fiction.
Classification: LCC PS3554.R425 I84 2020 | DDC 813/.54–dc23

ISBN 978-1-61254-464-9
LCCN 2020907784

Printed in United States
10 9 8 7 6 5 4 3 2 1

For more information or to contact the author, please go to www.RichardDresser.com.

For Rebecca.

introduction

I was born in a midwestern college town where my family lived for five generations. Two branches of the family—those of my grandfather and his brother—would get together every Sunday at my great-grandfather's house. He was called the General, and he ruled the family. Being the youngest has its advantages. They'd forget I was there, and I'd be under the table hearing some pretty twisted tales. I'd try to figure out what they were talking about, but they interrupted each other all the time and disagreed about everything, so I got more and more confused. Plus, I knew they weren't telling the whole story. They all had secrets.

The family started falling apart in 2019 around the same time when the country was cracking up. I thought there must be some kind of connection, a mystery at the center of it, and if I could solve it, then I'd know who my relatives were and why they did what they did. It would be nice if there was a single answer to the mystery but, spoiler alert, there isn't. I discovered a whole lot, but I'm not sure I actually solved anything.

What I did find out is that there is a killer in my family. That's what changed everything and made people take sides and basically tore the family apart. It wasn't exactly a secret, since the whole country found out about it, but it sure was news to me. And I dug up a whole lot more than what ended up in the newspaper and on TV. It turns out people will tell you just about anything if you take the time to listen. Who knew?

Since my family would argue about even the basic facts of family history, like when I was born, I thought the best way to get to the truth would be to talk to each one of them alone. It wasn't easy. They'd want to know what others had said so they could disagree. That's how they were, looking for an argument even when the other person wasn't there. But, overall, I think they tried to be honest even when it didn't make them look good, which it usually didn't.

I assembled everything in chronological order, which is harder than it seems because they had completely different memories of when things happened. Sometimes they'd disagree by years. I had to use my best judgment, which meant deciding when things *probably* happened, who was telling the truth, and then tossing out the stuff that was too boring, dumb, self-serving, or mean even for them, which would be enough for a really long and unnecessary sequel.

If any of them has a problem with what I've done, I'd like to quote my grandpa: "Fuck 'em."

HLW

the families

The General and his wife (deceased) had two sons,
Paul and Garret.

Paul's family

Ruth (his wife)

Mickey (their eldest son)

Kate (their daughter)

David (their younger son)

Garret's family

Hadley (his wife)

Terence (their eldest son)

Isaac (their younger son)

Ella (their daughter)

part one

LOUISE
(age fourteen in 2035)

I decided to start with my great-uncle Paul. He was always the easi-
est one to talk to, mainly because he always did all the talking. My
earliest memories are of Paul telling me stories. Starting when I
was about two years old, he'd talk to me as if I was a well-educated
adult who'd lived all over the world and understood references to
things like Sacco and Vanzetti and the infield-fly rule. Plus, he's
the only one in the whole family who didn't look nervous when
I announced I would interview each one of them, and that they
had to tell me the truth because I'd find it out one way or another.

1. fall 2019

PAUL
(Ruth's husband, age fifty in 2019)

Can I say something before I talk? I admire what you're doing, Louise. But a word of caution: there are people in the family who will not make it easy. For starters, my brother, Garret, won't talk to you. For legal reasons, due to certain violent actions, he probably can't; also, the English language has never served him well. He knows plenty of words but never seems to find the right ones. He'll come over for dinner and say three words: one of them is "hello," another is "goodbye," and the middle one is "yes" to a beer. I love him, but he's always controlled his entire family, so I can't imagine you'll get much from his kids. They'll do whatever he wants. He was unbelievably strict—which is a nice word for borderline abusive—when they were little and, well, you've seen the results. Ruth and I never believed in spanking or threats or time-outs, we wanted our kids to discover who they were, which wasn't always who we wanted them to be, but that's what makes life infuriating. Or interesting, depending on how you look at it. I know Garret was horrified—behind our backs, of course—at our child rearing, which he'd say was typical liberal coddling that destroyed the nation. He's dead wrong about this and just about everything else, but I do love him, as I believe I mentioned.

My side of the family presents a different problem. They— we—don't shut up. Ever. So, you're going to have a major editing job picking your way through the gems to find which ones gleam the brightest. You can always come to me when you know some-one's lying, or, as in Garret's case, not saying a damn thing.

I'm impressed that you want to find out what our family is all about, but that's a tall order, and life is all about low expectations. What I'm telling you is what I used to tell David's Little League team when they needed an assistant coach and Ruth volunteered my services. I'd yell from the bench, "Aim high but prepare for disappointment!" I think it really landed with most of the players, especially in the late innings.

I don't know where you want to start this thing. Everything changed, of course, on November 9, 2016, when we woke up from our nightmares to find out they were real, but the country didn't truly unravel until 2019. I was teaching at the university, the most popular professor in the history department, according to RateMyProfessor.com. I hate all that competitive "who's the best" crap that pits professor against professor and frankly means nothing. It's one more distortion to an honorable profession, so I steer clear of it. But the facts are that I was number one, year after year, in a very large prestigious department, and the student eval-uations were off the charts. I can show them to you sometime if you're interested. Maybe you'd like to include them in your book.

DAVID
(Paul and Ruth's younger son, age fourteen in 2019)

You want me to pretend you're not there, Louise? I've been doing that for years. No, seriously . . . 2019? Wow. Okay. Great. Let's start out when I was in my awkward stage. Which went on a really, really long time. Some people think it never ended. Here we go.

Freshman year of high school, a bunch of us would eat lunch together and hang out at someone's house after school. We were so deeply uncool we didn't fully understand how uncool we were. But we had our little group, and that's all we needed. That fall there'd been some bullying, nothing too awful unless you're the one getting bullied, but it became an issue when the Parents Association got involved. Parents have a kind of genius for making things worse, especially when they get together as a group. They had emergency meetings that led to the Stop Bullying Now (SBN) club. One day, it was just *there* as if it always had been. They'd stop you in the hall and make sure you weren't getting bullied, which always felt vaguely threatening.

My older cousin, Terence, a junior, joined and then one by one my friends signed up, which meant they'd all eat lunch together and have goon training after school, so our group shrunk down to me and Jeremy. I wanted to join SBN, but my parents wouldn't let me. I told them Terence was a member and they said, "Terence's parents have different ideas about these things." Which sounded weirdly formal, since they were talking about my aunt Hadley and uncle Garret.

RUTH
(David's mother, age forty-eight in 2019)

Listen, Louise, I don't know about the others, but if I'm going to take the time to do this, I'm going to tell the truth. Which means talking about, well, adult things I've never talked about with you. I know you want me to pretend you aren't here, but you are here, and if it's too uncomfortable for you I'll stop. Okay, I had to say that. 2019, huh? Lots of memories, not many of them good . . .

What pissed me off back then was people saying, "What can we do?" It was so plaintive, the language of defeat. That's what I'd hear at my book club from these earnest, well-meaning women in designer jeans and two-hundred-dollar blouses. "Well, ladies, we could start by discussing the book." I'd chosen *It Can't Happen Here* by Sinclair Lewis, about a fascist takeover of the USA, but half of them hadn't finished it because they were so paralyzed with worry that it was happening here. The one thing we agreed on was a serious assault on one bottle of wine after another, which meant the meetings got louder and wilder with confessions of infidelity and marital problems and financial terror and children cutting themselves and stealing mommy's meds and getting bullied or bullying others and cheating on tests and we knew this privileged life we had was hurtling to an end. We were scared to death.

DAVID

One Monday morning, my last friend, Jeremy, told me he couldn't eat lunch with me anymore because he'd joined SBN. His parents thought he needed at least one extracurricular activity, so he could get into a college they could mention to friends without fear of humiliation. So, our group was down to just me, which cut down on the conversation at lunch but not by much. The worst of it was I had no one to hang with after school.

RUTH

The election was only a year away, and of all the most important elections ever, it was the most important election ever. If it went the wrong way—well, we couldn't allow ourselves to even think that, which is why it was all we thought about. I considered those book club women lifelong friends but, as it turned out, the only one I ever saw after that night was Pam Rayner.

On the night we weren't discussing *It Can't Happen Here*, I got so frustrated with the helplessness and despair I slipped out the back to my Subaru and drove away forever. But I'm grateful to my book club because it stopped me from pretending our lives were even a little bit normal anymore. On the way home, I decided to do something that mattered, to show the frightened, medicated ladies that it was possible. I knew it would be tough convincing Paul because he talks a big game but is naturally cautious. I could have said fearful, but that's not fair. But kind of true. But I didn't say it.

When I got home, David had gone to bed. I poured one more glass of chardonnay because it was Tuesday and told Paul we were going to be a stop on the Underground Railroad and take in refugees. He just smiled and said, "Honey, that's never going to happen."

PAUL

Ruth was totally receptive when I pitched the idea of taking in refugees. That's when things were heating up at the border, people ripping babies from mothers and putting them in cages and sending families back home to be killed in whatever circle of hell they were trying to escape. Red Hats were on the loose performing their civic duty terrorizing brown-skinned people. Being a stop on the Underground Railroad felt like the least we could do.

DAVID

My parents were all about being open and honest unless it was something that mattered. Then they'd whisper in the other room, so I knew something was happening. My older brother, Mickey, was a freshman at the university, and he'd come for Sunday dinner, and my sister Kate was a senior in high school, but she'd worked out some independent study scam so she was never around, plus she had a boyfriend at the U. But, for Sunday dinner, we were all there and my dad said, "We're going to have someone living with us for a while," and my mom explained about taking in a refugee and how we can't tell anyone. She asked if I was okay with that and before I could say anything, Kate said, "What if he's not? Would that make any fucking difference?" And then they were off, everyone talking at once, forgetting about me.

MICKEY
(David's older brother, age nineteen in 2019)

Just to be clear right up front, there's something I can't talk about. And you won't get it from anyone else because I'm the only one who knows the truth about what went down. Actually, there's one other person who knows. But that person is sworn to secrecy and would face dire consequences if it ever came out. So, there you have it. I swear I'll be dead honest about everything else. If that's cool, then I'm good to go. 2019? Seriously? You had to start there?

What I always loved about football is that my parents hated it. The brutality, the concussions, the militaristic conformity, it challenged all their beliefs. They would have liked to prevent me from playing, but as good liberals, they wanted me to make my own choices, even if it killed them. And it nearly did. But they never missed my games. I didn't appreciate until much later how hard it must have been for them to sit in the stands with that drunken bloodthirsty mob, praying I didn't get hurt. The other reason I played football is—and it's better if someone else says this—I was really fucking good. I was a wide receiver, fast with soft hands, and I loved the mass psychosis in the stadium when I scored. So, when the whole Underground Railroad thing was happening at home, my head was someplace else. David was the one who had to deal with it.

DAVID

When my dad asked me to help him get the room in the basement ready for our refugee, I was all over it. He even let me use power tools. As a shy, recently friendless, uncoordinated fourteen-year-old, I was just glad to have something to do.

KATE
(David's sister, age seventeen in 2019)

Louise, I think you probably know some of what happened to me—sorry, "happened to me" sounds as if I had nothing to do with it, and frankly, I have no one to blame but myself. Which I hate because blaming others has always been so satisfying. I can spend entire afternoons gathering airtight evidence in my head against loved ones for letting me down. But I try to be better than that now, and sometimes I am. So . . . 2019? Lifetimes ago. But sometimes it feels like last week.

One of my missions back then, when I wasn't saving the world, was saving David. It couldn't be good for him to be spending so much time with our parents, and he didn't seem to have any friends. What kind of a childhood is that?

DAVID

I always thought I had a happy childhood. But it's not as if I had another childhood to compare it to.

RUTH

All three of my children—*our* children, sorry—are smart. But David might be the smartest, even though you wouldn't know it by the way he talks.

DAVID

Freshman year I took a hard look at what I'd have to do to get out of high school early. That's why I studied all the time.

KATE

I was still in high school but I had a pretty loose schedule thanks to my guidance counselor, Mr. Groom. He was a churchgoing family man with solid midwestern values who prided himself on how he connected to the kids. He had a big framed photo of his family of five, all of them smiling wildly in their disturbing holiday sweaters. I proposed making a documentary about the evolution of bullying at our school from the innocent days of throwing some dork's briefcase out the classroom window all the way to the vicious, online, suicide-inducing bullying of today. My pitch was pretty emotional, and Mr. Groom signed off on my very independent project (the film, sadly, remains in preproduction).

It meant I could spend lots of time at the university with Glenn, this awesome senior I was dating. We'd take David to concerts and movies and rallies, and the air was crackling with drugs and sex and revolution. It was like David suddenly had a couple of bad parents to offset his good parents.

DAVID

After school one day, my mom took me down to the basement and introduced me to Dr. Morales, our refugee. He got out this tiny chess set. Once I got the hang of it, we'd play every day.

KATE

My boyfriend, Glenn, was a revolutionary right up until he got the call from his dad to go back to Cleveland to run the family's discount furniture store, Bedding'N'More. He went from organizing demonstrations and turning over police cars to developing new price points for living room sets, which was an eye-opener for me in terms of commitment to a cause. It wasn't until much later I found out what had happened to Glenn. But he taught me about radical politics and uncivil disobedience, and when he left, I was determined to prove I didn't need a guy to make shit happen.

DAVID

My parents got me a classic wooden chess set, which we set up on a table in Dr. Morales's room. I read chess books and practiced online and got pretty good, but I never could beat him. There are adults who'd let a kid win once in a while, but Dr. Morales wasn't one of them. After one game when I was sure I had him but didn't, I saw his smug little smile, like beating a kid eighty-nine times in a row was something to be proud of. He said, "David, when you beat me, you will know you earned it." I went upstairs and told my mom I wasn't going to play anymore.

The next day after school, I hung out in my room studying so I could get out of high school early. That went on for three boring days. Mom finally said, "You could at least say hello to him. Dr. Morales spends so much time alone." So, I went downstairs and the chess board was all set up as if he knew I was coming. It was the best game I'd ever played, and I thought I'd win because even if I screwed up at the end, he'd give it to me to make things right. But he beat me and smiled that smug little smile. I didn't cry. Beating him became my life's mission.

Later that night, I woke up when I heard a whirring sound coming closer and closer. I looked out my window, and there were these two helicopters with search lights. Our town was starting to feel like a place I'd never been before.

PAUL

It must have been Sunday dinner with Mickey and Kate when David asked why the helicopters were there. I said, "To keep us safe." David was a worrier, and I didn't want him to worry.

KATE

Suddenly, this Guatamalan doctor is living in our basement and helicopters are sweeping the town to roust out refugees, and they tell David the helicopters are keeping us safe? So, I told David that Dr. Morales is considered a criminal because of the racism of our government, and no one can know that he's living in our basement or we'll go to jail. Which freaked David out because my parents had spun it like they'd brought home a rescue puppy.

RUTH

I told David that Dr. Morales would be staying with us until his wife got here. Then they'd go to the next safe house, and the next, and when they made it to Canada, they'd be okay. We were no longer living in a country that welcomed anyone from anywhere. He asked if we were going to jail for taking him in and I said, "No, but it's very important that you don't tell anyone he's here."

PAUL

Kate and I had some knockdown arguments about David. I'd ask her how she knew so much about raising children—did she have some she forgot to tell us about? Then she was out the door, slamming it so hard the windows shook. I'd be relieved she was gone and then couldn't sleep until I heard the door opening at 5 a.m., praying it was my daughter and not the police telling me what happened to her.

RUTH

Being an optimist, Paul thought things would get better when Kate got older. But she was always a mystery to him.

KATE

When I had a problem, I'd never tell my dad. I'd never tell my mom, either, but that's normal.

RUTH

Back when Kate turned fourteen, we had no idea what to get her for her birthday. Paul pointed out how obsessively she listened to music—especially his massive vinyl collection—and suggested a guitar. I had my doubts since back then she'd bounce from one grand passion to another, but when she ripped the wrapping off a very economical Yamaha guitar, she was, for the first time in her life, speechless.

I still treasure those few moments of silence.

DAVID

There was a lot of tension at school because the Stop Bullying Now club was stopping people in the halls and giving them a hard time. I think they saw themselves as border patrol agents in training and it was pretty clear the nonwhite students got stopped more than anyone else. There used to be a lot of laughing between classes, but now we just kept our heads down and hoped we didn't get stopped. My cousin Terence, who was kind of my hero, was an officer in SBN. He used to tease me at school, but now I didn't even exist.

So, it was weird when he dropped by the house after school one day with a football. We went out back, and he told me he really wanted to beat the adults this year and that I could be the hero. I used to dread going to the General's house on Thanksgiving because of the football game. It was kids against adults, and the adults always won, and I was the worst kid except for my cousin Isaac who wouldn't play anymore, which made me the worst. But Terence had this secret play we practiced over and over, and every time it worked, he'd be high-fiving and telling me I was the man. The next day at school I said, "Hey, Terence," when I saw him in the hall, and it was like he didn't recognize me.

PAUL

My brother Garret's family took the football game way too seriously, maybe because they were all pretty good players and, except for my son Mickey, we were hopeless.

DAVID

That morning, I was down in the basement playing chess with Dr. Morales, and we both knew this was the day I'd finally win, but he was dragging it out as long as he could. Most adults would have conceded and let me finally win one but not him. My mom called that it was time to go, so we stood up and looked at the board, and I asked if he thought I was going to win. He said, "We'll pick this up later, David." The guy never gave me a break.

We got to the General's house, and the adults were boasting how they're going to kick our butts. Terence wouldn't even look at me because he didn't want to give a hint about our secret play.

TERENCE
(David's cousin; Garret and Hadley's eldest son,
age eighteen in 2019)

Louise, I don't know if my dad will even talk to you, so I better step up for my side of the family, right? Anything you want to tell me?

LOUISE

No.

TERENCE

Got it. So, ever since Afghanistan, my life is a jigsaw puzzle some asshole dumped on the floor, and I'm crawling around trying to fit a few pieces together. People tell me stuff I did, and I say, "No shit? Are you sure that was me?" Years later, David and I talked about that day, so I don't know what I'm remembering and what he told me. I just know it was a close game and the General's up on the deck in his Adirondack chair and he yells, "Next touchdown wins!" Which pissed everyone off, cause both teams knew they were winning by a lot.

DAVID

We're in the huddle and Terence says, "Me and Dave got this one." If I used grammar like that, my dad would have spanked me (metaphorically, which still hurts). I knew if I messed up, it would follow me forever. What I had going for me was low expectations from everyone, so I'd been preparing for this moment my whole life. The snap goes to me, and I make this huge fake pretending to throw to Mickey, and Terence comes back and I lateral the ball to him. Mickey's in the clear screaming for the ball, and Terence fakes the pass to him, and I'm all alone on the other side of the field in my comfort zone: forgotten and ignored. Terence fires the ball, and it bounces off my hands and floats in the air in front of me. I can still see it. The rest of my life is up for grabs, so I throw myself forward, and it lands in my hands just before it hits the ground, inches over the goal line.

Everyone goes nuts. My dad hugs me and then Mickey and Kate and my mom and even Uncle Garret. Terence grabs the ball and slams it in my gut and says, "The ball is yours, Davey, you're the man." I've still got that ball. It's a pretty great sports memory for someone who doesn't give a damn about sports. I retired after that game. You probably read about it in the papers.

RUTH

Years later, I came across a video that Isaac had made of that game from the deck standing next to the General. I asked David if he wanted to watch it and he said, "No, it'll never be as amazing as I remember it." But it was. I watched it by myself and cried. The whole family was together then.

KATE

David was the kid you forgot about because he did everything right and never got in trouble. But getting all that attention that day, you could see how much he needed it. He couldn't stop smiling. The General always made a toast before dinner, and it was usually about the military and the country and family and faith, but this time he ended with something like, "And thank you, God, for David's catch, a moment we will all remember." Everyone yelled, "Amen!" and started cheering.

DAVID

People would joke about how quiet I was, but in my family if you put yourself out there even a little, someone was always waiting to knock you down. I wasn't used to being the center of attention, which is maybe the reason I screwed up.

MICKEY

We're leaving, and my aunt Hadley is trying to get people to take pie, and my mom is saying, "No, we'll just eat it and hate ourselves," and it's all that end-of-the-party banter.

KATE

Uncle Garret was making one of his borderline-offensive jokes about women to provoke me when I heard David say, "Can we bring pie home for Dr. Morales?" Uncle Garret's face tightened. And then the conversation picked up as if nothing had happened, but of course everything had happened. David didn't seem to know what he'd said. He just wanted to do right by his friend Dr. Morales.

DAVID

We pull into our driveway, and I suddenly remember I'm about two moves away from checkmating Dr. Morales. I didn't know how much fun winning was because it had never happened before, and now twice in one day! I go running into the house, then down to the basement, and the door to Dr. Morales's room is open and it's dark, so I turn on the light, and the bed is turned over and the table is on its side and the chess pieces are all over the floor and there's no Dr. Morales. All I could think was, now I'll never beat him.

I went upstairs and my parents weren't there, and I kind of panicked and ran around the house calling to them and then I saw them in the backyard holding hands and looking up at the night sky. I went outside and said, "What are you looking at?" They held me so hard it hurt. We could hear the helicopters coming closer and closer with their searchlights probing the town. That's the first time I remember seeing my parents scared.

KATE

My cousin Isaac was allergic to everything, missed tons of school, stuttered, plus he had some kind of learning disability. He was a year behind his brother, Terence, but he might as well have been at a different school. Terence was a tough guy. High school kids were scared not to be his friend. I'm not sure if he had any real friends. Isaac was lucky to have a mom, my aunt Hadley, who understood him and protected him from the violence in that family. But no one protected him from the violence at school.

My brother, David, told me how Isaac got up on stage at a talent show in the high school auditorium, and students were screaming and throwing stuff at him, and he stood there all alone with his guitar and sang "Blackbird" from the White Album. David said it was awesome. As soon as he finished singing, the bullies from SBN started clapping and cheering. No one could believe it.

DAVID

I didn't tell Kate what happened after Isaac sang. You'd think he'd love being popular for one minute of high school, but he held up his hand and everyone went quiet. He had a bad stutter, except when he sang. That's why he started singing so young, to try to beat the stutter, which he never did. So, when he starts to talk, he's stuttering and he goes, "We all have to decide if we're going to be *in* the mob or *stand up* to the mob. I say fuck the Stop Bullying Now club."

He walks off the stage totally calm while kids are screaming at him. I was scrunched down in my seat, knowing in my heart I could never be as brave as my cousin Isaac.

ELLA
(David's cousin; Garret and Hadley's daughter,
age fourteen in 2019)

Louise, the only way I can tell my story is if I close my eyes so I can't see you. Don't take it—I was going to say "don't take it personally," but how else could you take it? You're my daughter. Anyway, I'm proud you're doing this, and I really wish you weren't. High school, huh? That's a fun, easy time for everyone, isn't it?

LOUISE

It would be great if you just talked about what was happening to you back then. Thanks!

ELLA

Sorry. When I was fourteen all I cared about was fitting in. Watching Isaac scared me because, selfishly—which is all anyone ever is in high school—having a brother do something like that was going to land on me. My friends were all looking at me like, "This sucks for you, Ella." But I was proud of him because we were all terrified of the Stop Bullying Now club and no one was standing up to them.

DAVID

SBN understood better than anyone how things worked at that time: *Rules are for losers. Never apologize. The truth is whatever you say it is.* They knew just how far they could go before the school administration would bring the hammer down. The way they terrorized Isaac after that assembly—pushing him into lockers, stealing his backpack, ripping up his homework, you know, clever high school antics—it was a shock, but after a few days it felt like that's how it had always been.

For a bunch of C students they were pretty sophisticated about using fear to control everyone.

ELLA

It was totally uncomfortable at our house in the morning before school. Terence would be strutting around in his SBN T-shirt, and Isaac would be quietly getting ready for another day of abuse, and I was mainly concerned with how I looked, what boys I liked, and if my friends really liked me. I once overheard my mom telling a friend that I should have been born in the 1950s, I'd fit right in. I don't think it was a compliment.

KATE

When David told me about our cousin Isaac singing "Blackbird" at school, I had this idea that he and I should sing at a family party. The two of us were always friendly enough when the families got together, but we'd never spent any time one on one. And I'm two years older, which is huge in high school, so he was a little freaked when I asked him to come over, but he showed up with his guitar, and I told him we'd rehearse a few songs to play at his dad's birthday. We noodled around until we found ourselves in this groove, and he started singing "One Hundred Years from Now" from *Sweetheart of the Rodeo.* I joined in, and we barely made it to the end of the song before I started laughing. He said, "What did I do wrong?" and I said, "Isaac, you are so fucking good, how did you get so good?"

He was breathtaking, actually, and the look on his face, it still chokes me up to think about it. I hadn't seen that look since he was a little kid, before the world worked its magic on him. That was one of the best times of my life, playing with Isaac and seeing him come to life. I was Emmylou Harris and he was Gram Parsons, and after "Dark End of the Street" we both were laughing because it was totally outrageous how our voices fit together.

RUTH

After Dr. Morales got taken, I wanted to sit down with Garret and Hadley and find out what had happened. I assumed that Garret had called in ICE after David blurted out that Dr. Morales was living at our house, but Paul said those helicopters were out every night, and it could just as easily have been one of our neighbors who ratted him out. You couldn't trust anyone back then, family included. The worst of it was how David took it to heart. We were finally able to convince him that what happened to Dr. Morales wasn't his fault.

DAVID

My parents worked so hard to convince me I wasn't responsible for Dr. Morales getting taken that I knew it was my fault. I carried that around for a long, long time.

PAUL

Ruth was dead set against going to Garret's birthday party. There was hardly anything you could bring up that didn't take a hard turn into politics, and Garret's family lined up on the wrong side. I talked about trying to understand them, and Ruth said she understood them perfectly, which is why she didn't want to see them. I had an unlikely ally in Kate, who said we had to go.

RUTH

We went to Garret's party, and it was making me crazy. I knew we were one drink away from everything blowing up when Kate and Isaac stood up and Kate said, "Uncle Garret, this is our birthday present." The two of them started singing and it was just so . . . unexpected . . .

TERENCE

My dad was always about old-school country so when Isaac started singing Johnny Cash, he was a goner. He just stared at the two of them, but I could tell he was feeling it. I knew I'd never get that from him.

KATE

When I saw Uncle Garret blink back a tear during "Precious Memories," I thought, "Yes! We've got you surrounded, you cold-hearted son of a bitch! We're going to make you cry in front of your family!" It's about the happiest I ever saw Isaac. His family got a glimpse of who he really was.

After we sang and the party was winding down, Garret said to Terence, "Didn't I tell you to clean up?" There was all this joyful birthday chaos in the living room of wrapping paper and wine glasses and cake, and Uncle Garret had this thing about clutter. It was frankly pathological. And he's staring at Terence with this look. Terence says, "I'll get on it after they leave."

Garret's voice drops to nearly a whisper and he says, "You'll get on it now." So poor Terence starts cleaning up like he's the help, and some of us naturally started pitching in, and there's Garret with that scary low voice saying, "That's Terence's job."

When you hear that voice, you don't ever forget it.

Aunt Hadley was my favorite. She was this beloved kindergarten teacher. Parents would pull whatever strings they had to get their child into her class. Kids she'd taught would keep in touch, drop by the school, visit her before they went off to college. There was just something about her, you wanted her in your life. It must have been hell for her when Uncle Garret went into the dark place.

ELLA

At school there were all these awful rumors about what they were going to do to my brother Isaac, which my friends couldn't wait to tell me. Isaac was so brave showing up day after day, and I think that was because of Kate. She saw something in him. She was the first.

KATE

I convinced Isaac to play with me at the university, just a few songs in the quad on a Sunday afternoon, but the students would stop and listen. Then we got invited to play at parties and in the student union, and we became a thing. At first, it felt weird to be tooling around with Isaac, but I realized he never tried to be anything other than who he was, which, when you're a teenager, is pretty heroic. People didn't know what to make of us until we sang, and then it all made sense. We tried our hand at songwriting and slipped a few originals into our set, which went over okay, so we kept writing and playing. We didn't have any big plan, it just felt like what we should be doing.

MICKEY

The big worry my parents had about football was concussions. I knew it wouldn't happen to me because I was nineteen and invincible, so when it happened, I tried to downplay it.

It was homecoming, the whole school had turned out. Near the end of the half, I made a pretty dazzling catch and was stutter-stepping to beat the first guy when I got blindsided by a helmet-to-helmet hit and went down like I'd been shot. They took me off on a gurney and even though I was out cold, they couldn't pry the ball out of my hands. Pretty impressive, right? I don't remember any of that, so it might be bullshit. The headaches that followed were real. I didn't want to admit how bad it was, but I had to take fall semester off. I was living at home and had to get out of the house, so I'd go to the campus library to read. Since football was off the table, I was taking a hard look at my life.

DAVID

Kate and Isaac made a few DIY recordings of the songs they wrote. The college radio station started playing "Look What Happened to You," which was kind of a break-up song to the United States. Isaac had gone so far into uncool he had come out the other side and had a following; nothing major, just out-of-it kids who finally had a hero.

MICKEY

There was this super-serious librarian I'd see every day, Dee. I'd try to get her to talk to me, but it wasn't easy. One day, I told her that post-football I needed a new direction and asked what I should read. She wrote down some titles, which turned into a significant reading list. She was tough and serious, so when I made her laugh, it was big. When I returned a book, she'd quiz me on it and if I gave a lazy answer, she'd call me out. I never studied as hard as I did for those trips to the library. I asked if I could buy her dinner to pay her back, and she took a hard pass. I wasn't used to getting shut down, but the way the wind was blowing, as an African American she knew getting even a little involved with me could mean trouble.

PAUL

Kate and Isaac were writing songs together, and there was one called "When the World Was New" that they couldn't finish. Every night we'd hear the beginning of it over and over. I'd whisper to Ruth, "This is how they break terrorists at Gitmo."

DAVID

The high school cafeteria was brutal. A lot of kids would hide out in the library so they didn't have to face the anxiety of trying to eat when you could get frozen out or mocked or bullied and have an upset stomach and the rest of your life ruined.

One Friday, Isaac was headed for what looked like a safe table when some jock came up behind him and cleverly flipped his tray, and all that fine public high school epicurean cuisine went flying. There was a moment when the whole cafeteria went silent, then Isaac turned and smiled at the jock. It was so unexpected and fearless and weirdly powerful that the jock didn't know what to do.

Then the goons started screaming and threatening Isaac the way they did after he spoke up at the assembly. It looked bad, so a bunch of us jumped up and rallied around him like we're going to protect him, but some of the bullies came after us, and we all had the same thought: *we're fucked.* They were the tough kids, and we were the kids who tested well.

It looked like ass-kicking time but then all those kids who looked up to Isaac as a heroic loser tore themselves away from their half-hearted bean and cheese burritos to join us, and we've got all the outcasts, the nerds, the freaks, the weirdos, the dweebs, the learning disabled—Isaac's people—and there were a lot more of us than them. Cause face it, the ultimate truth about high school, which makes it the ultimate truth of human existence, is that more people *don't* fit in than do. There wasn't even a fight. We just milled around pretending to be brave, and the teachers took over, and things lurched back to the free-range insanity of high school normal. Those of us who jumped up to save Isaac had a bond like we'd gone to war, and we realized there were more of us than them. But it didn't stop the way they treated Isaac.

3. winter 2020

PAUL

Mickey's concussion scared the hell out of us—sitting in the stands in the middle of bedlam watching him get wheeled off the field. Ruth and I were both thinking, What if he isn't the same? And of course, he wasn't. Even though we spent a whole lot of time pretending he was.

MICKEY

When I went back to the university for spring semester, I got a job at the library. That's when my new friend Dee realized my one great talent: I am fucking relentless. She'd replaced football as my great passion, and now she was my supervisor. I was a very eager new hire.

PAUL

One Friday afternoon with everyone counting down to the weekend, I said to my American History class, "If we kick out everyone who isn't a citizen and we don't let anyone else in, what does that do to our country?" Silence, then this earnest, grade-grubbing, front-row freshman, Kelly, said it was a good thing because white people could be in the minority by 2045, and if we don't take care of our own people, who will? There was a groundswell of support for the courageous work of the administration to keep out immigrants who were taking our jobs and committing hideous crimes while refusing to speak English, although their music can be pretty awesome.

That's when I read to the class what the US Office of Strategic Services concluded were the primary rules of Adolf Hitler: "Never allow the public to cool off; never admit a fault or wrong; never concede that there may be some good in your enemy; never accept blame; people will believe a big lie sooner than a little one; repeat it frequently enough and people will believe it." Sound familiar?

I could see the rage and contempt rising on the faces of Kelly and her cohorts. The African American, Asian, and Hispanic students didn't say a word. Students of color were losing scholarships for reasons made unclear in a blizzard of fine print, but the message was obvious: We don't want you here. That year the earth was shifting under my feet. My work had never seemed so important.

MICKEY

The university was getting a shitload of money from the government for the new psych center, and from the start, it was a mystery what happened there. Word got out that students could make extra cash by volunteering for educational tests and then flyers appeared with a challenge: "Do you have the courage to face the real you?" There had been rules against using students as subjects of testing, but there was a major governmental push to render the country as unregulated as its leader. So, students were now vulnerable to rapacious loans and mysterious research.

PAUL

When I started teaching at the university, I assumed it was just a step along the way before grander things, but the longer I taught the more I wanted to stay. Financial security was a concern, given the constant whiplash of the economy with trade wars and tariffs and pandemics and isolationist policies that kept the country in a state of fearful agitation. I'd found a safe harbor doing something I loved, and tenure meant we'd make it through the storm until things got back to normal.

MICKEY

My librarian friend, Dee, and I were spending all our time together. I couldn't get enough of her. Her advisor told her they didn't have a diverse enough range of students for the study at the psych center and suggested she consider it. The study was supposedly aimed at developing breakthrough educational approaches for the underserved, which was hard to argue with if it happened to be true. Dee had big plans about grad school and wanted to remain in good standing in her department, so she volunteered. I was opposed to it, but she said she didn't have a choice.

We talked endlessly about the study. What we never talked about was the excitement we felt being together. We'd never even kissed. The week before she went in to the psych center, we got into our first serious argument. She was convinced I couldn't ever understand what life was like for her as an African American woman at the university. I said I thought she was afraid of what she was feeling for me. That's when she threw me out. It wasn't until years later I found out the real reason she signed up at the psych center.

KATE

My boyfriend Glenn had a falling-out with his family over his politics. They cut him off financially and he was scrambling for cash, so when the psych center opened, he was one of the first who signed up as a subject. It didn't seem like a big thing, just bogus educational testing in exchange for beer money. He went in for three days and afterwards, when he got a call from his dad, he high-tailed it back to Cleveland to take over Bedding'N'More, the family business. It seemed strange, but those were strange days. Of course, we had no idea they'd get even stranger. We'd get nostalgic for last week, when things were better.

MICKEY

I was falling in love with Dee, and when she said I couldn't possibly understand what was going on with her, I knew she was right. So, without telling her, I signed up for the testing. You had to commit to three days, and I arranged it so we'd be going in at the same time, even though she didn't know I was doing it.

KATE

As I later understood it, the whole thing at the psych center was about interrogation and coercion. As soon as you signed up, they did a deep dive into your personal history, then turned you upside down and shook everything out, so you were vulnerable right from the start. After check-in, it was what you probably thought it would be: bland educational testing. Then, by degrees, you were put in more and more charged situations. They were fine-tuning methods of getting whatever version of the truth they wanted, smashing you into a million pieces and putting you back together slightly reconfigured.

Glenn used to say the problem with paranoia is that it never goes far enough; whatever they're doing is much worse than whatever you imagine. They had the goods on him—he'd gone to a campus shrink—and they used the most intimate parts of his life against him.

MICKEY

When I got out of the psych center study, it was midnight and I wandered the campus for hours talking to myself, but I couldn't understand the point I was trying to make. My mind was spinning, and I felt like I'd never make it back to solid ground. Early in the morning I went to Dee's dorm room, knocked softly, she opened the door, stared at me and said, "What happened to you?"

I said, "The same thing that happened to you."

I thought she was going to slam the door in my face, but she just grabbed me and we were both sobbing, trying to understand what had been done to us. Even with the horror of what we'd been through, it was incredibly exhilarating. I mean, how often do you tell the truth without any concern for how it makes you look?

That night Dee and I slept together, and for all the sex I'd had, this was the first time I made love. We tried to be discreet because the whole country was hurtling forward into the past where an interracial relationship meant danger. My mom says the concussion changed me, but that diminishes everything else. Getting dinged in a football game is nothing compared to connecting with another human being on the deepest level.

4. spring/summer 2020

PAUL

One Sunday night, I mentioned to Mickey I was going to the antigovernment campus march and would he like to join me? I thought he'd be all over it, but he said very slowly, as if he was explaining time zones to a small child, "Dad, the campus demonstrations are sanctioned by the university. They exist only to promote the lie that this is a free society and the system works." I pointed out that so far, the system *does* work, but he said it's been corrupted and turned against us, so working within the system is fueling the tanks that are about to roll over us.

He had an edge I'd never seen. That was the first I heard about the march being planned in DC to protest the massive election-year military parade featuring tanks and missiles and everything else a weak, damaged, unloved commander in chief would want.

KATE

Back when we were still doing Sunday dinners at the General's house and my brother Mickey was a senior, he gave a speech announcing that he'd decided to go to college at the U. He'd been recruited everywhere, so it was a big deal that he was going to stay in town and play for our team. He milked the moment for all it was worth, and the family was cheering as if he had just scored a touchdown.

As for me, I had big plans to go to a fancy East Coast college when I graduated high school the next year, but with my dad still at the U I'd get free tuition, so it made sense to go there. I got my cheers—not as loud as Mickey but nothing to be ashamed of—and when things died down my cousin Terence stood up. We were in the same grade but our paths never crossed. He wasn't much of a student, and no one knew if he'd even graduate, but I guess he felt like he had to make an announcement about his future.

RUTH

It kind of broke my heart when Terence made his little speech. He was stiff and tongue-tied, nothing like Mickey and Kate, who thrive on being the center of attention. When he announced he was enlisting in the Marines, there was silence for days. Then we all cheered because what are you going to do? Paul was the one who went over to Terence and shook his hand.

KATE

Terence kept looking over at his dad, who couldn't give it up for him, and I'm thinking, *Jesus, man, you're going to go get your ass shot up in Afghanistan to make your daddy proud, and he won't even shake your hand?*

LOUISE

I'd put off talking to my Grandpa Garret. My great-uncle Paul had convinced me that Garret wouldn't even talk to me because of something criminal he'd done. And, honestly, I was a little scared of him. He'd never yelled at me the way he did with his own kids, but I was always super polite around him, just in case. I'm pretty sure he thought this project of mine was dumb, and I didn't want to hear him explain why. But it was turning into the story of Paul's family, which wasn't right. For the sake of my family study, I made myself sit down with Garret.

GARRET
(Paul's older brother, age fifty-two in 2019)

Here we are, Louise. Finally. Guess you've talked to just about everyone but me. Which is okay. But you haven't got the real story if you've been talking to Paul. I'm not saying my brother's a liar, but he sometimes feels limited by the truth. It gets in his way. And it makes him look pretty bad, considering what happened. But I do love my brother.

MICKEY

The weekend after my cousin Terence announced his plans to enlist, I took him out to celebrate, as if what he was doing should be celebrated. He kind of hero worshiped me, which I find to be a solid basis for a relationship. Once I went off to college, we didn't see much of each other, and David would tell me about Terence being this tough hombre in high school, which sounds kind of sad, but going out drinking seemed like the right thing to do. I mean, who knows if he's ever going to come back home?

I was wasted and sleep-deprived from the political organizing with Dee, and here's my cousin going into the military. As a soldier in the post-2016 era, you couldn't kid yourself you were defending freedom. If you were honest, you knew you were just a pawn in whatever fever dream they cooked up to distract us from even worse shit they were doing.

But we didn't talk about that, we talked about the family and football and the cottage in Canada where we used to go. There was a big hole in the conversation where politics would be if I was talking to anyone else. We started playing pool, and there was a moment when he looked across the table and said, "Mickey, am I doing the right thing?" He looked like a little kid who'd gotten lost in the woods.

PAUL

It was a beautiful day for the campus march. The streets were jammed and we chanted and held signs and felt hopeful for a change. Then I saw my brother. By the way Garret was watching the goings on, it was clear he was working campus security, even though he was out of uniform. He shot me a tight, condescending smile like I'd see when we were kids and he was stoking my rage. So I'd go after him, which would give him license to beat the shit out of me and then, under questioning from the General, blame me for starting it.

We marched some more, but my hope had been blasted into vapors by my brother and I saw the march for what it was: so upbeat and innocent it could have been the Boy Scouts of America celebrating the Fourth of July.

GARRET

Let's be clear: I love my brother. Did I already say that? When folks meet Paul, he bowls them over with his decency and kindness. That changes a bit when you get to know him better. The mystery is how a man who knows so much can be so naïve. It might be as simple as the fact that he never served. As a clumsy, nearsighted kid with asthma, he got chosen to be the smart one. The expectation from the General was that I would enlist, which meant I was in the business of protecting people and Paul was in the business of being protected. I came home from the Gulf War in '91. Paul was in graduate school and headed for an easy life with Ruth, which got bankrolled for too many years by the General.

Anyway, it was just perfect seeing him marching along with his students, chanting and holding up their little signs. That oughta fix everything, right?

Me and a couple of buddies started a home security business with no help from anyone. We hit some bumps, but after a few years it took off. Then we got the contract for university security when they were privatizing. I'd see Paul on campus with a bunch of undergrads hanging on his every word. He was just eating it up. I was dealing with the other side of campus life, sexual violence, and random crime, which is a damn sight worse than you think.

So, him and me worked at the same place. For me, it was a war zone, for him, it was the University of Paul.

PAUL

Four of us in the history department would meet for beers at Clancy's Pub, no jukebox, no TV, no games, no cover, no students, no place better. It was understood that we could trash the university, the history department, our colleagues, our students, our loved ones, each other, and ourselves. We had what our students lobbied for: a safe space. So, it wasn't anything odd when I asked the others how they were dealing with the outbreak of white nationalism on campus. The group got quiet, which seemed strange since we were a close, opinionated, hard-drinking bunch, but they were suddenly on guard. I let it drop.

Later, when my friend Cal, the department head, was driving me home I asked about tenure. I'd put in my application and heard nothing. He told me this was a tough time with the university under pressure to monitor "left-wing faculty bias." He was staring straight ahead when he said, "My hope is that things will be different after the election."

I didn't realize until that moment how much I'd been counting on tenure, a bit of security in a world spinning out of control.

GARRET

After Election Day 2016, getting together with my brother Paul's family got rough. In their minds, we were the fools who got conned. They didn't have to say it; it was all over their faces and in the super polite way Ruth would avoid saying anything that might get us riled.

From my point of view, they were living in the past. The world had changed. The migration of desperate people was real—do we let them all into our country? Religious freaks want to kill us—do we put a target on our back? Half the world's starving—do we give away what we've got so we have nothing? When I looked at our big houses, our safe communities, our top-notch schools and all the food we can eat, I'd feel so damn lucky because the rest of the world doesn't have that.

Why did Paul and his family have such rage for the system that provided it? Paul had read all the books, but he hadn't seen what I'd seen in the military, how the rest of the world makes do. It's like he hated the few of us willing to take hard steps to protect everyone. And you couldn't talk to him because he knew he was right.

5. fall 2020

DAVID

My mom was dead serious about Halloween. She'd spend weeks on her costume, and one of her great disappointments was when I announced I was too old to go trick-or-treating. That year she was a witch with spectacularly disgusting teeth, and she tried to rope me into scaring trick-or-treaters with her, but even *I* was too cool for that, like what if one of my few friends came by?

It was getting late when the doorbell rang, and my mom opened the door doing a guttural moan for one last scare, and there was this Hispanic woman standing there in a cape. I asked what she was supposed to be, and she said, "His wife."

RUTH

They were supposed to let us know she was coming but we had no idea until she was at the door. With Halloween and everyone in costume, no one had noticed her out in the neighborhood. She was relieved to be in a safe house, but then I had to tell her that her husband had been taken.

PAUL

Ruth was so consumed by Anjelica's arrival that it was days before we talked about what was going on with me. It was pretty clear my academic career was in serious jeopardy, which was more than a blow to my ego; we needed the money. We were doing fine, but it was month-to-month fine, not secure-future fine.

ELLA

The day I found out I made cheerleader, I came home super ex-cited and saw my mom sitting in a chair in the backyard looking at her garden. It was one of those chairs no one ever sat in, so she looked out of place, like she was waiting for something. I started babbling about my cheerleading triumph, and what a huge thing it was for a sophomore to get chosen with all the beautiful and sophisticated juniors and seniors, and how a couple of my friends were saying I had a shot at being Winter Queen, which was the big prize at the Snowflake Ball, this major, all-school dance in February.

The way she smiled, I knew something was wrong, like she was looking past me into the future. She'd been to her doctor and got bad news. She was always so optimistic that hearing her say "bad news" was shocking. Then she said, "Ella, we all have to go sometime." I blurted out, "I always hoped Daddy would die first."

TERENCE

When I deployed, I didn't know how sick my mom was. I mean, I knew she was sick, but no one put a clock on it, and her and my dad were like, "Just carry on, Terence, okay?" This was one more thing to not talk about. My dad was freaked because life without my mom was going to be fucking hard for all of us, him the most.

RUTH

Anjelica was alone in the basement, pregnant in a stranger's house, husband seized by ICE, and helping her through this trauma was one small way I could do something positive. When Mickey told us he was going to the march in Washington, I told him to please be careful. He said, "Mom, don't you get it? The days of being careful are over."

PAUL

The military parade in Washington was the Great Leader's attempt to pose as a strong commander in chief, so as to boost him in the election. Mickey asked me to go with him to protest: "Taking down the government is a wonderful father-son activity." Even knowing what happened, I wish to hell I'd gone.

MICKEY

It was a huge rush for me and Dee when we joined that enormous crowd in Washington that was finally taking a stand against the Ruling Party. Back then, we thought being morally superior to the Great Leader would bring him down. We didn't understand that the sleazier and more corrupt he was, the more his people loved him. We were making him stronger.

RUTH

I was watching the march on TV with Paul and David when Anjelica called from the basement. It was all happening at once. We were saving the country and bringing a baby into the world.

MICKEY

When the Great Leader's military parade got canceled because millions of us blocked the way, there was a scream of joy I hadn't heard since football. Our work was done, but nobody wanted to leave. We were chanting and hugging and promising to keep fighting until we got our country back. But we'd done our job too well.

Weak men tend to overreact.

PAUL

David wanted a ride to his friend Brian's house, and Ruth was in the basement where Anjelica was giving birth, and I was just about to turn off the TV when it happened.

RUTH

While Gabriel was being born in the basement, I heard Paul calling to me. I rushed upstairs to see the National Guard attacking the crowd and stomping people when they went down.

PAUL

The tanks from the military parade started rolling through the crowd, and you could hear the screams. I remember David on the phone politely telling his friend he couldn't come over.

RUTH

I tore myself from the carnage on TV and went down to the basement to be with Anjelica, where I could do some good.

MICKEY

It was a mad scrum of desperation to live. Whoever was beating us and shooting us and rolling over us with tanks were probably scared kids like many of us, but when the commander in chief gives an order, you carry it out. I thought I'd missed out on the experience of war by not enlisting, but it turns out, all I needed to do was visit our nation's capital.

RUTH

I crouched in the basement comforting Anjelica, who had to stay out of sight so she and her baby wouldn't be seized by ICE, while upstairs Paul was drinking himself into oblivion watching the bloody battle in the streets of DC. That was the world Gabriel was born into.

TERENCE

It's tough work keeping the country safe. Most Americans never see it up close. That way they can sit back and complain about what fucking monsters we are, the ones who put ourselves on the line. But look at the results. How many democracies have lasted as long as us?

MICKEY

People were wandering dazed through the streets, bleeding, looking for loved ones, spooked by what they'd seen. There were buses going back to the university, so Dee and I hopped one. You'd hear people sobbing and someone would suddenly have an outburst about the fascist motherfuckers, and then there'd be long periods of dead quiet rolling through the night. We'd talked all the way to Washington, but now there was nothing to say.

GARRET

Up until they attacked our troops in DC, we could find ways to get along. This put it right in our faces: there were two sides, no middle ground, and we're going to fight each other to the death.

6. fall 2020

PAUL

When we heard the Great Leader was going to address the nation, Ruth announced she wasn't going to watch. "This is his plan," she said—"to keep us in a constant state of fear and agitation and always be at the center of our lives."

RUTH

I was out walking, and the streets were empty. I felt virtuous for being above it all, but then a block from the house I suddenly started to run, so I wouldn't miss a minute of the speech. So much for my big pronouncement. I got home and Paul said, "When did calling him 'the Great Leader' stop being ironic?"

PAUL

I banged down a tumbler of Knob Creek and made my prediction. He's going to admit this whole thing is a branding exercise gone awry so for the good of the nation he's resigning. He's sorry about, well, pretty much everything he's ever done. He plans to have a final fling with a porn star, publicly demand to know what the hell the evangelicals were thinking by supporting someone so morally bankrupt, then join a monastery and live out his life in celibacy and silent prayer to try to atone for all the pain he's inflicted on innocent people.

RUTH

I told Paul to shut up. I try not to do that, but sometimes it's necessary.

PAUL

Strangely enough, my prediction was wrong. He read off a tele-prompter, which always made him sound like English was his second language, and he didn't have a first.

RUTH

When he launched into a tribute to our sacred right to vote, I could feel my heart pounding. No, please. Not this. Then he said it. *Massive voter fraud has been uncovered. Voting machines have been compromised by radical socialist elements within our nation. Without free and fair elections, this is not our country. I will do whatever it takes to ensure that every real American's vote counts. We will win this battle, and it will only require the brief, temporary postponement of the upcoming elections. I have instructed Congress to vote on this immediately for the sake of our nation.*

PAUL

He talked about how he had incontrovertible evidence the demonstration in Washington was organized and financed by the Russians. Except he didn't say "inconvertible evidence," he said "big beautiful evidence from top-notch people." Only his strong actions had saved us from armed revolution.

RUTH

All this was regarded, like everything else, as an issue with two valid points of view. Polling indicated that half the country was fed up by violent protests, and the hacking of votes and the elections should be postponed to preserve our democracy.

PAUL

In the days after the announcement everything was different but it all looked the same, people heading off to work, kids playing ball, frat parties spilling into the street. But you could feel it in the air, something had shifted. My anger turned to sadness. What a charmed life we'd had in the good old USA, and now we're sleepwalking through the ashes.

MICKEY

I was involved with We the People, a progressive group that was all about social justice, and I couldn't wait for the first meeting after DC. I figured, now we take it to the next level. The leader started talking about registering voters in the African American community, and I couldn't believe it. I said, "Our government has declared war on us. They have taken away the elections. You really think this is about *voter registration?* This is about taking the battle back to Washington and showing these evil motherfuckers we will never stop."

They looked at me like I was off my meds and started talking about how we had to mobilize, since the election would be in a few months. I got it. Knocking on doors was safer than going back to the streets. Afterward, as Dee and I headed to her dorm room and I'm railing about how they're not seeing what's happening, she said, "I'm going to Detroit to register voters. I hope you'll come with me." It felt like our relationship depended on it.

RUTH

Paul's biggest problem used to be that too many students would sign up for his courses. His tour de force on the sixties got so popular they moved it to this huge lecture hall, and he had video clips and scenes from movies and perfectly curated music, and he was on fire. I'd sneak in and stand in back, and Paul would take us on this thrill ride through the war and the madness. His course politicized a whole lot of students who wished they'd been born sooner, but he'd tell them, "This is your time. This is your battle to fight." That course turned out to be his downfall, with the crackdown on left-wing bias. Paul was never any good at academic politics, and he'd say things to be provocative that wouldn't have mattered a few years ago but now were evidence in some mysterious case against him.

PAUL

On the Election Day that wasn't, I placed wildflowers on the grave of my mother at Lakeview Lutheran. Like most things I was doing at the time, it wasn't planned, it just happened.

DAVID

Things got tense on the home front. My dad had his classes cut back, so he was banging around the house with lots of executive time, watching almost as much television as the Great Leader.

RUTH

One night, I woke up to singing. I couldn't figure out where it was coming from, so I got up and wandered through the house. It was a lullaby that kept pulling me closer and closer. I went downstairs and realized it was coming from the basement. I was halfway down the steps and there was Anjelica holding baby Gabriel as she sang. She saw me and stopped, but I smiled and motioned for her to continue. She was singing so softly, how could I have heard it up on the second floor with all the doors closed?

Like everything that mattered, it was beyond understanding. Gabriel finally fell asleep and she put him in his cradle. We sat on the sofa together not saying a word, and I noticed the little things she'd done to make our basement the warmest, most inviting place in the house. I never could have found her strength, enduring the loss of her husband, building a home with her baby in a stranger's basement in a police state where going outside could get her arrested. All I could do was hug her and hold her, and then we kissed.

PAUL

I think I knew Ruth was falling in love with Anjelica before she did.

RUTH

Raising the baby with Anjelica mattered more than anything else. One little life brought into all this cruelty and madness, and we would protect him and help him grow.

DAVID

It used to be we'd eat dinner as a family and instead of grace we'd each say what we were grateful for. Then Kate started saying things like, "I'm grateful for oral sex," and Mickey would say, "I'm grateful for skinny dipping with sorority girls." That's when we stopped being grateful before dinner. After they moved out, I'd have to come up with something I was grateful for, which was impossible since I was in high school.

RUTH

Paul and I had had this long, beautiful, intimate, hilarious conversation that had gone on for years. It started the night we met at a dinner party that was devolving into charades, which caused Paul to sneak out the back and I followed. We were as giddy as if we were cutting school, sitting in his car talking until a honking horn hours later meant we had to move so others could leave the party. Now, after years and years of love and marriage and children, we'd drifted into silence. I had more to say, but I couldn't say it to Paul.

PAUL

Where were the experts to analyze the data in the black box of my marriage to determine why it crashed? Maybe it came down to pilot error preceded by years of neglect.

7. spring 2021

PAUL

There's nothing more hopeful than a new baby, and the happiness after Gabriel was born slammed into the sorrow of the life I'd known coming to an end. Walking down the steps at 117 Poplar was an emotional kill shot. One day I'm living in a cozy house with people I love, and the next, I'm unpacking my suitcase in a downtown rooming house and opening a refrigerator where people label their food. It was clearly time to economize, so I downscaled from Knob Creek to Heaven Hill and read the failing *New York Times* at the library.

At first, I kept to myself, but my fellow exiles were a generally friendly bunch, finding divine hilarity in their free fall into the abyss and nurturing unlikely dreams of a return to normalcy with prodigious drinking in the living room, with the boiler clanging in the basement. After a few cocktails, it felt almost like family, except we didn't know each other well enough to cause real pain. Like drunks since the beginning of time, we'd try to top each other with our tales of misery. I was in bad shape, but the competition was fierce.

DAVID

I had to get past the weirdness of visiting my dad in his rooming house at 276 Brook Street. He'd made friends with this guy, Ted, who was in his sixties with a big laugh, a few lonely teeth, and three or four ex-wives (he was positive he had never married his third) who would call to remind him of all the ways he'd failed them—which made for lengthy, one-sided conversations. My dad would hang out with Ted on the porch with their drinks, competing about who had the darkest take on the news.

PAUL

The university cut back on my course load, but I still had my legendary lecture on the sixties. I wanted my students to face what was being lost, but they had everything they'd always had: parties, gym access, friends, fraternities, sororities, a bottomless daddy-fueled bank account, Netflix, football games, gut courses, sexting, uppers, downers, parents who wanted to be their BFF, and an awesome, forgiving god to watch over them and be their BFF when Daddy was in Cabo with his work wife. It was their self-satisfaction that infuriated me. I was done with political correctness. I told them, "This entire class is a trigger warning for future devastation, and yes, there's a safe space waiting for you: it's your coffin when you die. Until then, everything is dangerous, relationships and jobs and friends and holding on to your humanity, and you'd better embrace the danger because this is what life is." Most of them looked annoyed, wondering if this would be on the final.

MICKEY

They announced the elections would be held in a month, and there were plenty of "I told you sos" from my ex-friends in We the People. By that time, I was involved with another group (which must remain nameless) determined to smash the university's complicity with our authoritarian government.

PAUL

The Great Leader's plan to destroy the environmental movement was straight out of his extremely limited playbook: he'd announce something ignorant and indefensible, humiliate his followers into supporting it, demonize whoever didn't, and make it a loyalty test. Half the country would spit out their mocha lattes in horror and the other half would delight in their horror. As long as the battle lines were so clearly drawn, he could do whatever he wanted.

His big idea was to sell off what remained of the National Parks and open them for drilling, starting with Bears Ears National Monument in southern Utah. There were a number of reasons Bears Ears was a perfect point of attack: it contained sacred Indian land, important archeological sites, endangered species, and had been designated as a national monument by the previous president, who was hated and feared for his decency. For anyone puzzled by the timing, this was the leader's response to Global Health Watch saying that without immediate action we'd be hit with massive food shortages, mass migration, cataclysmic weather events, more pandemics, polluted air, and, not to get too technical, we'd be completely fucked—all of which the Great Leader labeled "socialist propaganda" from his golf cart.

RUTH

What the government was doing was obscene. We kept saying we're better than this, but every day we proved we weren't.

KATE

Isaac was slogging through the end of high school, and I was wondering what I was doing at the U. When I heard about a festival at Bears Ears to protest selling off the national parks, I went to

Isaac's house and made my pitch to his parents that Isaac and I should play at the festival. Why should this gentle soul with such an amazing gift get bullied at a school that won't protect him, when he could be out in the world starting his life and doing something that matters?

Hadley got it. She wanted to see Isaac happy while she still was around to enjoy it, and Garret would do anything for her in the time she had left. I couldn't quite believe they agreed. Garret followed me outside and said, "Isaac needs a lot more help than you think." And I said, "Yeah, well, he's a lot stronger than you think." Uncle Garret broke down and made me promise to protect him. I'd never seen him scared.

MICKEY

I didn't tell Dee what I was doing in the radical movement because it could get her busted out of school. She wanted to register people in Detroit to vote because the delayed election of 2020 was our last best hope. When I said it would never happen, she got angry and said with all my privilege I could afford to be cynical and not work for change. Everything I said came out wrong, which was too bad, since I knew I was right.

I ended up going with her to Detroit even though I had a queasy feeling we were running out the clock, which doesn't make sense when you're losing.

GARRET

I didn't want Hadley to worry, so on the day of the Festival at Bears Ears, I set her up with the entire second season of *The Crown*, while I was in the basement switching between FOX and CNN. I was hoping to see Isaac and Kate perform, but the music part of the coverage got bumped for the protest, which was a bunch of Indians and environmentalists with their chanting and their signs, and then a bunch of regular folks showed up to protest the protest. Working class people who'd get jobs from the development of the area. The economic side tends to get lost in the yelling and screaming from the left. But there was my son Isaac, right in the middle of the damn thing.

KATE

We were stunned by the size of the crowd at Bears Ears. We shouldn't have been, since more than half the country was on our side. It's just that the other side had the power.

GARRET

I went in to check on Hadley and she said, "You need to watch this, Garret, you need to see what they're doing." Screw *The Crown*, she'd been watching the news the whole time. My wife and I watched TV to find out what was happening to our son.

KATE

We played "Look What Happened to You," a favorite of literally tens of people across the nation. Then Isaac stepped up to the mic and said, "I have an important announcement. I know a lot of you are worried about the fate of the world. I'm here to tell you it will be just fine. What's ending is the human race, and maybe that's better for life on earth."

Even with his stutter he was pretty powerful, and some people applauded the end of the human race. During our last song, fights started breaking out, but it was odd because usually there's a fight in one place and other people get involved, but this was isolated fights in different parts of the crowd that started at exactly the same time.

GARRET

You can do everything right but the fact is, you put yourself in a situation like that and you're trusting your life to the actions of a mob. A mob is not rational. A mob will kill you and never feel a thing.

KATE

A bunch of us from the festival were staying at a Holiday Inn Express, and that night, we converged in the breakfast room with beer and whiskey and dope, feeling lucky we'd made it out. Nobody could believe how disciplined the opposition was. I mean, if we could organize like that, we'd overthrow the government in an afternoon and still make happy hour.

There was a weirdly intense freelance journalist named RJ Manning getting in people's faces, and everyone was opening up to him. I had a hunch he was working for the other side, so when he wormed his way over to me, I proposed that he fuck off. He demanded to know what was wrong with me. I told him we didn't have time to get into that with the detail it required. I was about to go back to my room when I saw Isaac talking to a lanky, long-haired guy who'd been lurking around the stage as if he had a job, which he didn't. I don't think Isaac had ever had a drink, but there he was sharing a bottle of red with this mystery dude who had "freeloader" written all over him.

As I was getting on the elevator, this RJ person hopped aboard, and we rode to the third floor in silence. I got off, he followed me down the hall. I wondered if I was going to have to punt his scrawny, undercover ass all the way to Colorado when he asked me why I wouldn't talk to him. I told him my hunch that he was working for the other side—based on the fact that they'd out-organized us and must have been getting their intel *somewhere.*

He started talking so fast I could hardly keep up: *Yes! The ones who attacked were National Guard troops disguised as everyday Americans upset with the protest. That was what the Russians did in Ukraine, use out-of-uniform soldiers to pose as local rebels. The Great Leader was stealing a page from Putin's playbook, or, more likely, the two leaders had talked strategy naked in a sweat lodge, playfully snapping towels at each other's butts, since they're such friendly lads and clearly on the same side.*

RJ was still there in the morning, deconstructing the madness. He turned out to be the smartest person who ever sat on my bed.

8. spring/summer 2021

PAUL

The Great Leader was ecumenical in his cruelty, but he took particular delight in the abuse of children. He put them in cages and stunted their education and fought tirelessly for their malnutrition and killed their spirit with violence and vulgarity and deceit. It was how he'd been raised, and now he was being generous enough to share it with the nation.

MICKEY

We were talking to these black guys on the steps of one of the projects in Detroit. They'd all gotten government warnings about the danger of trying to vote without a valid passport and helpful suggestions to skip the line and vote on their phone. They saw through the scams but didn't want to get busted for being a black voter in the Great Leader's America. Dee said she'd be at the polls and that she was a lawyer—she wasn't, but she was making a point—and she'd personally protect them. I was doing my best to help out, but my problem—well, one of them—is that I have trouble faking it. When I'm excited everyone knows it, and when I'm going through the motions it's pretty obvious. Dee said, "If you don't want to be here, you should leave." Then I had to convince her I wanted to be there, which wasn't easy because I didn't.

Later we're talking to a guy coming out of Food Giant and Dee gives him the pitch about voting and he says, "Frankly, lady, I don't see the point." And I blurt out, "I'm with you, brother."

Dee gives me a look and says our only hope is at the ballot box, and if I can't get behind that, I should leave. We're staring at each other, and if I'd reached out and held her and tried to explain myself, it all might have turned out differently. But I didn't. She turned and went over to talk to a couple of women getting out of their car.

I'm standing there in the Food Giant parking lot watching the best part of my life end. But man, I was so sure I was right.

KATE

The next morning in the breakfast room, I worked with RJ getting people's stories and building the case that the brutal organized response of "the locals" to our Bears Ears protest was actually a government-directed hit. RJ knew his story needed to be airtight because the Great Leader was the most prolific liar in the history of lying, which is, of course, the history of the human race.

Isaac and his new friend finally showed up, shaky and hungover. They took their time figuring out how to turn the knob so the Cheerios would drop into their Styrofoam bowls. I went over to make sure Isaac was okay, and he introduced me to his new friend Neil, who seemed like a guy who could wreck your life without meaning to. Isaac was practically an adult, what could I do?

RUTH

I started off on a walk, and it was so crisp and clear I found myself thinking, *How many more days like this will we ever have?* I went back inside and told Anjelica to bundle up Gabriel and put him in his stroller. It was two blocks to the park and everyone was out walking and jogging and skateboarding and playing soccer, and you could just feel how much we all wanted to seize this moment and hold it close. Anjelica was wide eyed, taking it all in. This was the first she'd seen of our town, and it looked pretty great. People smiled at us and made faces at Gabriel, and we bought ice cream from the truck, and I kept thinking, *America, I love you to death, and you're breaking my heart.*

KATE

Nobody wanted to leave our Holiday Inn Express commune and go home. There was a roadhouse ten miles away, and we'd pile in cars every night and go play our music and get drunk and convince ourselves we were keeping the resistance alive. I was up against an academic deadline, and my advisor was emailing me that I was in serious danger of flunking out. With the weight of everything that was happening, a college degree seemed quaint, but the way I was raised made it hard to write off an education. RJ was finishing writing his story and was going back to New York. We were spending a lot of time together, and he told me I should have my name on the story with him, and I was so surprised and touched I told him to shut the fuck up. I don't know why I've never been asked to write endearments for Hallmark cards.

I drove him to the airport and he made me promise to come see him in New York. I wasn't out of short-term parking before I started missing him so much my whole body ached. Back at the Holiday Inn Express I told Isaac it was time to go, and for the first time I got pushback. He told me to stop acting like his mom, and I said if I was acting like his mom, I'd be sick and dying. Which was such an awful thing to say, I tried to suck it right back into my mouth. Blurting out hideous remarks is one of the downsides of being me, but everything else is pretty great.

Isaac admitted he was terrified of military service and since he wasn't working or going to college, he was sure his dad would make him enlist. I tried to reassure him that his father had long since given up on him, which made him feel a little better. He promised to come home in a week.

GARRET

I had my hands full at work, but it was a blessing because it took my mind off Hadley. And Isaac. I was meeting regularly with the university administration about how to deal with campus radicalism, which was growing like a cancer. My security company was on the line. I'd sold the administration on what we could do, and now we had to prove it. What made it tough was the fringe element stirring things up. You get a bunch of eighteen-year-olds away from home for the first time, they can be convinced of just about any left-wing nonsense. And there were professors who did just that. So I'm trying to make the students, their parents, and the administration happy and keep 'em all safe. It gets real complicated when family is involved. I had intel there was a major radical action in the works, and I was worried.

I wanted to tell Paul, but he'd have gotten up on his high horse and gone public, and I couldn't take that chance. The stakes were too high. And Paul never understood the situation.

KATE

When a week went by with no word from Isaac, I made a Skype call. He was drunk and Neil was in the room, unseen. There were private jokes and laughter at my expense, which pissed me off after all I'd done for him. He said he was playing at the roadhouse every night and building a following and people needed to let him be whoever he wanted to be. I said, "Fine, Isaac, but if you aren't home when your mother dies, you'll carry that for the rest of your life." I was cast against type as a responsible adult, so my performance wasn't very convincing.

9. fall 2021

TERENCE

I was sure when I deployed I'd never see my mom again, but I got back home and there she was, bravely hanging on. She wanted me to take some courses at the U, but I don't need a class to feel dumb, I can do that all by myself. So, I worked for a buddy with a moving company and spent a lot of nights in bars hoping I'd run into someone I knew, but when I did I wished I hadn't. I hated being alone, but people made it worse.

It was my dad of all people who came to the rescue, offering me a gig at his company. So, I finally made it to college as a security guard. If more parents got a glimpse of what was going down on campus, they'd save the sixty grand a year and push little Timmy into the military, which was way safer.

Me and my dad bumped heads at home, but we were pretty good working together. I was still a disappointment, though. Which didn't bother me much, except when I thought about it, which was pretty much every day and more when I drank, which was pretty much every night.

PAUL

The shock of the 2020 election being delayed had worn off, and we lived with the next election being forever a month away.

TERENCE

One night I decided to check out the VFW. I was scared of turning into one of them boring drunks at the bar going on about the war, but I had to do something. I get my beer and see some vet telling a story to a bunch of guys laughing their asses off. It's my old friend Bobby, who lived across the street until his family moved away when we were kids. He sees me and says, "I guess they let any dumb fuck in here." He comes at me screaming he's going to kill this candy-ass, creep motherfucker, and when the other guys grab him he starts laughing and hugs me and says, "Where you been, brother?" Turns out, he deployed the same time as me. We got together most days after that, just like when we were kids. He'd come in the house like he was a member of the family, which he kind of used to be.

ELLA

We had a little party for Terence to welcome him back, but it was really for my mom. Terence said, "Mom, I've got a surprise." He opened the door and Bobby came in, and you could see her light up. The two of them always had this bond.

GARRET

I remember saying to Hadley, "So many of us come back messed up, but Bobby's just like he was when he was six years old."

She gave me this look and said, "I don't think he is."

TERENCE

Bobby and I had a regular thing of getting together Saturdays to call local veterans to make sure everyone was okay. The weekends were the hardest, when we'd wonder why we were still alive and our friends weren't. I'd call the vets and just check in, but Bobby would get on the phone and rag on 'em and give 'em shit and make 'em feel like they had a friend.

MICKEY

There was this one week when I was pretty sure I was being followed. After a late class, I spotted the guy. He hesitated like he was deciding whether to duck behind a tree or come over to me. It was Terence. We hugged, and I suggested we get a beer. Trying to find a bar where a vet and a notorious student radical could drink together wasn't easy in those days. Then I remembered the bar where my dad used to go with his faculty friends. It was every bit as boring as he said; no wonder he was a regular. We had some beers, and Terence told me about Afghanistan, and then he said, "I guess we both know what it's like to get attacked." He knew I'd been at the DC protest. I always liked Terence, and I had to remind myself he'd been tailing me.

TERENCE

When we were kids, my family had a cottage in Canada with Uncle Paul's family, and we'd go up for a few weeks in the summer. Back then, Bobby was having a rough time at home, so we invited him to come with us on vacation. I remember showing him all the secret places and teaching him to water ski, and he told my mom it was the best time he'd ever had. We made big plans for next summer at the cottage, but that's when my dad sold his share to Uncle Paul, and we never went back.

KATE

Now that my parents' marriage had blown up, we didn't go to the General's house for Sunday dinner anymore, so I'd catch up with Mickey on campus. I told him the deal with Isaac, how he was in a bad situation in Utah and how I'd promised Uncle Garret I'd bring him home. We had a school break coming up and Mickey said he'd drive to Utah, get Isaac on a plane, and then kick back with friends in Oregon.

I was surprised he hit on this plan so fast, but looking back it made perfect sense.

ELLA

One night, I was hanging out with Bobby and Terence, playing pool, and my mom told me to go to bed, which kind of pissed me off since I wasn't a child, but we were all being nonstop nice to her given the situation. Maybe an hour later, I woke up to hear this tapping on my window. My bedroom was on the first floor right next to the driveway. I was a little scared, but I pulled back the curtains, and Bobby was standing there in the moonlight, smiling like he just had the most amazing idea.

I was half-asleep but I opened the window, and he hoisted himself up and climbed into my room. He didn't say a word, just lay down on my bed. I was so groggy, I lay down next to him and he whispered, "So what is it you wanted to tell me?" We had to bite the pillow we were laughing so hard, but we couldn't make a sound because if my dad walked in he might get the impression that his sixteen-year-old daughter is in bed with a twenty-one-year-old Marine.

He started kissing me very gently, and there was something almost innocent about it. Almost. It felt insanely good. Most of Terence's friends ignored me, but Bobby talked to me in a non-bullshit way like he was actually interested in what I had to say. Having someone pay attention to you when you're sixteen is a pretty big deal. Actually at any age. We just snuggled and kissed and that was the start of the first adult relationship of my life, although I guess it wasn't *that* adult since it involved crawling in windows in the middle of the night.

GARRET

Even when he was small, you could always trust Bobby. Once after grocery shopping, we all got in the car and he said, "Mr. Weeks, I have to go back in the store." I asked him why, and he held up a pack of chewing gum he'd lifted. He couldn't let himself get away with it.

I said, "Do you want me to go in with you, Bobby?"

He said, "No, this is something I have to do myself." He was maybe seven years old. We watched him walk back to the store, this little kid, all alone, trying to do the right thing, and I remember wondering if my kids would do that.

ELLA

Part of what made the nights with Bobby so exciting was the danger of getting caught. One night, we heard footsteps stopping outside my bedroom door. We held our breath and then they went back down the hall. We started laughing and then they came back, and the door started to open, and Bobby slid down under the covers. My mom was standing there, and I pretended to be asleep and she said, "Remember when you were little and you'd have a nightmare and I'd lie down next to you until you fell asleep? I miss that." She was at the wrong end of a bottle of chardonnay, which probably wasn't a good idea given her medication. She told me how much she loved me, and she was gone. Then Bobby climbed out the window, and he was gone too.

TERENCE

My mom rallied. Seemed like every day she got stronger. She'd be the one to beat it and not even make a big deal about it. Self-pity was not a thing in our house. Or any pity at all.

10. winter 2021

PAUL

I was doing my morning jumping jack on the porch of 276 Brook Street when Cal came bounding up the steps with an idea of how to get me tenure. He couldn't promise anything, but it was so devastatingly brilliant, he was sure he could pull it off. He said I was the best professor in the department. I told him I wouldn't fight him on that, and however it worked out he'd always be my friend. I think that relieved him. We all needed each other more than ever back then. We shook hands and made plans to talk when he got back from vacation in a week. He had to work late that night doing assessments in the psych center to make extra cash.

ELLA

One Friday night in the winter, I was invited to a party that was hugely important to me for a whole lot of reasons too embarrassing to go into. But Terence was working with my dad, and Isaac was still in Utah, so if I went out then Mom would be alone. Terence said I had to stay with her. All I could think about was how hard I'd worked to build the social capital to get invited to the party, and now I was supposed to lose it by babysitting Mom, who was doing just fine. How could out-of-it Terence ever understand that? It was one of the worst fights we ever had. He said, "I'll know if you leave, Ella, so don't." That was the first time I told my brother to fuck off. It felt so good, I wondered why I'd waited so long.

PAUL

I was so fired up about Cal's tenure plan, I decided to cut back on the cocktail side of life. That night, I worked out at the gym, huffing and puffing on the elliptical, watching a revolving panel of excitable insiders convincing each other, "This time it's different, he must resign." Then I got sushi and went back to my room, feeling virtuous about my brand-new healthy lifestyle. That's when I heard it. Jesus Christ. I didn't know what it was, but I knew it was big.

ELLA

My mom must have heard my argument with Terence, so she asked what I'd have been doing if I'd gone out. I was deep in this annoying teenage phase of guarding my secrets—such as they were—from the family. It's pretty hard for me to think back on not talking to my dying mom. But that night, I told her about this group of girls I used to be best friends with when we were little, who'd iced me out ever since freshman year, and I never knew why. Lately they'd been almost nice and invited me to this party, which would have been a major social breakthrough. She asked me if I liked them, which stopped me cold. I'd never even considered that. My mom said, "Well, Ella, I don't think you're missing much tonight."

The house was usually so chaotic but that night it was just the two of us, and it was snowing harder and harder, and we made hot chocolate and sat by the fire. If I could have just one minute back from that night, I'd be happy for the rest of time.

GARRET

What happened that night changed everything. This is the hardest goddam thing to talk about, Louise. I'll do my best.

I knew this terrible thing was going to happen. I just didn't know when. I'd worked so hard finding out everything I could, but I didn't have quite enough information to make a move. The clock was ticking, and I couldn't tell anyone. You act too soon, you blow it. Or you wait too long, which is what I did.

TERENCE

Worst night of my life. And I've had a lot of bad ones. My dad finally told me what was happening. If there's anything good that came out of that night, it's that me and my dad shared the guilt. We couldn't talk about it with anyone else. We didn't talk much about it with each other, now that I think of it.

DAVID

I was downtown with a couple of friends, nerding out at an arcade. The boom was so loud it shook the building, and we went running outside, and it looked like the sky was on fire.

ELLA

Mom got tired early, so she went to bed, and I'm hearing from my friends about the unfolding drama at the party and how everyone's going to stay over because of the snow, and there are exciting possibilities—Tyler Cole had finally broken up with Sheila Nyland and was gloriously lonely—and they're trying to convince me to sneak out for a sleepover, and I decide that's what I'm going to do because when will I ever have this chance again? That's when I heard it, and then they're all texting *WTF* . . .

DAVID

I'm running down the street and everyone is totally freaked, and it's like I'm in someone's disaster movie.

ELLA

I heard my mom calling from her bedroom, kind of moaning—a sound I'd never heard before—and somehow my idiotic decision to sneak out was connected to the boom, which was connected to the moaning. Everything was happening at once, and it was all bad. I went into my mom's room, and she said very softly, "Ella, it's time to call the ambulance." She'd aged years in the hours since she'd gone to bed.

I called 9-1-1, but it took forever for the ambulance to get through the snow. Two EMS guys come into the house looking shaken and I'm thinking, *Get it together, guys, isn't this what you do? Bring people to the hospital?* I rode with Mom in the ambulance, and we're skidding on the icy roads. I'm holding her hand, and it seems like they're taking the longest route. At that time in my life I was not one to speak up, but I was so scared I said, "Why aren't we taking Franklin?"

One of them said, "A building blew up at the university."

That's why I couldn't reach my dad and Terence. I kept calling and calling, while Mom is slipping away, and it's snowing so hard we can hardly see where we're going. The only one I reached was David.

DAVID

When Ella called, I headed over to University Hospital. The streets were madness, sirens and smoke and cops everywhere and people screaming. Nobody knew what had happened, but it felt as if there must have been massive loss of life. I get to the hospital, and it's weirdly quiet. Where are the victims?

I rushed into my aunt Hadley's room, and there she was, hooked up to all kinds of tubes, and it was only my cousin Ella with her. She always seemed so sophisticated in high school, at least compared to me, which is setting the bar pretty low, but she was standing by her mom's bed and she looked like a little kid, totally helpless. When she saw me, she came rushing over and hugged me, which she never did. It wasn't that we didn't like each other, we just traveled in different circles, and I was probably a social embarrassment. But, at that moment, we were together, and it was huge.

There was a young doctor hurrying in and out, and Ella asked him what they were doing for her mom and the doctor said, "Frankly, based on her medical history, the best thing we can do is let her go." Which might have been true, but it was a knife in the heart.

There was this moment when Ella just stared at him. Then she reared back and punched him in the chest, hard, and said, "You have no fucking right to say that." I probably should have done something, but I was too shocked, I mean, Ella was the sweetest girl, and here she is, slugging a doctor and saying "fuck." It was kind of great, actually. The doctor apologized, while he was backing out of the room, and she's saying, "Do your fucking job, doctor."

It felt like we'd been abandoned, and it was up to us to do whatever had to be done, which wasn't supposed to happen for years. That's when I decided to be a doctor. I would save people like my aunt Hadley and get adored by people like my cousin Ella. My whole life changed that night.

Ella went over to the window to pull herself together, looked out and said, "Oh, my god, I can't believe it."

ELLA

Isaac was getting out of a cab and walking through the snow to the hospital entrance. His hair was long, and he was so thin and had this really unfortunate beard, but it was magical. He just . . . appeared. When he came in the room, Mom's eyes opened, and she managed a smile. I always suspected that Isaac wasn't of this world, but that night proved it.

Later on, my dad and Terence showed up, so the whole family was together. We were talking to Mom, who was lying there, eyes closed, and Terence said, "Can she hear us?" For some reason, we all turned to Isaac, who said yes. So, we kept telling her how much we loved her and that it was okay to go.

At one point, David said, "I should call my parents."

My dad and Terence looked at each other, and my dad said, "That's not necessary." The way he said it, that's when I knew something else was going on, but I didn't know what. I just knew I'd never seen my dad and my brother look the way they looked that night.

KATE

Isaac called and said, "My mom left us last night." He thanked me for getting him to come home and see her one last time.

I said, "You can thank Mickey. Where is he, anyway?" He said Mickey had gotten him on the plane and then headed out to see friends in Oregon.

Isaac suggested we sing at his mom's memorial, which turned out to be the best thing we could have done.

PAUL

The people who bombed the psych center were careful there would be no loss of life. The violence was a response to the university working with the government on a secret program that would no doubt be used against anyone who opposed them. What the bombers didn't know was that my friend Cal was working late that night at the psych center so he could get his vacation in. Cal was a good man in a tight spot, like many of us at that time. He was the one fatality. I never found out what his plan was to get me tenure.

GARRET

There were four people who bombed the psych center. Over the next week, me and Terence worked around the clock to track them down. We didn't have time to grieve over Hadley; we were exhausted and out of our minds. It wasn't just bringing the terrorists to justice, it was saving my company's contract with the university.

Ruth offered to plan the memorial, which was a big help. There was a lot of tension between our families, but we always stepped up for each other. Not everything has to be about politics. Ella was taking it the hardest, and it was good for her to work with Ruth.

KATE

When Isaac and I sang at Aunt Hadley's memorial, Garret started smiling. I hadn't seen him smile in months and months, since Hadley's diagnosis. There was something about Isaac that was so joyful when he sang, you couldn't resist. I remember watching Terence watching his dad watch Isaac. There was Terence, the ex-Marine, working with his dad and being the best son he could be, and somehow Garret couldn't give it up for him. We sang all these songs that Hadley loved, and we finished with everyone joining us for "We Shall Overcome." It wasn't the song their family would have chosen, but that was what Isaac and I were feeling after Bears Ears. We were killing it, and Isaac kept looking over at me smiling, like, where did this come from? We never sounded better, and I remember feeling guilty that I was so happy and excited about our future while we were mourning Isaac's mom.

But that's what Aunt Hadley would have wanted, to give us a ray of hope in the middle of the sadness to keep going with our music. I wouldn't have done anything different, even if I'd known that would be the last time we'd play together.

GARRET

I couldn't find the words to talk about Hadley. I just stood up and told about meeting her on winter break when she was back from Teach for America in East Liverpool, Ohio. It was a tough situation out there with school problems and kid problems and problems in the town. But they loved her. She got Christmas cards from folks out there right up to the end.

PAUL

I didn't say anything at Hadley's memorial because I was afraid I'd slip up and tell the truth. Which wasn't what people wanted to hear. East Liverpool, where she taught, was one of the most polluted towns in the country. There was a massive waste disposal facility and no regulations, which has been the mantra of the Ruling Party for ages. There was benzene in the air, which is why she got leukemia. She paid for that time teaching with her life.

Like most of the horrors of the times, it was completely preventable.

ELLA

Whatever was going on with my mom's friends—marriages headed south, divorce, kids in trouble—they'd come by the house to talk to her. There were so many times a friend would come in sobbing, and later, I'd hear this explosion of laughter from the kitchen. I was a little kid standing outside the door, and I couldn't hear what they were saying, but when they started laughing, I'd laugh along with them.

After the memorial, one woman after another pulled me aside and said, "You know, Ella, *I* was your mother's best friend."

PAUL

We were a wreck from saying goodbye to Hadley. When her memorial was over, I hugged Garret and said, "Anything I can do for you, brother, just say the word."

He just looked at me. "Tell me where Mickey is." I told him Mickey had gone to Utah to get Isaac on a plane and then headed to Oregon to see friends. He said, "When you hear from him, you need to tell me."

part two

11. winter 2021-22

PAUL
(age fifty-two in 2021)

Garret always thought Ruth and I were way too lenient with our children. Pushovers, as he once put it. Liberals without any rules. As opposed to his psycho-drill-sergeant approach to child-rearing, which made growing up tough for all of them. He was always looking for what our kids did wrong, as some kind of proof that his way was right.

For years, he didn't have much to work with, since Mickey and Kate and David all got good grades and went to fine colleges and had plenty of friends, while his Terence and Isaac and Ella were struggling. But things were changing. Our kids had their issues, and Garret couldn't wait to go after Mickey when he had the chance.

RUTH
(age fifty in 2021)

When Paul told me that Garret was circling around Mickey, asking all these leading questions, it was all I could do to not confront him. Mickey was a radical and liked to stir people up, and Garret hated all that. He couldn't wait to, I don't know, put him in his place. I remember thinking what a terrible reaction it was to Hadley's death, for Garret to become even more of a bully.

GARRET
(age fifty-four in 2021)

They'd found three of the bombers. There was only one left. I was pretty sure I knew who it was. But what I had still wasn't rock solid. It was cops in Minnesota who got lucky and caught the three. I decided it was on me to get the fourth. I *needed* to do it. To make up for how I'd dropped the ball. So I could maybe live the rest of my life without torturing myself. I felt guilty I was thinking more about catching Mickey than about losing the only woman I ever loved.

TERENCE
(age twenty in 2021)

On weekends after calling the other vets, me and Bobby would shoot hoops, get in a pickup game. He was driving me home after we kicked ass in a two-on-two on the town courts. I was going on about how awesome we were—especially me—and Bobby was pointing out that the two guys we beat were about twelve, and I was saying, no, man, they were at least fifteen. We were just bull-shitting, laughing, and Bobby got quiet, which happened, like, never. I said, "Hey, are you okay?" There was silence, then he apologized for not speaking at my mom's memorial. I told him, man, it didn't matter, it was just whoever felt like talking.

And he said, "I knew I couldn't talk about her without crying."

When me and Bobby were kids, him and his parents lived across the street and we did everything together. His dad, Gene, had been in the Merchant Marines, retired, so he had lots of free time. He rode a Harley and took us hiking, and there was a place way out in the woods where we camped a bunch of times. It was a huge deal when me and Bobby were allowed to camp there by ourselves. We didn't find out till morning that his dad was camped out nearby, just in case.

Gene was the one dad in the neighborhood who made time for us. One morning when we was maybe eight years old, Gene got on his Harley and off he went. I remember talking to my mom about it, and she said, "When a man leaves on a motorcycle, he doesn't come back."

So, Bobby was stuck with his mother who was kind of nuts. My mom would send me across the street and say, "See if Bobby wants to go swimming with us." Or come over for a cookout or go to the movies. I was this clueless little kid who didn't understand that my mom was making Bobby a member of our family. But *he* knew, and he never forgot.

After a few years, Bobby's mother couldn't afford the house, so they moved away and we lost touch. But for the hard times after Bobby's dad left, my mom made sure he had a family. When he told me this, I just lost it. I mean, that's how she was, just do what's right and don't make a big fucking deal about it.

RUTH

I'd always been so wary of Sunday dinners at the General's, but now I found myself missing them. I even missed the General, who could be such a dictatorial blowhard. He was living alone in that big, drafty house with an ever-changing team of caregivers.

One afternoon, I found myself driving over to see him, which I never would have done if I'd thought about it. It felt odd to be there without the rest of the family, but I rang the bell and Geri, an African American caregiver, took me inside to the library, where the General was slumped by a dying fire, reading Heroditus. He bounced right up and was so genuinely glad to see me, I felt small and selfish for never thinking to visit him before. I told him how much I missed the family parties at his house, and he said he never thought there'd be such bad blood in the family.

We talked to each other in such a real way, as we never had before. I promised I'd come back to see him, and I did. The family was splitting apart just like the country, but I made a point of visiting Ella and the General. We'd find ourselves talking about the way things used to be, with football games, Easter egg hunts, Christmas Eve, Sunday dinners together.

It had only been a few years, but it seemed like some innocent, long-ago time that was gone forever.

ELLA
(age sixteen in 2021)

After my mom died, things changed with Bobby. He would still tap on my window and climb in my room and get in bed with me, but the closer we got to each other, the more I could see that with all his joking around he kept almost everybody at a safe distance. I was one of the few exceptions. One night, I said something about my mom, and he started to tear up and tried to make a joke of it, and I said, "Bobby, it's okay, you can be who you are with me." When we kissed after that, it was different. I guess we were falling in love.

Sometimes we'd just whisper in the dark for hours and then he'd climb back out the window, and other times, as soon as we lay down together, we'd start kissing and touching and undressing each other, and that winter we had nights so magical nothing in my life has come close. Two naked bodies squished together on a single bed, not able to make a sound for fear of getting found out. He'd say, "Ella, if I ever hurt you, I'd never get over it." And

I would tell him this was the absolute best thing in my life, which it was.

I started to see the struggle he was having. Part of it was about me—he was so happy being with me, which paralyzed him with guilt—and the other part of his struggle was something else.

TERENCE

Bobby was always talking shit about going to California and opening a surf shop, kind of a stretch for a guy who'd never surfed and wasn't crazy about the water. It was just part of his rap, like how when he made his fortune, the first thing he'd do is get a new best friend.

The Saturday he didn't come over to call the other vets, I made the calls myself, then left a message for Bobby: "Hey fuckface, you missed the calls, you selfish prick." As soon as I did it I felt bad, but that's the way we talked to each other. I was working the next few days, and when I tried again and he wasn't there, I started to wonder.

ELLA

When Bobby disappeared, the whole family slipped into panic mode. Terence and my dad were trying to remember if Bobby had said anything to suggest where he went. I was in my own scared place, but it was worse because I had this secret. If I admitted what had been going on with Bobby, he'd be excommunicated from the family. But I was like them, trying to remember if there were any signs.

Our last night together, he had been almost giddy, like the first time with me. But then I thought of this moment in the dark when he whispered, "Ella, you're like your mom, you see pain no one else sees, and you make it better." He went on about how it's too bad more people don't have that gift, and I should always know how much I meant to him. But then he was slipping my T-shirt off, and I was unbuckling his belt, and that moment was gone to make way for the next one. How could I have told my family that?

TERENCE

I kept thinking about Bobby's dream of going to California. This is how he'd do it, no goodbyes, just disappear, and then I'd get a call to get my ass out there because he's got a place near the beach, and the girls are awesome, and we're going to start a surf shop together.

He knew I was stuck. If I didn't get out, I'd get old in that town. I might turn into one of them drunks at the VFW that scared me so much.

GARRET

We talked to Bobby's mother—ten minutes and I was surprised he hadn't left sooner. She lived on another planet. Bobby was a miracle for turning out like he did.

TERENCE

Bobby'd been gone a few days, long enough so you worry but short enough so you try to convince yourself not to. One morning I saw there was a message from him on my phone, and I thought, California here I come, baby. The message was just this creepy groaning sound, then nothing. Me and my dad played it over and over but couldn't figure it out. I felt like I knew the sound but couldn't place it. He said, "At least we know he's alive."

ELLA

I couldn't think of anything but Bobby. I was tanking tests and so distracted, one of my teachers insisted I talk to the guidance counselor, who asked if everything was okay at home. *Yes, Mr. Groom, everything's perfect except my mother just died, and my secret Marine lover has disappeared. Oh, and I might be pregnant.*

TERENCE

That winter, we set all kinds of records for snowfall. The college shut down, people were stuck inside, the shelters were full, and old people were at risk. It was like we were getting punished for something. Whatever it was, we deserved it. The plows were going all the time trying to keep the streets open, but everyone was burning out and losing it. There was a shooting over a parking space, and one of the guys driving a plow for forty-two straight hours broke into a stranger's house and went to sleep on the sofa.

One night I woke up and heard strange sounds, so I went outside to check things out. The trees were groaning in the wind and I was thinking, *Where have I heard that sound before?* I stood there in the snow listening and then I knew. I went inside, bundled up, and got a toboggan out of the garage and started hiking.

It was a long way out in the woods to where Bobby and I had camped as kids. That's where I found him, hanging from a tree. I climbed up and cut him down, put him on the toboggan, and the two of us headed back home.

ELLA

There have been entire years of my life that slipped by, and I can't remember what I did. And then, there's the winter when my mom died and Bobby died and I was pregnant and the country was blowing up. I could openly grieve for my mom, but everything with Bobby was a secret, including how hard his death hit me.

How did I deal with it? I started going out with Tyler Cole. The only way I could do it was to pretend I was someone else, and the strange thing was how easy it was. I'm either a totally dishonest person or a brilliant actress. Or both. I played the part of a carefree sophomore instead of a shattered pregnant kid who woke up every day terrified.

One night, Tyler had dinner at our house and I was amazed at how convincingly we portrayed a normal family. I made passable fajitas and we talked football and horror films, but my body was telling me a decision had to be made.

GARRET

I had a breakthrough in the case. All the hunches I didn't act on were true. I was mad at myself for not taking action but glad I finally had confirmation. It was a hard truth, but a helluva lot better than not knowing.

I put the pieces together about Mickey the day before Bobby's funeral. Bobby was like family. And he meant everything to Hadley. No way would I stay away from the funeral just because of who I'd run into.

TERENCE

How do you say goodbye to your best friend when he goes out like that? When you've been with him every damn day, and you never saw the signs? I told my dad I didn't need to go to a goddamn funeral to remember Bobby. He just said, "I'll be in the car. Come out when you're ready." In my dad's head, he was giving me a choice.

PAUL

Ruth and I went to Bobby's funeral together. Anjelica stayed home; it was too dangerous for her to be out with all these people, especially military-type people. I held on to Ruth during the service, and we walked out of the church holding hands.

It wasn't until we were outside that I saw Garret. He was coming over to us, and I could feel my stomach clench, and Ruth squeezed my hand so hard it hurt. My own brother—that was the effect he had on us. He stood right in front of us so we couldn't get past. I tried to lighten things up, telling him, "If people didn't keep dying, we'd never see each other, Garret." Which was wrong on so many levels and for so many reasons, as Ruth helpfully pointed out with a single look.

ELLA

People were getting up and talking about Bobby and I'm sitting there thinking, what if I faced this crowd and said what I haven't been able to tell a single soul? *Since Bobby's life is over, I think you should know the truth. I loved Bobby with all my heart. He sneaked in my bedroom window on many nights and we made love and we shared everything, and I think I'm going to have his baby. Oh, and I'll never love anyone as much as I love him.*

It was so clear in my head that I was scared I would suddenly get up there and say it. I was actually holding on to the pew so I wouldn't.

RUTH

There are many times when Paul is an absolute lifesaver. This wasn't one of them. Garret just kept staring at us, and then he said in this soft voice so we had to lean forward to hear him, "I think you should know. They've caught three of the bombers. The fourth one is Mickey."

PAUL

Growing up, Garret punched me in the gut, hard, many times. This one was worse. I said, "That's not true," but my voice didn't even sound like me.

Garret said, "I'm going to find him." Then he was gone.

RUTH

I think we already knew. We just couldn't face it. Garret made us live in reality, which wasn't always my favorite place to be back then.

PAUL

We headed straight for the car. Ruth gave me a ride back to the rooming house. In all the years of our courtship, marriage, and separation, it's the only time we were both crying at the same time. Usually tears are a tag team event for us.

RUTH

Year by year, living with the truth had gotten harder. Now it was intolerable. Our family had landed smack in the middle of a civil war. The one most in the middle was Ella. She and I had worked so well together planning Hadley's memorial, and she and David were suddenly close since they were together during Hadley's last hours. But Ella was loyal to her own family, and politically, well, at that point you couldn't talk to any of them. We all stayed in our own camp.

KATE
(age nineteen in 2021)

At first, none of us believed that Mickey could be involved in that kind of violence. Then I'd see footage of the DC march, and the tanks rolling into the crowd, and I'd think, *He's right, we're at war, and we need to fight back or everything we love will be gone.*

RUTH

Anjelica and I had to be careful. She didn't have papers, and if they grabbed her she'd get deported, so we picked our spots going outside. Apart from her legal status, we had to be on guard because same-sex relationships were under fire. Legal protections were gone—the Supreme Court made sure of that—which meant it was open season for the Red Hats, who were doing the government's work.

It was safer in our university town than in other parts of the country, but there was a chill in the air if you were holding hands with your girlfriend. We were happy to stay home and marvel over Gabriel, the most perfect child who ever lived. I'd look at my own kids, Mickey dead or on the lam, Kate at loose ends, and David lonely and just trying to get by, and I'd wonder what kind of parents Paul and I had been. Could we have done more to guide them to a successful place, or was our curse the times we were living in?

ELLA

I was going crazy bouncing between my fake, bubbly high school persona and the cold desperation I felt when I was alone. I finally went over to Aunt Ruth's house. She had told me, "I can never replace your mom, but I'll always be there for you, Ella." I was just about to knock on the door when I heard laughter inside, and I thought, when was the last time I heard people really laughing? Ruth was so happy with Anjelica, I could feel it as soon as I went inside.

We had tea, and I told her about my situation, and she gently asked me what I wanted to do. I told her I didn't see how I could do right by a baby. Getting an abortion is, of course, a huge decision, but at that time the government was working overtime to make it even harder. There was a nationwide abortion freeze ("pending further study until we can get a handle on the situation") with heavy legal penalties, so you had to know somebody, and you had to have money. There was an organization called LifeSacred, which was building a database of doctors who performed abortions and pledged to kill one member of each doctor's family if they continued. Kind of an eye-for-an-eye approach to an established medical procedure, and you had to be twenty-one to purchase contraceptives, so there were many girls in my position, but I have never felt so alone.

Ruth told me she was plugged into this underground network for taking in refugees (like Anjelica), and there were people who'd know where I could get an abortion. So much of what we'd taken for granted was now against the law, as if the Taliban had ridden into our town, and you either conformed to their sixth-century beliefs or got beheaded. What touched me was how people were organizing to take care of each other at great risk.

Ruth turned out to be like my mom: you could bring her a problem that stopped you cold, and you'd leave feeling better.

TERENCE

Ella was acting even weirder than usual. In the past she'd have talked to my mom, but now she had no one.

ELLA

Typical night, I'm lying on my bed sobbing and there's a soft knock on my door. Terence comes in and he says, "Are you okay?"

And being a jerky little sister, having the world's longest teen-age breakdown, and a little too stuck on my new favorite word, I said, "What the fuck does it look like to you, Terence?" He turned to leave, and I said I was sorry and blurted out that I was going to have an abortion. I could see him putting the pieces together— little sister, sex, pregnant, holy shit!—then he said he'd take me to get it done. I told him he didn't have to do that, but he said I needed protection.

The attacks on doctors and their families were all over the news and this LifeSacred group was leading the charge. Weaponize mercy and things get scary. The day we went to the clinic, I was glad he was there, but however you do it, it's the loneliest trip a girl's ever going to make.

TERENCE

I was totally opposed to abortion but my sister needed help, and what kind of brother would throw his bigshot opinions around at a time like that?

ELLA

We drive the whole way in silence until I say, "Terence, please don't ever tell Dad about this." We're in the parking lot of the urgent care clinic where my brave doctor is waiting, and there's one other car in the lot, and the driver is checking us out. Terence and I are thinking the same thing: that dude is up to no good. The longer we wait, the worse it gets. The guy finally gets out of his car, hand in his pocket, and he's coming right toward us. Terence whispers, "Bring it, motherfucker," and gets a handgun out of the glove compartment and opens the door. I say, "Terence, no!" but he's already out of the car, fearless, facing down the danger. He must have been one hell of a soldier.

They're staring at each other, and the guy finally says, "It's my wife; going full term could mean her life." His voice is shaking.

Terence says, "It's my sister, and she's just a kid."

The guy says, "Good luck, brother."

Terence says, "You too." He gets back in the car, and we sit there a minute and he says, "Now we know who Tyler Cole really is." I just looked at him, like what are you talking about? He says, "He's responsible for this, and he leaves you in danger?" I burst out laughing, can't stop, and Terence is staring at me wondering exactly how crazy his little sister is.

I finally say, "Tyler is not the father." He keeps looking at me, and I force myself to say, "It's Bobby. Bobby is the father."

Terence's face starts twitching like he's trying not to cry, then he's pounding the steering wheel so hard I'm scared. His best friend offed himself without telling Terence about this huge thing with me happening right under his nose. No wonder he felt betrayed. He finally calmed down and said softly, "It's Bobby's baby," like he was just trying out the words.

TERENCE

The thing I remember saying is, "You still want to go through with this?"

ELLA

If anyone else had given me a ride to the clinic, I'd have done it. But Terence and I were both in love with Bobby, and this baby was what he left us. We sat in that parking lot a long time. I finally said, "Let's pick up a pizza on the way home." We're driving home and Terence says, "When your baby is born, Dad might notice and then you'll have to tell him." I whacked him on the arm, and we both started laughing.

TERENCE

Years later, I said to Ella, "It's lucky I went with you that day."

And she said, "That wasn't luck, Terence, that was you doing the right thing. I can't imagine what my life would have been if you hadn't."

ELLA

Louise, when you told us you were going to interview all of us about the family, I promised myself I wouldn't tell the truth about your father. I spent years hiding it from myself. But now . . .

LOUISE

You have to tell me. And you have to pretend I'm not here. Remember?

ELLA

Yes. It just isn't easy . . . this part of the story . . .

LOUISE

I'm not here. It's just you talking. Now talk, please.

ELLA

Okay. Back when Bobby and I were—I almost said "dating," but the fact is, we never saw each other outside my house—I was totally obsessed with the high school social scene and popularity. My friends would try to fix me up with boys, and I always said no. I had the love of my life, I wasn't looking for anyone else. I was living in two very different worlds. It would have been perfect if I could have brought Bobby into my high school world, but I couldn't.

After I made cheerleader sophomore year, some of my friends started telling me I had a serious shot at being voted Winter Queen at the Snowflake Ball, the big deal, all-school dance in February. I—like practically every other girl—had secretly imagined what it would be like to win. But I couldn't win if I didn't go, and I couldn't bring Bobby as my date. That became a pretty big thing for me. Honestly? As pathetic as it sounds, I was feeling sorry for myself.

At that time, Tyler Cole and I were just friends. So, I was surprised when he asked me to the dance. This was my chance at the crown. I said yes before he could even finish asking me.

Then I had to tell Bobby. I couldn't hide how excited I was. I was just gushing about how my friends actually thought I had a chance to be Winter Queen. I don't like to think of myself as ruthlessly competitive, but maybe I am. Anyway, Bobby said all the right things, how I should go and have the time of my life, but I could see he was hurt. Or maybe scared that I'd leave him. Because by then, what we shared went so deep for both of us. I told him I loved him—the first time I'd actually said that—and he smiled a pretty sad smile. Like I was saying it just so he wouldn't feel bad when I went off on my glam date with all my friends and he was left alone.

Once Tyler and I got to the dance, I was telling my friends to shut up about my chances of being Winter Queen. My friend

Gina, well on her way that night to becoming my ex-friend Gina, told me that if the voting's close I would probably get a break because of losing my mom. I was so shocked, I didn't say a word.

What happened was, there were two absolutely gorgeous senior girls who hated each other. And, basically, they split the vote, and I had a strong sophomore turnout, which was enough to win.

I went up to get crowned, and the whole school was cheering, even if half of them were secretly gnashing their teeth because *they* didn't win, and I thought, if nothing good ever happens to me again, I'll still die happy. And of course, I cried, which is required in those situations. It was the night I'd dreamed of.

I never saw Bobby again. That's when he disappeared.

12. spring 2022

PAUL

Friday, end of class, I announced the weekend assignment: a think piece about why the talking points of the Ruling Party are so often echoed in the manifestos of mass murderers. Kelly and her cohorts glared at me. According to RateMyProfessor.com, I was once the most popular professor in the history department, but my ratings—which, as you know, I honestly don't care about—were dropping day by day.

Afterward, walking to the parking lot, a TA came running up to tell me that a fellow professor named Jody Simons—a classroom hack exploring new frontiers of mediocrity, who'd taken over as department head after Cal's death—wanted to see me in his office. Jody was a rapidly aging boy wonder. He navigated the brutal, bloody, hand-to-hand combat of university politics with charm, guile, good looks, and a finely tuned sense of what ass needed to be kissed for his fraudulent life to continue.

Jody didn't waste any charm on the likes of me. No greeting, no bullshit small talk, no how's the family, he just said that my application for tenure had been denied. I never had a reason to hate Jody, but now I did, and that felt good. There he was, a smooth-talking smugster wallowing in unjustified authority.

"On a personal note, Paul, what's going on with you? I hear you've been engaging in revolutionary rhetoric in the classroom." I explained that if we pretend what's happening makes sense, then we're collaborating with the fascists. Every day we must fight against creeping normalcy. He smiled at my foolishness.

I was suddenly aware of a disturbing smell, which surprised me since Jody had always been such a neat, well put together fellow, and then it occurred to me that living in the rooming house had taken a toll on my wardrobe and hygiene. I'd become the guy you move away from on the bus before he can hit you up for spare change, or worse, sing "Hey Jude." Jody asked if there was anything he could do. I said, "Tenure would have been nice, you fucking traitor." Not exactly a Mr. Chips ending to my teaching career.

ELLA

During those long months of my pregnancy, I'd be trudging the halls to my next class, feeling fat and sick and ugly and wondering why I was still in school. Whenever I wavered, Ruth was there to make sure I kept my eye on the prize. I would get my diploma and go to college and have the life I wanted. I'd just have to work a little harder and be a little more disciplined than my classmates. I was spending more and more time with Ruth and Anjelica, who made raising a child feel like the most important thing you could do. A baby meant hope, and there wasn't much of that around.

The terror was when I was alone. There were other girls in school who'd gotten abortions—everyone knew who they were—but I was the only one that year who was actually going to have her baby. I thought that would make me an outcast, but instead I got invited to parties, and kids I didn't know would fist-bump me in the hall. I guess I was seen as a rebel who was doing things her own way, or maybe they were right-to-lifers who saw me as a girl who'd screwed up but was doing the right thing. After all my desperate efforts to be cool and popular, it had finally happened, and I had no interest at all.

PAUL

The university didn't fire me; they just made it clear I had no future there. My few remaining small classes were taken from me, and I was left with just my big sixties lecture. They could still make money off me.

With fewer teaching responsibilities, I had plenty of time to obsess about Mickey. In addition to the horror that he'd done the bombing and killed my friend Cal, I had the selfish hurt that he'd planned it and pulled it off and I never had a clue. How well did I know my own son? By then, the three other bombers were awaiting trial. Mickey had either made it to safety or gotten killed along the way.

The uncertainty was impossible to live with. Maybe if Ruth and I still lived together we could have talked about it, but she was consumed by her love affair and a baby, which makes you live in the present, while I was slogging through the rubble of the past, looking for answers. It was Kate who told me about Mickey's girlfriend, Dee.

ELLA

When the time came, my dad and Terence drove me to the hospital. They were a wreck, jittery and nervous and competing over who could be more helpful, which was exhausting. Ruth was waiting at the hospital. She sent them off on some bogus mission, and I knew I'd be okay.

DAVID

I made it through high school in three years, as planned. I didn't know anyone from the class ahead of me, so I didn't go to graduation. If my parents were still together, they probably would have insisted I go, but everyone was flying blind. I just wanted out of everything connected to my town, my high school, and my family.

RUTH

David worked so hard with all the chaos around him. He wanted to go to New York for college, but he was so young and had no idea how much he'd miss us.

KATE

RJ's energy was terrifying. I told him if he was any more intense he'd get locked up, and he said if he was any less intense he wouldn't be so fucking good. I loved how arrogant he was, refusing to play modest about his talent. People have accused me of arrogance but it was just an act I tried to pull off when I was feeling sad and worthless. I can't help it if they fell for it.

RJ was in New York hustling his story and I was at the U, studying hard so I could go to law school and fight the daily destruction of the land. Marches and music weren't going to get the job done any more than Mickey's tragic journey to the dark side. I was on a mission to get the EPA back to protecting what was left of our land, which meant the Ruling Party would have to accept science, a subject that confused and enraged them.

PAUL

I met Dee at the Student Union for coffee. I told her I couldn't get past the hurt of knowing I wasn't as close to my son as I'd thought. How could he could get so deeply involved in this violent radical group without me having a hint? She admitted she felt the same way. He'd told her he was going out to Oregon, but had sneaked back into town and done the deed and disappeared with no goodbye, so what was their relationship all about?

She was both in love with him and furious with him, which made grieving even harder. I squeezed her hand and thanked her for seeing me. We knew we were being watched and anything interracial was suspect.

RUTH

The families were so violently at odds, I didn't tell anyone I was visiting the General. One day he said, "How come my son Paul never comes to see me?" I mumbled about how busy he was, and the General said, "Well, Ruth, I know things are good with you and Paul because I've never seen you happier." The look on my face gave me away and he said, "What the hell is going on?" I told him that Paul and I weren't living together, and he said, "Is that why you're so happy?"

I took a deep breath, decided it was cowardly to lie about what mattered most in my life, and told him I'd fallen in love with someone else. He nodded, and I said, "She's made me very happy."

He stared right through me and I thought, here it comes. Then he smiled. "You've always been full of surprises, Ruth. Maybe that's why I like you so much." Usually he gave me a quick, avuncular goodbye hug, but this time he held me tight.

PAUL

Ruth kept telling me to go see my dad, but since I had nothing to do I could never find the time. And I didn't know how to explain myself. After all those years when he could boast about me, I was done professionally, my marriage was over, and I was living with a bunch of drunks in a downtown rooming house. And I knew there's no way he could ever accept Ruth and Anjelica.

Then he had his fall. Squirrels were invading his bird feeder, and he went rushing out with a squash racquet. A soldier to the end.

RUTH

I got the call that the General was on his way to the hospital. I called Paul and Garret, and we all met up in the ER, and that's how the brothers started talking to each other again.

GARRET

Me and Paul were a pretty good team when we had to be. Growing up with a mother who had mental problems, we had to watch out for ourselves.

RUTH

I went to see the General when he was back home from the hospital. He was a bit shaky, not the force of nature he'd been. We found ourselves talking about that football game when David scored the touchdown, and he said, "We should have a family party."

I said, "You mean before we sell the house?"

That was the first time it had come up. He was quiet for a while, then the two of us started talking about his future, and I could tell he was getting mentally ready to move. We made a plan for him to go into an independent living facility I'd found called Blue Hill. When I got in my car, he was standing on the steps waving goodbye with his white handkerchief. It was a grand, silly gesture he always did when people left after a party, and now he was doing it for me.

GARRET

Me and Paul decided the days of our father rattling around that house were over, so we found a place to move him called Blue Hill.

PAUL

Garret and I have spent much of our lives at odds, but I'm proud we were able to talk our dad into selling his house and moving into an independent living place I found called Blue Hill.

RUTH

Emptying the house landed on me. It was overwhelming. The General had lived there forever, and when his wife died, she'd been transitioning from collector to hoarder.

PAUL

What a job it was moving him out! But we worked together and got it done. That's what families do. Sometimes.

ELLA

I named you—I'm sorry, "her"—Hadley Louise, but saying "Hadley" was too painful, so we called her Louise. I never knew how my dad felt about me getting pregnant. He swallowed it along with his grief about Mom, but day by day I could see him falling in love with baby Louise. There was a bright new life in a dark house, and she demanded that we pay attention.

I'd bring her over to visit Ruth, who'd been married and raised three kids, and I'd hardly even dated, but there we were being moms together. I told her I wasn't sure I wanted to go to the General's party. Ruth said it was my decision, and I should do whatever I wanted as long as I went.

DAVID

I assumed it would be just my mom and I going to the party, but then I saw that she and Anjelica were packing up Gabriel, and I was told to load up all the baby equipment. Go someplace with a baby, you're an invading force. I wasn't as concerned with ICE as I was with the relatives. I whispered to my mom, "So, we're all going?"

She said, "It's a family party. This is our family." I shrugged, like, you're the one bungee jumping; I hope you measured the cord.

PAUL

Once Ruth and I split up, I sold my car. I'd spring for the occasional Lyft if there happened to be a free meal on the other end, but for the most part I was the guy who walked everywhere talking to himself. Yeah, that guy.

DAVID

We were maybe a mile from the General's house when I saw my dad trudging along. I said, "Mom, should we pick up Dad?" She hesitated, then suddenly pulled over and backed up fast. He had to jump out of the way, so he wouldn't get run over. He came up to the car and she said, "Hello, Paul, would you like a ride?" He said, "No thanks, it's a pretty nice day." It wasn't, but whatever. Mom pulled forward without checking the traffic, and cars had to honk and swerve, and several helpful motorists weighed in with a middle finger just in case we weren't feeling like assholes. I guess Mom was more anxious than she let on.

We got there, and we're all in the backyard dreading what the General will do when he meets Anjelica and figures out what's going on. Nobody talked about it, but you could feel the tension.

The families hadn't been together for ages, and Mickey's a terrorist, and we disagree about everything political, and now this.

The door opened, the General came out, went straight to my mom, gave her a hug and introduced himself to Anjelica. Never missed a beat. The three of them started chattering away like old friends, he removed Gabriel's nose, and we all breathed again.

ELLA

I was upstairs, panicked about what the rest of the family would think of me with a baby. I looked out the window and saw Ruth and Anjelica laughing with the General, so I picked up Louise and said, "Honey, we're going in." It's amazing how much strength that tiny person who turned out to be you gave me. Sorry, honey, I know, you're not here.

LOUISE

Just so you know, you're the only one who keeps doing that.

ELLA

Again, I'm sorry.

RUTH

I was talking to Terence when he said, "Who's that guy?"

I said, "That's your uncle Paul." Paul was in his own world, ambling up the driveway singing to himself.

Terence kept staring and said, "What happened to him?" He hadn't seen Paul for a while, so the shabby clothes and buoyant haplessness were a shock.

KATE

Isaac and I talked about how awesome we were playing music at his mom's memorial, and he suggested we start up our act again. I told him I was going to New York to see RJ, and I'd call when I got back.

RUTH

I couldn't stop thinking about Hadley. She was the one who held our families together, and I wanted to do that myself but knew I couldn't. I was suddenly overcome by my own sadness and inadequacy, and that's when I felt an arm around me. Isaac said, "My mom would be so grateful for all you're doing for Ella. She'd be lost without you." How did he know what I was thinking?

I said, "Isaac, you're just like your mom, you never miss a thing."

TERENCE

All week I'd been looking forward to this party, and now I'm a ghost, the kind of person you don't talk to, and nobody did. Then it hit me. The last real thing that happened to me was a firefight in Afghanistan. Right now, I'm dying on the battlefield and everything since, including this party, is what my poor brain is dreaming before slipping over to the other side. It's not real, I'm dead, I'm fucking dead, and no one can see me because I'm not here. My heart's pounding and I'm thinking, I have to talk to someone who will tell me the truth. I got out my phone to call Bobby, and I'm just remembering that he's dead too when my dad calls everyone in to dinner.

PAUL

The General made a toast thanking Terence and Garret for their service and said we have to fight the enemy whether it's overseas or here at home. He was looking at me when he said it.

RUTH

Paul always deferred to his father. I don't know why he picked this moment to make a stand.

PAUL

I said, "Am I the enemy, Dad?" Everything stopped.

The General gave me this tight smile and said, "You'll have to answer that question yourself, Paul. Everyone working against our government is the enemy."

I said, "Given that this government is taking away our freedom and our rights, I think anyone *supporting* the government is the enemy."

RUTH

I said, "We don't need to do this," and the General said, "I'm afraid we do, Ruth, we're at war. Those of us who served know that in a war you're on one side or another, right, Terence?"

We all looked at Terence. He was eating his mashed potatoes with his hands.

KATE

It was so fucked up. Poor Terence was busted in this crazy private moment, and my dad, who was always the great peacemaker, wouldn't let it go. He said, "I'm not on your side, Dad. This country is in a death spiral, I won't be part of it."

The General said, "You didn't serve, Paul, you hid out at the university. You have never once thanked me or Garret or Terence for our service."

DAVID

My dad took a big slug of wine and said, "Thanks, guys. I forgive you for your service. You didn't know any better. But you sure as hell should know better by now."

KATE

I thought Uncle Garret was going to jam a fork in Dad's head.

RUTH

As much as I wanted Paul to stop, I was proud of him.

GARRET

My brother's radical socialist left-wing rant played like gangbusters at the university, but there was no place for it at that table with three veterans. I said, "Paul, look what your precious ideology has led to. Look what your own son has done."

RUTH

When Garret said, "You raised a terrorist, Paul. I think it's time you took responsibility for that," people gasped. I know I did.

KATE

When Uncle Garret said, "Your son is a murderer," the night was over. I mean, how could we sit still for that?

PAUL

When Garret called Mickey a psychopathic killer, I felt it necessary to point out that there was more blood spilled on his side of the table. "Whatever Mickey did, he was trying to save the country from people like you."

KATE

My dad stood up, and it would have been an awesome exit except he said, "Come on, Ruth, we're going home." In that moment, he forgot they were separated. My mom was caught off guard and, weirdly enough, it was Angelica who took charge. She said, "I'm sorry, but we must leave. How can we eat together if we are at war?"

She was so easy to misread. She came across as sweet and quiet and accommodating, but she had such fire in her soul. Watching her seize the power in a roomful of strangers, I completely understood why she and my mom were together.

RUTH

Nobody tried to stop us. We went outside and stood in the driveway, Anjelica, Gabriel, David, Kate, Paul, and I. Paul finished his wine and threw the glass into the woods by their house and said, "That was a fun family event, except for the family."

We were laughing when I turned and saw Ella looking out the window at us. I froze. Out of that whole awful day, that was the most awful moment for me.

ELLA

It happened so fast, the banter, Grandpa's toast, the argument, and then they were gone. We were inside with the meal we'd

111

spent all day preparing, and they were out there laughing. It was shameful.

I started clearing the table and my dad and my brothers helped. When we came back from the kitchen, Grandpa had gone to bed. We were all upset, but I think it hurt Isaac the most.

13. fall 2022

PAUL

It had been two years since the 2020 election was postponed, and there was an unfamiliar bipartisan push to finally make it happen. That was when the majority leader lurched into view, an odd, croaking humanoid who bore a striking resemblance to a *Tiktaalik*, the first fish to walk on land some 375 million years ago. He was perfect for the times, whip smart, amoral, and fixated on fulfilling every twisted brainless musing of the increasingly demented Great Leader. He blocked the Senate from taking up the motion to mandate an election and made a rare opening statement.

With the emotional range of a cat box and the integrity of its contents, he announced that an election in 2022 would throw off the four-year cycle that was sacred to our democratic system. Instead, the future of the country would be determined, as the Founding Fathers decreed, by voters in the election of 2020, which would be held in 2024. People didn't know whether to be relieved or follow through on their plans for death with dignity.

KATE

RJ's piece revealing that soldiers disguised as counterdemonstrators had beaten up and shot protesters at Bears Ears under orders by the Great Leader landed in the failing *New York Times*, and then it was everywhere. I went to New York and up to his room at the Warwick, where he'd reached a state of pure mania, bouncing back and forth between the room phone and his cell. He was on fire, everyone wanted him and it was all too much, so I left.

He followed, reluctantly abandoning the phones as if they were crying babies who needed his attention.

As we walked to Central Park, he was talking faster and faster about sources telling him the government's plan to shut down all domestic protest. Bears Ears was a warm up for the Free Speech Initiative, which he believed was linked to the opening of reeducation camps. I finally said, "RJ, I have to go. This is your moment, and I'm in your way."

He said, "You can't leave. We're getting married."

I burst out laughing, not the most gracious response to a marriage proposal.

DAVID

My dad was busted down to one class at the university, and my notorious brother, Mickey, was either dead or on the lam after blowing up the psych center, and my uncle Garret and cousin Terence were running campus security like the SS, so maybe it isn't surprising I decided to go away to college—Columbia, where I got super focused on being a doctor and lost myself in the work. But every once in a while, something would yank me back into the world, like the shooting at my old high school.

People say, "I could never imagine it would happen here," but we all knew it was coming. Here's a surprise: the shooter was an isolated kid who spent every free moment in white nationalist chat rooms, got bullied at school, and had parents with guns they didn't lock up. He'd had a run-in with bullies from the Stop Bullying Now club and decided to fight back.

It shook me up, thinking of those familiar halls splattered with the blood of kids just trying to get through another miserable day of high school.

PAUL

It was getting to be a regular thing, visiting my mom's grave on Election Day when there was no election. For some reason, standing there in the cemetery, I'd remember the times when she was a real mom, taking care of me and laughing and telling me what a wonderful little boy I was and how happy I made her.

Not the way she was the rest of the time. A cold-eyed stranger.

DAVID

I was on what I thought was a date with this girl Sophie from my dorm. For me it was the first romantic possibility since I'd come to New York, for her it was an economy move, since her meal plan didn't cover the weekend.

We're at this joint Tacombi finishing our tacos, which she'd been inhaling like she was going to the chair, when I told her about the shooting at my old school. She stopped chewing long enough to say that the way to stop adolescent violence is by teaching kindness. Maybe because she'd made it clear she wasn't interested in me as anything but a casual friend who'd presumably pay for her tacos, I went off the rails and told her what she said was delusional, knee-jerk, liberal bullshit. Can mass shootings be stopped? Yes! And not through Kindness Workshops! Put serious limits on guns, up the age of purchase, get tough with background checks, and stand up to the Ruling Party's demonization of everyone who doesn't look and think like them. Since we don't even try to stop mass shootings, we must want them to happen. We have a fucking death wish. And a country with a death wish deserves to die. I went on for about ten minutes like an unmedicated Kanye or my dad during cocktails, getting more and more enraged.

I finally stopped, breathless, and Sophie was staring at me like it was a 9-1-1 situation. Then she said, "Jesus Christ, Dave, you and I really need to get to know each other better." College was so much more fun after that.

KATE

RJ liked bars even though he never drank, so we went back to the hotel. He ordered a burger, and I told him I needed time to think about his marriage proposal. He said, "Oh, just say yes, Katie, you know you're going to." The man never lacked for confidence.

I was on my third and final last drink when he was overcome by exhaustion. We went up to bed, and he was mumbling about how to fix the electoral college, and then he was asleep. Around 3 a.m. his moaning woke me. I called the front desk, and they got EMS.

ELLA

My old boyfriend, Tyler, had a sister wounded in the school shooting. I visited him and there weren't any words for what was happening, so we just held hands. It was such a surreal autumn with this sense of grief and panic and impending doom, we didn't think anything of the fact that we hadn't seen Isaac for days.

KATE

RJ's last hours were so consumed by pain, it was a blessing when he went.

DAVID

Kate and I were supposed to have breakfast at her hotel. I was in the restaurant thinking, how typical, I'm on time coming by subway from the Upper West Side, and she's late coming by elevator from the third floor.

There was a crush of media in the lobby, which didn't seem unusual. In New York you were always in the middle of breaking news. Then I saw her walking through the lobby, leaving.

KATE

RJ had OD'd, which I couldn't get my head around. He didn't drink or get high, and he went running every day in this sick, obsessive way, or maybe that's just what I think of anyone who exercises. I couldn't get through to the doctors, not being next of kin—although I would have married him, just as he said—and in the swirl of paranoia, anyone trying to get information about RJ was suspected of working undercover for the media or the government or the Russians or the right-wing fear machine or the socialists, so, I got ignored, which pissed me off.

I was headed out to escape the madness when David grabbed me and said, "Did you forget? We're supposed to have breakfast." He'd been in his airtight student bubble and had no idea what was happening. We went to the coffee shop, and I explained RJ's kickass story revealing the government's Putin-inspired strategy for smashing protest and the insane media onslaught and how he'd OD'd. But it didn't seem believable—like finding out Mickey bombed the psych building—and you think, what did I miss? Did I even know this person?

David listened to my rant and said, "RJ was poisoned." As soon as he said it, I knew it was true. That's why the doctors wouldn't talk to me; the overdose story was being concocted to explain why this suddenly major voice against the administration died in his moment of triumph.

DAVID

Kate thought it was a brilliant insight, but I was just going off what she said. She told me I was the smartest one in the family, and I was going to be an awesome doctor. She'd always been stingy with compliments, and it felt wrong to be wallowing in the wonder of me with her boyfriend having just died, but I couldn't help it.

I don't have a lot of those moments.

KATE

The only person who could have gotten to the truth of this mysterious death was the one who died. RJ would have made sure the autopsy saw the light of day, but I certainly wasn't up to the job. I didn't know what to do, so I stayed on at the Warwick and became friends with the bartender, Eddie.

One night he told me there was someone who wanted to talk to me. I didn't want to meet anyone who wasn't bringing me a drink, but he was right there at a booth in the corner, an anxious, tweedy guy nursing a Diet Coke. Turned out, he was a doctor who'd seen the toxicology report. They'd found traces of gelsemium, a rare poisonous plant used by the Chinese for assassinations. Also the Russians.

PAUL

When the investigation/cover-up was complete, the Great Leader looked straight into the camera and told us that RJ Manning did not die in vain, his death was a wake-up call. The brilliance of the Great Leader was that he could express compassion but convey the exact opposite: the *real* wake-up call was that it was now open season on journalists.

KATE

On one side, there was hard evidence in the toxicology report that RJ had been poisoned with a substance used by the Russians. On the other side was the Great Leader saying RJ had died of an overdose. The truth was a partisan issue and instant polls revealed the overwhelming belief that RJ was an addict whose death shone a harsh light on the pervasiveness of opioid abuse. They had the winning narrative so the Great Leader announced Project New Day to lead the war on addiction, featuring federal rehab centers all over the country, the first one honoring RJ Manning and bearing his name.

I was invited to attend the ceremony in the Rose Garden and I thought, will I ever get another chance to confront these sociopathic motherfuckers? But it would have conflicted with happy hour at the Warwick.

RUTH

I couldn't stop worrying about Kate and the war on journalists. There was only one person who'd make me feel both better and worse, which is exactly what I needed.

PAUL

She wanted to meet for lunch, probably so I wouldn't drink, as if I'd ever defer to the hands on a clock to make such a momentous, personal decision. I got there early, and she breezed in, her standard fifteen minutes late, looking effortlessly sensational, and it was just like old times except she'd fallen in love with someone else, and I was a bitter, aimless, has-been drunk. I couldn't get enough of her.

If I had to identify our major problem, it's that I was in love with her, and she wasn't in love with me. It hadn't always been like that, but she had somehow moved past the romance—hard to believe, although easier when I'd catch a glimpse of myself in a full-length mirror straight out of the shower—but she still liked me and that was something to build on.

She was upset about how journalists would respond to RJ's murder. Was calling out the Great Leader on his laughably obvious torrent of lies worth your life? Especially when much of the country seemed to have happily put down roots in his lunatic kingdom where up was down, and we could zoom back to the glory days of whiteness if we locked up enough brown people. If enough people bought the fantasy, did that make it real?

Were we the ones deluding ourselves with reality when it didn't exist anymore?

RUTH

I told him we should do this again, and he said, "It only hurts when we say goodbye." I watched him trudging back up the hill to his rooming house. He'd always taken long sabbaticals in his head, but now it looked like a permanent residency.

KATE

David found me in the bar, which didn't take much detective work. He said I had to go home because I was running through my money and Mom and Dad were upset and he was in the middle of his finals and tired of making up reasons why I wasn't home.

DAVID

Kate was all over the place emotionally, and she did the worst packing job since I came home early from summer camp (fake mono). But I think of that day with her in New York fondly because that's when I stopped being just the annoying little brother. And she liked that I always let her handle the talking part of the conversation.

RUTH

Kate moved in with Anjelica and me, which filled me with dread. She immediately reverted to the most unappealing traits of her adolescence, with sullenness, mood swings, crying jags, and point-less arguments. She never put a dish in the sink and always left the bathroom a wreck and sucked the oxygen out of every room she walked into.

Given what she'd been through, I didn't feel as if I could throw her out. But boy did I think about it.

KATE

It was great for Mom and me to spend time together. I wasn't ready to move back into the dorm, and it had been so long since the two of us could just hang out together. She and Anjelica had a life that was mainly about the baby—and let's face it, that's pretty boring—so they were glad to focus on me for a change.

I kind of dreaded telling Mom I was moving out because I knew she'd be disappointed, but she put on a brave face and im-mediately offered to help me move to the dorm.

RUTH

We were ecstatic when Kate moved out—we got our life back!— but I worried about her constantly. Leading her long parade of boyfriends going all the way back to middle school—starting with Timmy Field, who had a shiny, metal smile and was half her height—was RJ. We never met him, she wasn't with him very long, but by the way she talked about him, I have no doubt he was the love of her life.

ELLA

After the disaster at the General's last party, the lines were drawn between our families. We didn't even talk about Uncle Paul's family, except when it came out that Kate's boyfriend died of an overdose in New York. All my dad said was, "I can't say I'm surprised."

TERENCE

My dad was deep in his own head back then. You'd be talking to him, and he wasn't there. Part of it was losing Mom. But the thing he'd talk about when he'd been drinking was Mickey. How he got away with it. And it was pretty clear he blamed himself for how it went down. After a few drinks, when it was just me and him, Dad would say he was going to bring Mickey to justice. That's how he'd say it. "Bring Mickey to justice."

With my dad, the softer he talked, the more he meant it. I remember as kids we were never scared when he yelled. When he got quiet, that's when we knew we were fucked.

Whenever he talked about Mickey, it was like a whisper.

KATE

I knew Isaac needed me and wanted to start playing music again, but after RJ, I just froze up. I couldn't help myself, so how could I help anyone else? What I didn't know was that his mystery friend Neil from Bears Ears was at a Motel 6 outside town.

ELLA

I joined a Mommy and Me group which made me feel consistently inadequate until I met another young mom, Nandita. When the good moms were humblebragging, we were the bad moms, exaggerating our failures and confiding that our babies weren't really that special and generally trying to crack each other up.

They didn't like us, and we didn't like them, and there's no greater bond than that. Nandita wasn't married either, had disappointed her first-generation Indian parents, was gloriously vulgar, super smart, and obsessed with pop culture. She was much more American than me.

All it takes is one person who makes you laugh and suddenly your whole life is bearable.

KATE

After the shooting at my old high school, you'd hear "thoughts and prayers" from everyone in power like a Greek chorus of meaninglessness. The Ruling Party pledged to regulate the video game industry, since that was obviously the reason we were killing each other. Guns had nothing to do with it.

I was raging about this to Isaac, and it all ran together with my grief about losing RJ, and I failed to notice how he was taking it to heart.

ELLA

I was about to knock on Grandpa's door at Blue Hill when I heard Aunt Ruth's unmistakable laugh. What the fuck? The families were supposed to be at war, so what were the two of them doing together? I headed back down the hall, and Louise started to cry. She was just a baby, but she wanted to see her great-grandpa.

I once asked Nandita where she got the strength to soldier on, being on her own with a baby and no money and no job and no family, and she said, "I'm the biggest coward in the world. I'd like to crawl under a rock, but Chandi won't let me."

The last thing I wanted to do was go in that room, but I had to do it for Louise.

RUTH

When Ella came into the General's room, I thought, how did we get to a point where she's afraid to see me? I told her I was glad she showed up because after that disastrous family party I wanted to apologize for my bad behavior. She said, "You sure you can finish that in one day?" Louise put her little hands out to me, and I knew we'd be okay.

GARRET

I got a call from my brother Paul, which caught me off guard since we weren't on speaking terms after the party. He told me to turn on Wisconsin Public Radio, Meredith Mason's show. I figured it was some kind of music thing, but it was our senator taking calls about the school shooting. Then I heard my son Isaac's voice.

KATE

Isaac asked the senator what he'd do to stop the shootings if it was his own daughter Molly who was killed. The senator told Isaac to leave his family out of it. Isaac said, "That's what every family with a dead kid wanted—to be left out of all this. But they didn't have that choice, and you don't either, sir. Your daughter Molly never made it to her soccer game."

The senator's voice went cold. "What are you saying?"

Isaac said, "You need to know what losing a child feels like, so you'll take action and make it stop."

Meredith Mason jumped in to say this needed to be addressed off the air. Then she played a Fleetwood Mac song.

TERENCE

One reason my brother Isaac had such a hard time in life is he didn't lie. Can you imagine surviving ten minutes of high school without lying? Most people thought Isaac was making a point to the senator. My dad and I knew he was in deep. We just didn't know how deep.

KATE

I'm convinced they were able to kidnap that child because of Isaac's pure soul. Look in his eyes and you trust him. Molly, the senator's eight-year-old, was supposed to get picked up right after school and driven to the soccer game by a friend's parents. Isaac and Neil had been scoping out the situation, and Neil, who was some kind of techno genius, hacked into their email. He told the parents that Molly wasn't feeling well and would be going straight home.

When Molly came out of the school to get picked up, Isaac and Neil were waiting in their rental.

GARRET

I knew Isaac and this Neil guy had the senator's daughter someplace. I'm telling everyone in charge that it's my kid and I can help. They didn't want my help. They had it all figured out.

TERENCE

My dad and I found out from the news just like everyone else. They wanted people to stay away, but hey, it's my brother.

KATE

My mom and I watched it on TV.

Isaac and Neil were holed up in Neil's room at Motel 6. It was on the second floor, and the camera would zoom in on the room, and you'd see the little girl at the window in her blue soccer uniform. The reporter said the kidnapper wanted to make a public statement directly to the senator.

GARRET

By the time the senator got there, it was getting dark, with a smattering of rain, and there were bright lights shining on the second-floor balcony outside the room where they had the girl, like someone was putting on a show. The crowd was getting bigger and bigger, and the National Guard was there, locked and loaded.

Nervous kids with guns in front of a mob, good plan.

TERENCE

The senator was sitting in his limo, and the crowd was getting restless. They wanted the show to begin. I looked in the motel window and saw Isaac on the phone talking to hostage negotiators, then the senator got out of his car and walked across the parking lot and stood there all alone, looking up at the balcony.

The whole thing was blazing with light and people went quiet.

RUTH

Kate and I were sitting on the sofa barely able to breathe.

PAUL

Ted and I watched on the little TV in the den of the rooming house.

GARRET

The senator was standing there in the rain, waiting for something that wasn't happening, so he turned to go back to his limo. That's when the motel room door opened, and Isaac came out on the balcony.

I don't agree with what he did, but I know why he did it, making this crazy Hail Mary to stop the endless slaughter of children. Looking at him in that harsh light with everyone watching, what I felt was pride. He was doing something that was absolutely wrong, but he was a hero. Unlike that coward Neil who never showed his face.

KATE

Isaac was explaining that he wanted the senator to stand up for Molly and every other child who went to school in fear that it would be their last day on earth. It would take courage, but it could be done. And the only way the senator could understand the urgency of this would be to feel the loss of a child himself and know that being careful and trying to placate the NRA and the Great Leader and the Ruling Party was no longer an option.

This was his moment and he needed to act.

TERENCE

Isaac is standing in front of the window while he's talking to the senator. The senator is nodding like he agrees with Isaac, but he's moving to the side, real slow. Isaac's moving along the balcony to keep talking to him.

GARRET

I saw it. I saw what they were doing, and I screamed *NO!* People turned to me like I was crazy. They missed what happened.

TERENCE

As soon as Isaac moved away from the window, the girl was no longer in danger. That's when they started shooting. They didn't fucking stop, either.

RUTH

We couldn't look, but we couldn't turn off the TV. We ran into the backyard as if someone was chasing us. Kate kept crying, "It's all my fault." We stood there in the yard holding on to each other. Through the window, we saw the TV endlessly replaying the horror, and we were afraid to go back inside. It was Anjelica who turned off the TV.

GARRET

Isaac's death didn't kill me. And it didn't make me stronger. It gave me enough sadness to last the rest of my life.

TERENCE

When things are tough, my dad doesn't talk much. I mean, he never talks much, but in hard times it's down to, like, nothing.

That's how our family is. We went home and didn't say a damn word to each other. We didn't know how.

KATE

It was about the hardest thing I've ever done, driving over to their house. I knew Uncle Garret blamed me, and I had to face him sometime. It might as well be now.

I made myself get out of the car and go up to the house and ring the bell, and then I waited and waited for god knows how long. I was about to leave when Ella opened the door. She said, "I'm sorry, Kate, but you can't be here." I saw Uncle Garret watching from the stairs. No one has ever looked at me like that. Ella closed the door in my face, which was the end of everything.

I was driving home when I blew through a stop sign near our house and got blindsided by a seventeen-year-old boy in his daddy's Land Rover, who'd had a couple of beers and was showing off for his girlfriend. If only he'd been going a little faster, I'd have died. I guess you can't have everything.

RUTH

I was on my way to see Paul—fifteen minutes late, right on time— when I turned left on Franklin and saw Kate's demolished car on its side next to the road.

PAUL

After an hour, I knew Ruth wasn't showing up. I left the cafe for the last time and started up the hill. Another chapter finished. That's when she called.

KATE

We Americans don't believe we should have to experience pain—that's what we export to the rest of the world—and we've got the drugs to back it up.

In one afternoon, I went from being trapped in the hot twisted metal of my CRV with a massive physical shock that shut down my body to floating euphorically above the pain. I never felt a thing. People shuffled in and out of my room, and when I drifted up to the ceiling and looked down on them I couldn't stop laughing at how shaken they looked. Didn't they get that dying's no big deal? It's not exactly a surprise ending for anyone over the age of four. I kept looking for the ever-popular white light to move toward, but sadly, it never came. I was stuck with the annoying overhead light in my semiprivate room.

RUTH

It was the same hospital where she was born. That was where she came into the world, a colicky baby with a lengthy to-do list, and that was where her life was ending.

KATE

After days and days, I could pick up a few words from my visitors, and then the words formed sentences, and with grim resignation I could understand what they were saying. There I was, back on earth, hardly my favorite place in the universe, but what choice did I have?

part three

14. fall 2024

PAUL
(age fifty-five in 2024)

Just when we'd accepted that we'd never have a chance to vote out the Great Leader, he landed like a bloviating dirigible in the Rose Garden to announce that security measures were now in place to ensure the sanctity of voting, and we would at last have fair elections. He celebrated himself as if he'd just invented democracy, and his robotic stooges slapped hand A against hand B, producing a clapping sound as they'd been instructed in the Presidential Toady Workshop.

It was finally here, Election Day 2024.

RUTH
(age fifty-three in 2024)

It had been so long since anything had felt normal. That must have been why so many people wanted to believe we were back on track.

DAVID
(age nineteen in 2024)

Two weeks before the election, the candidate of the Opposition Party was arrested on a rape charge, a perfect example of how the terrible things the Great Leader knew to be true of himself were the things he found in others.

PAUL

Days before the election, the Majority Leader emerged from his dusty crypt to ram through the Great Leader's Big Beautiful Tax Act of 2024. Everyone who voted would get a giant tax rebate. This ham-fisted theft of the election was rushed to the Supreme Court, which approved the national bribe before adjourning to its annual Judicial Retreat and Golf Tournament at Mar-a-Lago.

KATE
(age twenty-two in 2024)

Election Day was always a big deal in town, but now it was over the top, a breathless orgy of flag waving and a celebration of all religions, as long as they were Christian, which suggested either ignorance or an ongoing belief in the Big Lie. Either was worse than the other.

ELLA
(age nineteen in 2014)

There was a parade with a marching band and speeches about the Constitution and a strange, violent pageant about Bunker Hill, in which brave white Americans defeated the British, who were portrayed by black people. I had to steer my uncle Paul away from it. As a historian, he'd have keeled over from a massive and justifiable heart attack.

There were long lines at the polls because if you didn't vote, you wouldn't get your tax rebate.

PAUL

Participating in this sickening red-white-and-blue circle jerk—this celebration of all the ideals that had been gleefully obliterated—was too much for some of us to bear.

RUTH

Of course, he won by the largest margin in history, which he would have claimed even if it wasn't true. But, sadly, it was.

PAUL

It wasn't until after the election that a closer examination of the Big Beautiful Tax Act of 2024 revealed that certain groups of people were ineligible for the tax rebate, including environmentalists, librarians, pediatricians, sculptors, yoga instructors, midwives, comedians, park rangers, mimes, herbalists, dog walkers, life coaches, glassblowers, vintners, psychiatrists, felons, architects, archivists, auctioneers, philatelists, podiatrists, social workers, branch managers, manicurists, software designers, social media influencers, character actors, folk singers, disc jockeys, safety experts, greeters, bouncers, literary agents, color commentators, magicians, optometrists, financial managers, managing directors, pitching coaches, tutors, editors, exterminators, wedding planners, fashion consultants, physicians' assistants, amateur thespians, professional gamblers, mediators, registered nurses, crossing guards, foot models, craft beer distributors, urban planners, pastors, restaurateurs, tattoo artists, bouncers, lactation consultants, photographers, journalists, photojournalists, public defenders, postal workers, acrobats, clowns, cartoonists, hair stylists, porn stars, graphic designers, executive assistants, guidance counselors, female impersonators, event planners, grief counselors, ornithologists, child advocates, performance artists, novelists, poets, screenwriters, bloggers, playwrights, journalists, advice columnists, memoirists, composers of atonal music, modern dancers, abstract expressionists, installers of solar panels, animal trainers, graduates of film school, organic gardeners, veterinarians, speech writers, neurosurgeons, sales representatives, game theorists, cartographers, facilitators, teaching assistants, chemists, nutritionists, bookbinders, travel agents, tax advisors, voice-over artists, masseuses, robot designers, tree surgeons, surrogate mothers, sommeliers, foreign exchange students, stuntmen, women referees, genealogists, regional planners, and the criminally insane.

Among the groups eligible for tax rebates were real estate developers, big game hunters, and golf pros. The Great Leader was hurt and angry that the Big Beautiful Tax Act of 2024 didn't bring the nation together. Once again, he was demonized by the fake media.

15. fall 2025

RUTH

When Kate returned to the university, I remember thinking how tough she is, how she has always been able to set her mind on something and make it happen. I never had that kind of ambition. Right after college, I got my masters in social work and ended up a therapist with a small private practice downtown. It was great in terms of being home when the kids got out of school, but for years I've been haunted by the notion that I should have done more.

Kate was different. She always had a maniacal drive, along with her many talents.

Anjelica and I invited her over for dinner, and she was almost her old self until she had a couple of drinks, and then she was slurring her words, rambling on about how she was going to be a lawyer and fight the power, and RJ would live on through her work.

It was all pretty grand and repetitive, and we couldn't wait for her to leave.

ELLA

One night, I saw the door to my bedroom slowly opening. I was too scared to do anything but lie still and hope Louise didn't wake up. Terence slipped noiselessly into the room and stood over me. Lying there defenseless, exposed, my brother's eyes boring into me, my childhood came back to me in a rush of buried memories. Not the adored-little-sister childhood we'd all agreed on: joyful Christmas mornings and carefree summer vacations in Canada and hot chocolate by the fire after skiing, all of it verified by photo albums and home movies and affectionate family stories.

No, what slammed into me was my real childhood. Terence hitting me, beating me, throwing me against the wall and me crying so hard he gave me a dollar not to tell Mom and Dad. I was such a good little girl, I jammed the abuse down into a secret place where I couldn't find it. And it worked, because our Christmas cards—along with Mom's cheery holiday letter exaggerating our many questionable achievements—made everyone feel just a little more desperate about their own small, imperfect lives. Why can't we be like *them?*

As a child, Terence was a daily disappointment to Dad and fit in nowhere, and I was the only person he could dominate. I suddenly understood why I'd maneuver not to be alone with him. Why I could never relax when he was in the room. Why I still had a discoloration on my knee from when I'd been thrown against a bureau as a child.

The grandfather clock in the hall downstairs was chiming 3 a.m. I kept my eyes closed and hoped he wouldn't kill me. I could sense him walking silently to check the closet and look under the bed, and then he was gone, gently pulling the door closed after him.

KATE

There is a moment when you could have resisted the smooth-talking seducer leading you into the darkness. You could have said no, I won't go with you—when he's whispering softly in your ear that he can make the pain go away— but you're hurting so much and you want to feel the bliss just one more time, so when he takes your hand you smile, even though he's leading you into blasted-out places you've never been, where you will do things you never imagined, and when it's too late and you've gone too far to find the way back, you'll see him for who he is, a cold-eyed monster who is bent on killing you.

And what you will remember is that moment when you still had a choice, when you could have resisted.

RUTH

I was getting ready to have lunch with Paul—running late, as usual—and I couldn't find the pearl earrings he'd given me on Valentine's Day a hundred years ago. I was about to give up when I realized all my best jewelry was missing.

When it hit me what had happened, I was so upset I had to sit down.

TERENCE
(age twenty-four in 2025)

When I got home from the war, I could work and carry on and make it through the day. I kept to myself and nobody knew. After Bobby died it got harder. I'd hear a sound and have to look in every room. Having a baby in the house took everything up a notch.

I had to make sure we were all safe. That was my job.

ELLA

I put a lock on my bedroom door. I couldn't have slept worrying he'd come in to check on me and Louise. One night, I was standing by the window rocking Louise to sleep. There was Terence in the backyard, in the moonlight, checking the perimeter.

I have never seen a lonelier man.

PAUL

We all pitched in to keep the rooming house free of dirt, rodents, and remorse. Tentative friendships formed, which isn't easy among people who have been let down by others or broken their trust, or both. Ted and I would take a leisurely post-dinner stroll to the park, and I'd deconstruct the political horrors of the day. He told the others that the professor was worth listening to, so a new evening ritual was launched—six or seven of us sitting around the fire in the living room, drinks in hand, as I held forth on my favorite subject, the great unraveling. With my reduced teaching load, I had time to do some serious preparation for these talks.

My makeshift class was pretty smart, featuring several grad students and alums who'd been hit with the contagion of bad luck wildfiring through the community and a motley collection of folks who couldn't live with their families but did just fine with the likes of us.

There was a lovely young woman, Julia, who showed up one night and made it clear she was just there until university housing opened up. By the time it did, she couldn't tear herself away from the fun we were having at 276 Brook Street. She heard me talk about how the Great Leader's much-adored fortune originated with his granddaddy's whorehouse and was raised to new heights by his racist slumlord daddy, all of which taught the Great Leader, at a tender age, that if there was ever to be love in his life he'd have to pay for it.

Julia promptly suggested filming my political raps to send to her brother Jack in Bangor, Maine. Go for it, I said, which means I have to take responsibility for what happened.

GARRET
(age fifty-eight in 2025)

My company's contract with the university was about to end, and I knew they were considering switching to OdinWatch, a big national security operation. We had blown it with the bombing at the psych center, so we had to be perfect moving forward. Terence is a sensitive guy, and he picked up on the tension. With him not sleeping, and everything else he was up against, it's probably not a surprise he overreacted after a football game.

TERENCE

The other team's fans are headed to their bus and there's a lot of drunk trash talking with our folks, and it's sort of good-natured and sort of not. I'm supposed to keep things under control.

Their mascot is waddling toward the bus in his owl suit, and our fans are yelling shit at him, and he turns and starts screaming this incredibly filthy stuff, cocksucker this and motherfucker that. It was upsetting to hear this from an owl, so I tried to get him to cool down and get on the bus, and he called me a "fucking psycho," which hit a little close to home. But I'm like, okay, man, just keep moving. He starts toward the bus, and then he turns and sucker punches me. I grab him and yank him toward the bus, but he's hard to hold on to because of the owl suit. I finally grab his beak and manhandle him onto the bus, and our fans start to cheer.

140

I thought it was no big deal but of course everyone got it on their phone, and some genius slowed it down and set it to music—"Some Enchanted Evening"—so it looks like I'm slow dancing with an owl. That's when it went viral.

RUTH

One evening in the fall, I was clearing the table and Anjelica was getting Gabriel ready for bed when I saw Kate coming up the walk, thin and tense as if she hadn't slept for days. I could feel my heart pounding and wondered if I'd have the strength to say what had to be said. She dropped down on the sofa and started talking about how hard it was being back in school. I told her she should take the rest of the semester off until she felt stronger. She said if she left she'd never go back, and frankly, she couldn't remember why she was doing it in the first place. "Why am I doing this, Mom? It's too hard."

Never in her life had anything been too hard. She said she wanted to stay with us until she could figure things out. I said, "Kate, I love you and I want to help you, but we have a problem. Some of my jewelry was taken."

She started to laugh. "Mom, are you accusing me of stealing your jewelry?" I told her I didn't know what else could have happened. She just sat there, blank, then she stood up and said there's no way she could come in this house ever again. She was crying when she headed for the door, and I stopped her and hugged her and told her how sorry I was and how stressed out we all were and how I never should have said such a thing, and of course she could stay with us.

I knew Anjelica wouldn't be happy, but we had to take care of each other, didn't we?

DAVID

Sophie and I were at a party with Columbia students drinking just enough, so they wouldn't worry about their future but could still get up early to study. Sophie was with a group watching something on a laptop. She called me over to check it out.

There was my dad on YouTube, whiskey in hand, giving a rant called "The History of the Future" in front of a maniacal crowd of misfits jammed into the living room of 276 Brook Street:

PAUL

Every time the Great Leader lied, his breasts would grow an inch. Needless to say, they were blooming like hothouse plants. At first, no one noticed, but then the protuberances became an unavoidable issue, so he was fitted with a special man-bra and, under repeated questioning from Fake News, one of the Great Leader's meretricious press tramps insisted that the Great Leader's breasts were perfectly normal for a stable genius of his age and anyone who thinks otherwise wants to hurt the Great Leader's chances of saving coal jobs and building a wall and Making America Great Again, the way it was when there were steamboats and slavery and pussies could be grabbed with impunity. But the breasts kept growing as fast as the Great Leader lied, so he stayed out of sight in Mar-a-Lago, although he was occasionally seen hunched over in a golf cart with Don King, Rodrigo Duterte, and a cheerfully lobotomized Lindsay Graham. His face could be glimpsed in a window in the White House with an eerie smile, waving mechanically, and rumors were rife on cable news about the size of the Great Leader's breasts, and finally his raging ego engaged in mortal combat with his fear of humiliation. The ego won and there's a rally estimated by his spokesbots to be 95,000 at a raceway in Georgia that seats 7,500, and with the entire nation watching, the Great Leader comes striding to the podium and the deafening cheers of his poorly educated followers freeze, and the raceway is in stunned silence at the Great Leader, his enormous pendulous breasts slapping against his mountainous belly, his orange hair ablaze in the spotlight, his skin a quease-inducing color not found in nature, and before he can speak, he hears the sound that has sent a chill down his spine since he was a desolate teenage racist bedwetter desperate for his Klansman Daddy's approval: laughter. It begins with startled chuckles and builds to a wave of insane hysterical howling, and finally an obese drunk seated next to his identical twin, both encased in "I'm With Stupid" T-shirts, bellows: "Show us your tits!" Others pick up the chant until the raceway is a crazed chorus of men, women, children, dogs, and ferrets, all howling, "SHOW US YOUR TITS!" And the Great Leader, ever eager to please his excitable base, unbuttons his specially constructed canvas shirt and tosses it to his inflamed followers, and there, for all the world to see, are the Great Leader's enormous swollen sweaty breasts, swinging free in the warm Georgia night, hanging below his bulging waist and growing ever larger as he reflexively lies: "This is the biggest crowd in the history of crowds!" He turns to address the screaming masses, but the sudden movement causes the monstrous, engorged breasts to swing hard and accelerate and spin him around, faster and faster like the dreidel game he adores playing with grandchild Arabella Rose, until the Great Leader is a mad blur of white breasts and orange hair and swollen heaving belly and wild, frightened beastly eyes, and his final plaintive thought before he careens off the stage to be stomped to death in the pit of hatred and resentment he created is: "Why are they laughing?"

DAVID

Sophie said, "What do you think of this guy, Dave?"

I said, "I think you're going to be meeting him at Thanksgiving."

TERENCE

I always kind of knew I'd get fired by my dad. The way he did it was weird, though, even for him. The two of us drive in to work together and he says, "Terence, I need to see you in my office." So we drink coffee and bullshit about the Packers' secondary and then he talks about how our town has been designated a Zero Tolerance Zone where it's unlawful for more than eight people to assemble, so the university has to take security up a notch, and my viral dance with the owl is a distraction in negotiations.

I finally say, "Dad, are you firing me?"

And he says, "Maybe I can bring you back if we get the contract."

He asks if I have any questions and I say, "Yeah, why didn't you just tell me at home?" He explained that he wants to keep work and family separate. As if, when we get home, I won't be wondering why my old man fired me.

PAUL

Once I hit on the feverish saga of the Great Leader and his bulbous breasts, word spread and the audience got bigger and bigger, until the living room at 276 Brook Street was jammed every night. People sat on the floor and hooted and hollered and asked damn good questions. I'd debate them and call them out and challenge them, and day by day I'd put more and more prep time into it. Even our landlord, Philips, would stop in. That was the first time anyone had ever seen him laugh. Ted, who used to fundraise for the Audubon Society and knew his way around shaking folks down for cash, would pick up pizza and a few cases of Old Milwaukee and people would donate what they could. My gone-rogue teaching style was perfect for a raucous, beer-guzzling crowd of loners in a rooming house during the dying days of the empire. I forgot about Julia, who was in there every night filming.

One afternoon, she found me on the porch rehearsing that night's rant and gave me a check for $9,678.81. What the hell? She explained she'd been sending the videos to her brother Jack, who'd started a YouTube channel that was blowing up. He called it *The Whiskey Hour with Dr. Paul Weeks.* It was nice he'd awarded me a PhD, much easier than the traditional route, but I couldn't understand why he was sending me the cash. What's with this jarring outbreak of honesty in our me-first-fuck-you era?

She told me Jack had no choice, having grown up in Maine, plus he was a full-time beekeeper and part-time clown, so he didn't need the money.

KATE

David turned me on to Dad's new career as an online professor and nutcase. My mom and I would watch it together and laugh our asses off. She said it was just like living with him, except you could turn him off when he got to be too much. Maybe an on-off switch would have saved their marriage.

16. winter 2026

LOUISE

I just want to point out that starting right around here, I'm old enough to remember some of what they're talking about. Four years old. It's kind of hazy, but the big thing is, at least some of the time I'll know if they're lying. Or twisting the truth a little. Up until now, I've had to just take their word for everything, even when I had my doubts. Which I did.

GARRET

When OdinWatch got the contract, we were sunk. I'd bet everything on working for the university, and there was no Plan B. I'd fired my own son for nothing, and now I had no job. The guy who handled the bids, Jim Bryant, felt bad the university was cutting ties with me for a big national company, so he asked if I'd stick around to help with the transition. It's easy to say yes when you have nothing else going on, but I didn't know he'd made that part of the deal. They had no choice but to hire me as a consultant.

PAUL

One night during the Q&A, a beer-swilling woman in back raised her hand—Kate. She asked why the Ruling Party was fighting so hard against environmental regulations, since they must be smart enough to know their own children will breathe the same toxic air and drink the same poison water as everyone else. I told her it was a mistake to assume any of them were even a little bit smart, but the reason they're hell bent on sucking every coin they can out of the earth is because they know it's too late. They have a good laugh watching us take out the recycling and put up solar panels and march in the streets, because it doesn't matter anymore. And the fact is, whoever has the biggest pile of money will be able to put off the deadliest effects of climate change the longest. Their children will wear the best gas masks and live in airtight domes and keep white civilization grinding on, while the rest of the world morphs into a fetid swamp of Big Gulp cups and sex toys and rotting bodies. Next question?

ELLA

I'd watch *The Whiskey Hour* in my room with the door closed. My dad and Terence would have melted down into a puddle of rage if they'd seen what Uncle Paul was up to. At first, I thought he'd snapped, but the more I watched, the more it seemed like he was the only sane voice I was hearing.

PAUL

Students from the U would show up at 276 Brook Street, and they'd tell me how lame the history department had become since I'd been busted down to just teaching the big sixties lecture. It was a teachable moment because I made them learn how to spell *schadenfreude*. They were lobbying to get course credit for attending my rooming house rants, which is what led to my old colleague Jody getting in touch. He was still running the department and wanted me to drop by and say hello after my lecture.

I was thrilled to see that Jody was aging miserably. His once-handsome face was mottled by an ominous stress rash, his beloved hair was falling out, and his paunch suggested third trimester. He looked battered and beaten, like he'd finished second in a cockfight, as he asked if I'd consider taking on more courses.

I like to think I'm good at lots of things, but I am truly brilliant at feigning genuine concern. I told Jody I cared about him and that whatever was going on in his life was certainly more important than my teaching career. He had no choice but to shine a light on the dank worm farm of his life.

A month ago he'd been overcome by uncontrollable crying jags, couldn't sleep or taste his food or correctly identify his children, and one night drove his car hard into the side of his house while bellowing "Born in the USA." So, he called a meeting with his lawyer, his accountant, his shrink, his herbalist, his aromatherapist, his stepfather, and his life coach, the upshot being he needed to cut back on his teaching, start meditating, sign up for kickboxing, and find a way to keep the students, faculty, and administration happy, so he could maintain his shaky perch as department head with the extra dollars it generated.

Bottom line? I was popular and he needed me to take over his classes, so he could make a run at regaining his mental health. As Jody put it, "Paul, you are the shit." I got all misty eyed.

Then I said no, just to watch his face start twitching. I told him I'd keep doing the sixties lecture.

RUTH

When Paul and I met for lunch, we talked to each other in a way that we couldn't when we were living together and raising kids and worried about money. We were inching toward a different kind of closeness. At first, it was amusing when Paul's fans would stop at our table. Girls would flirt pretty aggressively, considering I was sitting right there, and Paul ate it right up along with his BLT. I mean, who doesn't like a major ego stroke, especially in front of your estranged wife? But it was hard to have deeper conversations with people interrupting us to tell Paul how awesome he was. When I brought it up, Paul said, "You liked me more when I was miserable"—which was annoyingly true. His whole happiness thing was hard to take.

PAUL

The online rants made my lecture even more popular. The lecture hall was huge and there was never an empty seat. The university set up a video feed to the lobby so students could cram themselves in there and get a taste of the magic. It was pretty great being me.

RUTH

Driving through town, I saw Paul ambling along in the sunshine with this beautiful young woman. He'd cleaned up and was on fire, and she was laughing at one of his lunatic-but-deadly serious observations. With perfect clarity, I said, "I am the past." It was a godawful feeling.

KATE

Living at 117 Poplar, I'd see my mom go off on these dates with my dad and come back upset. Once she snapped, "It's so like your father that it takes the world ending for him to thrive." I suggested they get might back together, which pissed her off, but I think she was glad to have me around to talk to about this stuff. I mean, she couldn't have talked about it with Anjelica.

RUTH

Things kept disappearing, and I kept making excuses. I hated how weak I was with Kate, but I was afraid if I called her out I'd lose her forever. One night, I invited Anjelica to walk to the park with me and when she asked who'd watch Gabriel, I told her Kate was there. Anjelica said, "I will not leave my baby with an addict."

Paul and I never used that word, as if saying it would make it true. I started to talk about all that Kate had been through, and when I was done Anjelica said, "She must move out, or I will move out."

So there it was. I'd be alone in that house with Kate, who was stealing and selling everything I owned. I knew if I thought about it I wouldn't find the strength, so I went to her room but she was gone. Maybe she'd heard Anjelica's ultimatum and couldn't face that conversation any more than I could.

PAUL

Being an exceedingly minor local celebrity had its perks. I suddenly had money (which brought me back to the Knob Hill shelf in my liquor store) and fans and a smattering of transgressive fame, which meant I had to guard my time. And, since you didn't ask, yes, there were women suddenly interested in sharing my bed. That's all I'll say. Except, because you obviously won't let it go, I'll just tell you it was the most promiscuous period of my entire life. Now can we drop it? Thank you. Between sex and bourbon and exercise and podcasts and teaching, there weren't enough hours in the day, so something had to go. I chose exercise.

It was a perfect situation, until Kate showed up with a lovely self-invitation to move in to 276 Brook Street. I said yes before I considered the implications. Where would she sleep? What would it do to my rollicking new life as a rooming-house dandy?

I talked to Philips, who said she could stay temporarily (and for free) in my room. I said, "Philips, for a notorious tightwad, you're being rather generous." But I was actually a boon to his business, since we'd started charging five bucks to get in to the rooming-house rants, and I was giving him a healthy piece of the action.

KATE

The economics of dope are pretty simple. Every day you need to scrounge up enough cash to get high. My drug of choice—thanks to the generosity of my doctors following the car accident—was OxyContin, and when I'd run through what they bequeathed me, I was in no shape to face the wreckage of my life sober, so it was game on, and the pills weren't cheap. I had nothing approaching a job or a future, and at that point, I was too chicken to steal from anyone but my mom (testament to a solid midwestern upbringing), so I started singing on State Street.

It's hard to look your best when your life is consumed by hustling pills, which might be why my version of "Both Sides Now" really got to people: this raggedy chick is living it. I'd sing it twenty times a day and the guitar case would be littered with enough bills to finance a tender night of Oxy bliss. The cash was good but even better was the street community. We tried to take care of each other, as much as addicts can pay attention to anyone but themselves.

PAUL

It was awkward at first, rooming with my daughter, but we got along pretty well, especially when she wasn't there, which was most of the time. It was a brief, stolen father-daughter time we could share amidst the ongoing tumult of family and country.

KATE

There was this one straight-looking dude who kept coming back to watch me sing. He stared like he had some kind of interstate-sex-slavery scheme in mind or maybe just a boring job at a bank, but it creeped me out. Finally I asked him, "What's your deal, man?" He suggested we take a walk, and he'd buy me a panini.

We're sitting on a bench eating, and he starts talking about how I need to get off drugs. I thought I'd been doing a fine job covering. I mean, there were no needle marks (because I'd promised myself I'd never ever shoot up), and I played every set on State Street as if it was Carnegie Hall. It didn't fool Dean. He said he was a drug counselor, and he was there for me when I needed help.

Over the next few weeks he seemed less creepy, which is not the same as falling in love, but when he didn't show up I'd wonder why. I'm packing it in at the end of another day of busking brilliance when he appears out of nowhere, all serious in an *I-feel-your-pain* kind of way and suggests another walk, but this time there were no paninis on the menu.

We go to his apartment, which he shares with six others. We walk past a towering bald woman playing the cello and into his room, and he asks what drugs I've been doing. I tell him just the ones I can get my hands on. That's when he opens his sock drawer and gets out a baggie with a pretty impressive supply of black tar powder. "One question," I say. "What the fuck?" Turns out he used to be a junkie before he was a drug counselor. He tests himself every day, knowing the bag of smack is over there winking seductively if he's interested. That's how he knows he has control and can handle any situation.

He lays out a couple of fat lines, takes a deep breath, snorts one up, and says, "I have power over the drug, the drug doesn't have power over me. Do you want to show the drug you have the power?" I tell him I'm steering clear of heroin since the reviews suggest it isn't that future oriented. We talk for a while and then start making out in a chaste sophomores-in-the-back-seat-of-daddy's-Chevy Nova way, and then I do the other line. We do a few more, and there's this mellow wave of warmth— and dare I say love—that washes over me. I couldn't remember what I'd ever been worried about. I say, "I'm ready to declare my major. I've tried everything else but this is it."

Dean wanted me to stay the night but there was a gentle rain, the streets were glistening, and I wanted to walk and walk and hold on to this feeling as long as I could. I said, "Dean, if I sleep with you it will be transactional, like I'm just doing it because you gave me the smack. I care for you too much to do that." He was so touched, he almost cried. I thought, *Fuck, I am ordinarily pretty inspired in the deceit department but now I'm unbelievable, I should run for office.* As I'm leaving Dean says, "Don't do it more than three days in a row, Kate. It's all about control." I told him I was lucky to have my own personal drug counselor.

What could possibly go wrong?

PAUL

I was sitting in a big rocker on the porch of 276 Brook Street watching the rain when Kate came up the steps and sat in the rocker next to me. She was so warm and affectionate, almost the way she was as a child. I mean before she turned five, when she was done with all that. For years, there'd been a gulf between us, but that night we connected.

She wanted to talk about family, specifically my mother. She needed to know why our family is insane. I pointed out that every family is insane, every family defies belief. When you see a loving family, it's generally a prelude to an inexplicable bloody massacre that baffles the neighbors who tell Heather from Action News that they were fine upstanding folks who brought over a fruitcake every Christmas while caroling with their six adorable children.

KATE

My dad never talked about his parents. Like some vets are about the war, it was too traumatic to mention. But that night, when I fell hard for heroin, nothing in the world could be so bad we couldn't talk about it. There was something about the two of us on the porch in the middle of the night watching the rain that got him going when I gave a little push.

His mother was warm and loving when he was little but then she disappeared for what seemed like forever. When she came back home, she was different. Remote, shut down, with angry outbursts. She slowly became more herself and struggled to be the perfect mom she'd been before, making elaborate little lunches to take to school. And then she went away again. That's what my dad and Uncle Garret's childhood was: their mother shuttling in and out of their lives. When she'd come back home, she'd have a frantic desire to make up for lost time, and the intensity of her love was frightening. Then she'd be spirited away again. The brothers were told she was going to the hospital, but they had to figure out for themselves it was the Mendota Mental Health Institute.

When my dad was fourteen, his mom came home and made a point of going to his jazz band performances and Garret's football games. For weeks and weeks, she was the mother they remembered—laughing, full of plans, involved in their lives.

One Friday night, my dad tagged along with Uncle Garret and his friends when they went out to the woods and built a bonfire and drank beer. The brothers moved in different circles and it was a big thing that my dad was included. He tried to keep up with the others, drinking so much he got sick. When they got home past midnight, they could see the General sitting alone at the kitchen table. Garret said to my dad, "I'll do the talking, you try not to puke."

They go into the kitchen and the General just stares at them, and they're ready to confess everything, when he says, "Your mother took her own life tonight."

My dad broke down telling me this. All these years he'd connected getting drunk for the first time to his mother's death, as if he was somehow responsible.

PAUL

Kate got me to peer into the fog and I started to see the hazy shape of things I'd been afraid to look at. I thanked her, and she gave me a hug. Later, I heard her playing her guitar and singing random lines like she was writing a song. I remember one line she sang over and over: "He don't know fuck-all about jack-shit." Then she tried, "He don't know jack-shit about fuck-all."

I was hoping it wasn't a tribute to her father, but either way it was quite a night for both of us.

KATE

Those first weeks of heroin were a wonder. I was falling in love with my abuser. I slalomed through the fear, grief, and self-doubt that had crippled me and plunged into song writing for the first time since Isaac. There was a warmth and safety in those nights, with just me and my guitar and my drug of choice. I stopped worrying about the future. This life was all I needed.

Sleeping with Dean was a small price to pay for my fix. He was as responsible as any dope fiend / drug counselor, and monitored my intake, sticking to his one rule about not getting high more than three days in a row. That necessitated my finding another connection, Jake, whose one rule was maintaining clean needles, which was critical because he had talked me out of my one rule about never shooting up, which made snorting seem like a harmless weekend hobby as opposed to the magnificent, heart-stopping leap into the cosmos that a needle provides.

We all had our one rule.

PAUL

After a couple of weeks of Kate whipping up French toast for breakfast and flirting with the guys and making friends with the women, she'd become the hit of the rooming house. She'd told me it hadn't worked out living with her mother but didn't give any details. The small petty side of me—which, full disclosure, isn't small, it's a bottomless pit of greed, envy, and insatiable need—was secretly glad that Kate and I were forging this new relationship while Ruth was unable to handle our brilliant, headstrong daughter. Sometimes Kate came to my rants, sitting in back with a beer. Even when the whole room was rocking with laughter, she'd just stare at me. She'd always been a tough audience.

When my kids were little, I was the funniest guy in the country, Don Rickles with an open-ended run at the Sands. Every joke destroyed. Kate was the first one who said, "Dad, that's not funny." She was six. My heart stopped. I was bombing in my own living room. I knew I had to work harder on my delivery or get new writers, and then the other two followed Kate's lead, and man, they were tough, like I had the 2 a.m. slot on open mic night at Mister Chuckles Comedy Club and my darling, apple-cheeked children were bitter, dead-end, drunken hecklers who didn't want to go home. Vegas became a mere memory.

KATE

One night, we were sitting on the porch and dad was talking about how year by year the human race is hurtling closer to our sell-by date, yet we focus on everything except the simple, profound matter of our own extinction. "Denial is the biological X-factor that will send us the way of the sad, flightless, all-too-trusting dodo bird: when confronted by a basic choice, we choose two-day free shipping over survival of the species."

I watched him laughing and drinking, and I pointed out that he's never so alive as when he's talking about The End. He said he'd observed the same thing in me, an apocalyptic yearning, which he suggested could be genetic. "Well," I said, "that lets us both off the hook. We can't help our excitement at the end of everything. But, Dad, I think you're drinking too much. In your rant tonight, you slurred your words for the first time." He knocked back the last of his whiskey and said he didn't think a practicing dope addict was in any position to counsel moderation. I was surprised he'd noticed.

I said, "I guess we're in a race to the bottom, Dad. And you know how much I hate to lose."

157

PAUL

We had dueling interventions, both abject failures, and I started slipping into old patterns, like worrying until she got home. One night I was drifting in and out of sleep and suddenly it was 5 a.m. and she wasn't there. I got up and went out for a walk. It was dark and cold, and when I came back shivering and was about to go into my room, the door at the end of the hall opened and she came out of Ted's room. We stared at each other and she said, "Hi, Daddy," in a small, hopeful voice like a child.

KATE

What's wonderful about my dad is also his worst quality. He can be a pathological optimist even when all evidence points to the contrary. I tried so hard to fit in at 276 Brook Street but I was drowning. And he couldn't see it. Or maybe he didn't want to see it because then he'd have had to do something.

PAUL

That afternoon, I was in the first-floor cell Philips called the library, even though you had to bring your own books. I was reading a massive biography of Mussolini when Ted squeezed in. There were two big leather chairs facing each other in the tiny room, so when he sat down our knees were touching.

He announced that over the past month he had fallen in love with Kate and they had been, as he primly put it, "intimate," but now there was a problem he wished to discuss. I put aside Mussolini with only 737 pages to go and braced for an awkward disquisition on how the yawning gap in their ages would be mitigated by the redemptive power of their love, but it was even more awkward than that.

When Kate left his bed in the morning, she'd taken the engraved watch his father had given Ted when he graduated from Muhlenberg, gold cuff links from his second wife, an autographed picture of Alfre Woodard, plus over 300 bucks he'd saved from admissions to my rants (which he kept forgetting to split with me). I promised to look into it.

The two of us were trapped in our big chairs, and it took an acrobatic move straight out of the Moscow Circus for Ted to extricate himself. I knew I had to take action, and I deeply resented it. Why couldn't I spend more quality time with the one person I loved unconditionally who was currently scrunched in a leather chair alone in the rooming-house library?

17. fall 2027

PAUL

The Great Leader had grown tired of speculation about who would follow him as president. He summoned the gelatinous, chin-free majority leader to the Oval Office, closed the door, and when they emerged twenty minutes later, they smiled like two enterprising hitmen who'd found the perfect spot to hide the body.

DAVID

When Sophie and I heard they'd scuttled the 22nd Amendment, and there were no more term limits, we couldn't even pretend to be shocked. This is where it had all been leading, President for Life.

Anyone in his way would, of course, be killed. It was more important than ever for us to graduate and get out into the world where we could make some small difference.

GARRET

My coworkers at OdinWatch couldn't fire me, but they made it clear they didn't want me around, so they ganged up to get me to quit. My coffee mug kept disappearing, I had to keep switching offices, I was excluded from meetings, and I'd get invitations to office parties after they were over. My childhood was perfect training for all this. When they go low, I get stoked. Plus, I couldn't afford to lose the job.

One day, my supervisor came down to my freezing basement cubicle and told me I had an assignment at Abrams Hall. He thought I'd say no, and they could fire me. Think again.

PAUL

After Kate moved out, there was a rhythm to my life I hadn't enjoyed since I was a legendary, full-time, almost-tenured professor. The lecture hall was SRO, students jammed into the lobby watching the live feed, and I was on a roll, talking about how two of our most intractable national problems have been carefully nurtured by the Ruling Party.

In the 1970s, Exxon's own scientists had known about the effects of fossil fuels on climate change, but the company buried the data and engaged, along with the Ruling Party, in a campaign to sow doubt about the science, just as the cigarette companies had done with the link between nicotine and cancer. Simultaneously, the Ruling Party had exploited racial division through the southern strategy and dog whistles about crime and immigration, which evolved into full-throated racist appeals. I encouraged my students to consider the country we'd be living in if the Ruling Party and Exxon had gone public with the truth about climate change. The planet would be healing. And if the Ruling Party had pushed for racial inclusiveness and universal health care and voting rights, we'd have a thriving democracy and the Ruling Party might even be in control through a legitimate appeal to voters rather than a fascist assault on democracy and the rule of law.

That's when my microphone was cut off. Bomb threat? Fire drill? No, the problem was political. A campus security guard gracefully vaulted onto the stage. "Hello, Garret," I said.

"Long time no see." Garret said if I left quietly, I'd be okay. The problem, I indicated to him, was the screaming students, which meant nothing would happen quietly. He told me to ask them to leave, so I stepped up to the podium and pointed out to my class that university security was helping us by providing a real-time example of how the state violates not only the law but the spirit of our precious and endangered democracy, and the students' duty was to fight back or else the country is doomed, and they'll trudge through the rest of their days in thrall to an ignorant, narcissistic, authoritarian madman.

Garret was hustling me off stage. "Good career move, Paul, inciting to riot."

GARRET

They started trashing the lecture hall, then they spilled out onto the campus, joined by students pouring out of every building to be part of the protest. I called for security backup as it spun out of control. The police came with tear gas and then the National Guard was called in. We did what we had to do.

PAUL

It turned out to be the biggest protest at the university since Vietnam, and I was declared an enemy of the state. I hoped I was worthy of the honor.

GARRET

I took the hit for the protest, and for the first time since I left the army, I was out of a job. I thought that was unintended consequences on Paul's part, but looking back I'm not so sure.

RUTH

Kate came back home, dirty, dead eyed, unkempt, went straight into the kitchen, and found a plate of vegetarian enchiladas, which she started cramming in her mouth like a wild beast. I said, "Kate, this can't go on. You need help."

She said, "No, I need a family that loves me." I told her she had a choice. Go into rehab or leave.

She went to the door, turned around and said, "Take a good look, Mommy. This is the last time you'll ever see me." Mommy. Then she was gone.

DAVID

Sophie wanted to come home with me for Thanksgiving, but I've always felt that a first visit with one's father in prison is a special time and should be done alone. So, there I was in the waiting area at Racine Correctional, figuring my dad would be broken down and desperate, but when he showed up to see me, he was at the top of his game. Thanks to incarceration, he was finally following doctor's orders to exercise, maintain a regular diet, and stop drinking. He'd set up a discussion group for inmates who wanted a break from TV to talk about how mass incarceration serves the Ruling Party.

It somehow made sense that he'd be enamored with prison life. He stayed upbeat till I asked about Kate. I'd thought she was fine, based on her glowing emails. My dad said, "Fiction has always been Kate's *métier*."

KATE

It wasn't just Dean who broke up with me, it was all six of his roommates. They had issues with me ringing the bell at 3 a.m., and apparently when I was visiting I didn't always respect the personal space of the others, at least that's what the gargantuan bald woman with the cello told me when she was explaining why I was never to come to that apartment again or the police would be summoned. I still had enough dignity to demand that if Dean was dumping me he had to tell me himself, so the cellist went off to wake him up.

Dean came downstairs bleary eyed and apologetic, explaining that dating an addict was hurting his career as a drug counselor and he hoped we could still be friends. I told him since we'd never been friends, I wasn't about to start now, and the only reason I'd spent time with him was because he was a dependable connection. It felt good to be so mean with Dean, blinking in his pajamas, but then I realized he was crying, which struck me as totally unfair. Wasn't I the wronged party? Shouldn't I be the one crying?

But I knew I'd hate myself even more if I walked away, so I hugged the cowardly two-faced son of a bitch, who, I was shocked to discover, I had come to like.

ELLA

Being a mom got a lot easier once I realized that everything I did was controlled by someone with an unformed brain who was inarticulate and unspeakably selfish. It was as if I'd given birth to the Great Leader except, unlike him, Louise was smart and warm and funny and endlessly curious about the world around her. I would die for her if need be.

I was thinking this way because of the danger that was lurking in the dark corners of our house and coming to a boil in the world she'd soon have to enter. One night, late, I heard Terence moving through the house, his footsteps loud and abrupt. He's in a panic, I thought, and then he was pushing on my locked door, and I said as firmly as I could, "Terence, do not come in here." He moved on down the hall, and I heard my dad's door open.

GARRET

Terence couldn't find his gun. He was terrified that someone had taken it and was going to kill "Baby Louise," who was five years old. He was so wound up, I told him not to worry about his gun because I had it. Then it all came spilling out, how I'd fired him from the company and ruined his life and somehow I was responsible for his mom dying, and then he came at me.

ELLA

Louise heard her adored uncle and grandpa fighting, and she started crying, but it wasn't a child's cry, it was a wail of anguish from the depths of her soul, as if she knew her safe and happy world had come to an end and life would never be the same.

GARRET

We both went crashing to the floor, and he got his hands on my throat demanding to know where I hid his gun, and I thought, *Is this where it ends? After all the horrible shit I endured in the army, my own son chokes me to death in the family room?* When he heard Louise cry, his whole body sagged and his hands loosened on my throat and we hugged.

TERENCE

That's the only time my dad ever hugged me. All it took was me trying to kill him.

ELLA

Louise was in charge of my much-needed assertiveness training. Before I was a mom, I was so sickeningly eager to please I'd hide in my room to avoid a confrontation. Now I'd look at Louise and think, "We're coming through so everybody needs to get the fuck out of our way."

That morning I went down to the kitchen where my dad was making coffee and Terence was sitting at the table checking sports scores on his phone. There was this awful heaviness in the air and I thought, these two jag-offs are so shut down they could just motor on through the day and never talk about what happened last night.

I said, "I will not allow Louise to grow up in this house."

TERENCE

It got real grim after they left. My dad was out hustling work and I'd get up late, walk all over town, and come back when it was getting dark. We'd go days without seeing each other. One afternoon, walking past the VFW, I started thinking about Bobby and how fucking much I missed him, so I went in to have a beer in his honor. I ended up honoring him a whole lot more than I planned, and just when I was about to leave, this black guy in a wheelchair, Ronnie, came rolling my way. He started talking about the new bartender, Floyd, like we was already in the middle of a conversation. Once I got a word in, I couldn't stop. I apologized for running my mouth, telling Ronnie how I was living with my dad, but him and me didn't talk, so I was making up for the silence.

Ronnie remembered Bobby from the VFW, and we toasted him a whole lot more. Ronnie was living with his mom and said it would be fine if I moved in with them. He let on she was the opposite of my dad, she never shut up, which was a different kind of problem. It felt good to be welcome someplace, even on the couch of a drunk stranger.

GARRET

Terence's stuff was gone, so after a few nights, I figured he had another place to stay. Ella texted to say she and Louise were living with her friend Nandita. I texted back that Terence had moved out, so it was safe to come home, but she didn't even respond.

I could hear Hadley saying, "Now you've done it, baby." Without the kids around, her death got real in a deeper way. I looked ahead in time and it scared the hell out of me.

I'd be out all day trying to rustle up a job, and at night I'd be visited by the people who weren't there: Isaac and Hadley who'd passed, and Ella and Terence who'd jumped ship, and Louise who I couldn't think about without tearing up.

The one I always came back to was Mickey. I prayed he was alive, so I could find him and bring him to justice. If I couldn't do that, then my whole life would be about one thing: not stopping the bombing when I could have. I couldn't go to my grave with that on my conscience.

With no job, I started doing my own investigating. I'd go by the police station so often it was like I worked there. They were glad to see me, at first. But I kept pushing, and they got short with me, and finally they'd act like I wasn't even there. The three other bombers were doing time, and that was enough for the cops. One of 'em finally told me I oughta face up to the fact that Mickey was dead. I told him he was wrong. Not that I knew for sure.

I stopped spending so much time with the local police. It was pretty clear they'd moved on. I couldn't move on. We live by the rule of law or we don't. And if we do, that meant finding Mickey wherever he was.

I finally managed to land a bullshit position back at Odin-Watch. Minimum wage to patrol the campus with rookies in their twenties. It was an insult but I didn't care. For the first time in my life, I was afraid of being alone.

TERENCE

Ronnie's mom talked faster than any human I ever heard, and she never stopped. But it wasn't just babble, she knew a mountain of shit about everything. I learned a lot drinking coffee at the kitchen table listening to her chatter on. Her laugh was so loud, the first time I heard it I reached for the gun I didn't have.

Ronnie said she used to teach English at the high school and was pretty normal, but when he got blown up in Iraq she turned into this monster caregiver. Ronnie had been all set to throw in the towel but she made him keep living. He didn't get a vote.

She ran a tight ship. No more bullshit walks around town, there were chores. We'd complain like we were nine-year-olds who had to clean our rooms, but we did everything she said. She had me doing odd jobs, fixing things around the house and cleaning up the yard. Ronnie did a killer impression of his mom, so after she gave me my marching orders and went about her business, he'd repeat the orders with a bunch of "dumb fucks" and "lazy pricks" mixed in, like he was the funniest kid in middle school.

One day, after she put me on yard detail, he finished his dirty imitation of his mom and she called from inside, "You know I can hear you, Ronnie." She was about the size of a salt shaker, but we were afraid of her.

ELLA

I always assumed I'd go to college and find something I was passionate about and meet an awesome guy and have kids and become a big success. But everything happened in the wrong order.

I met the wonderful guy and he died. Then I had a kid and didn't go to college, and never found that thing I was supposed to be so passionate about. I was living with Nandita and our kids and we survived, but shouldn't life be about more than just getting by?

TERENCE

I'm driving back to Ronnie's house with his meds when I stop at the light on Prospect. For some reason I look at the car next to me at the exact moment the driver turns my way. It's Isaac. He's got that half smile he had as a little kid, like he knew something he couldn't explain. My first thought is, Isaac doesn't have his license. Then it hits me: Isaac is fucking dead. And maybe I'm insane or drove into a different reality, but I know for sure that's him.

The light turns green, Isaac drives on, and I'm frozen until the asshole behind me swerves around and cuts me off and Isaac's car disappears into traffic. I floor it, and there's a flashing blue light so I pull over, figuring it will only make matters worse to tell the cop I'm trying to catch up to my dead brother who isn't a very good driver.

ELLA

I'd think about poor Terence struggling through every day, lost in his head, and feel guilty I didn't even know where he was. Maybe the reason I hadn't done anything to help him was because of what he'd put me through as a little girl. Nandita said, "If I were you, I'd probably be glad that he's suffering." As soon as she said it, I knew it was true. I told her I was going to be a better person, and she said, "Does that mean we can't be friends anymore?"

KATE

Robert Frost was a liar. He said, "Home is the place where, when you have to go there, they have to take you in." He left out: "Unless you're a raging dope fiend." I had no place to go. I tried crashing at the dorms but the ID thing was stricter than in the old days, the penalties rougher, and everyone was afraid of getting busted in a Zero Tolerance Zone.

One night, a homeless guy in a top hat told me about a new food source. I followed him to the Franklin Café, and he led me around back to the dumpster where we dined on preowned cheeseburgers. It started to rain and he turned to me, chewing furiously with teeth that were mostly a memory, and said, "It's a fucking hard life, but at least we stopped the socialists from taking over." He'd been foreman in an auto plant and was a huge fan of the Great Leader, whose trade magic resulted in the plant shutting down, which wiped out the guy's savings, destroyed his marriage, and dropped him down in a parking lot in the rain with a used cheeseburger and a hopeless dope addict. But didn't this beat the hell out of whatever the socialists would do?

TERENCE

Driving back to Ronnie's house with my speeding ticket, I tried to make sense of seeing Isaac. I was on the edge of something. Either I was going to be saved, or this was the end. I was fine either way.

18. spring 2028

PAUL

I got released in April. I'd made the most of my time in jail, and, having beaten the evil scourge of alcohol, I was more than ready to celebrate with a drink or two. It was a fine spring day when I Lyfted back to 276 Brook Street, where Philips was installing bulletproof windows. I'm sure he was glad to see me, but he hid it well. "Things are different, Paul." And they were. The old gang had moved on. Ted had joined a monastery: decent grub, a strict but fair deity, and an oath of silence, which freed him from the pitfalls of relationships and the English language.

I parked myself in the living room, the scene of past glories with *The Whiskey Hour with Dr. Paul Weeks*, and looked forward to the annoyance of getting bothered by my fans. But there was a new crop of shattered residents shuffling through, clearly over-matched by life in these United States. Julia suddenly appeared, anxious because her friend with a truck was late. She was finally moving into a dorm, which had been her original plan until she fell victim to our rooming-house hijinks. I asked about her brother Jack and whether we could crank up the online rants, but she said he'd recently been named one of the top five clowns in Belfast, Maine, and was going all-in on his clown career, which left no time for beekeeping or YouTube.

Julia kept furtively looking around as she whispered to me—well aware that students could get a generous tuition waiver for informing on enemies of the state—that she was hoping to transfer to Bates because the university was no longer the one she'd applied to. The Great Leader's travel ban meant talented international students could no longer get into the country, campus protests (you're welcome) led to martial law, and now the university, along with other college centers of the resistance, was facing the Educational Freedom Act of 2028, mandating a curriculum in line with the stated goals of the country, which meant the feckless ravings of the Great Leader would be drilled into the fertile minds of students all across the nation. "The Tweets that Shaped America" would no doubt turn up on a syllabus before long.

My salad days of rooming-house rants were over. 276 Brook Street had become a target because it once was a hotbed of the resistance, which is why local Red Hats would drive by howling racist slogans and shooting at the building in support of America and all it now stood for.

RUTH

I met Paul for lunch, feeling guilty I'd never visited him in jail. But we couldn't talk about anything remotely personal until after he held forth on his latest theory. He was convinced that time was actually speeding up. So many changes were coming at us—technological breakthroughs, cataclysmic events, and the cosmic vibrations of the planet—that our perception of time was being transformed. We're leading a dog's life, moving more and more quickly from infancy to adulthood to old age to death, and while we fully experience each stage, it slips by faster and faster in an increasingly mad rush. In the 1920s, life expectancy was shorter but the experience of life was longer. He thought, with this acceleration, we were hurtling toward the end of the species or at least its transformation into some kind of digitally enhanced creature that was no longer quite us—one of his favorite themes, which for some reason always made him laugh.

PAUL

I told her we'd kicked the shit out of the Cro-Magnons and the Neanderthals and all the other competition, tamed the land, and built a world to satisfy our every craving, which meant, with our superior strength and intelligence and nothing in our way, what doomed us was our own selfishness. Nothing could stop our ravenous appetites, not religion or government or war or yoga or violence or love or paleo or porn or 12 steps or smoothies or cross-training or cross-dressing or cannabis or simple good-will. We had to have it all, and hence would have nothing. Our lives would spin ever more quickly, warping time, and the story of humanity (abridged)—which started when our brains got big—would end with the last human, a bald, toothless, grizzled three-year-old of indeterminate sex, moaning and whimpering as it gummed its way through a soggy Big Mac next to the silent, empty 405 freeway before rolling on its back, choking on its own vomit and expiring—fade to existential black, a fitting coda to a species that probably should have sought professional help somewhere along the way.

RUTH

I said, "Paul, the problem with lunatics is they say just enough that makes sense so you buy the whole deal, which is a huge mis-take." He liked that. And then we were able to talk like any other separated-but-still-in-love-couple-with-troubled-kids-and-a-same-sex-relationship-who-wish-they-could-change-things-but-don't-have-a-clue.

I told him Kate had been living with me, but I threw her out because she was stealing, but, pathetically, I'd have put up with it if Anjelica hadn't threatened to leave. Paul admitted he'd thrown her out after she slept with his friend Ted and stole his stuff. Neither of us knew where she was. Paul said, "Either this is tough love or we are the worst parents in the world."

KATE

One lost day on State Street, I was playing "Bridge Over Troubled Waters" (by request of a moon-faced Baby Boomer), with a better chance of hitting Powerball than the high notes, when a well-dressed woman stopped. She said, "Katie, you probably don't remember me, I'm your mother's friend Pam Rayner." Of course, I remembered Pam. Big house, perfect life. Pam was also genuinely nice. She asked how I was doing, which seemed obvious since I was so thin a decent wind would carry me away, passersby averted their eyes, and, dead giveaway for the perspicacious, I hadn't bothered to cover up all my needle marks. "Perspicacious." I blame my parents for words like that rattling around in my cranium. It's their fault I never wrote a hit song: *"If I'm so perspicacious and you're so mendacious, why don't you steal my love?"*

Pam was watching my blank face, waiting for my response. I was surprised to hear myself describe a rewarding life of taking courses at the university, dating a wonderful grad student, and playing music for the sheer joy of it. Pam squeezed my hand and said, "Katie, I have a guest house if you need a place to stay." She wrote down her phone number and put twenty bucks in my guitar case.

I was surprised to see that I was still capable of embarrassment.

ELLA

Nandita never acted as if things were great. We were two young mothers with no college, no job skills, little money, estranged families, and nonstop stress. All of which added up to more laughs per day than I'd ever experienced. We worked when we could and took care of each other's kid and had dinner parties where the guests brought everything. We'd tell them twelve people were coming and invite six, which meant high-quality leftovers for weeks. Nandita made me realize how much energy I'd wasted pretending things were better than they were. Why? So other people wouldn't worry? What about telling the truth and letting them live with that?

DAVID

One night, late, my phone's buzzing. I answer it half asleep, and this voice is talking to me with all the sincerity of a robocall. I'm about to hang up and go back to sleep when I realize it's my uncle Garret. He's asking me about school and whether I like New York. Huh? He had never ever called me. So we're talking on the phone for the first time, having this weird, stilted conversation, like a job interview headed south, and then he says, "David, I'm wondering if you've heard from your brother Mickey."

So that's what this is all about. I'm thinking, *Even if I had, I sure as heck wouldn't tell you, Uncle Psycho.* Calling me in the middle of the night to lean on me to give up my brother. But I was polite. I said I hadn't heard from Mickey but if I did, he'd be the first one I'd call.

KATE

One gloomy morning, I wandered into a pawnshop called Rick's Olde Gold with my guitar. It was too cold to sing on the street, and I needed fast cash. As soon as I stepped in the door, I was blindsided by the memories. When I was in high school, Glenn and I would prowl around this shop in search of weirdities. I remembered how excited we'd been panning for coolness, but now it was a straight-ahead transaction: a fistful of bucks, and my beloved guitar was gone.

As I walked out into the slush, I knew I was entering a new phase, giving up the last thing I cared about in order to get high.

ELLA

Terence told me he had to get out of his friend Ronnie's house because his mother never stopped talking. He'd been sleeping in his car to get some peace, but Ronnie's mom would come outside in the middle of the night and bang on the window, and when he opened it she'd be midsentence with no sign of stopping, so even the driveway wasn't safe.

Then he told me he'd seen Isaac stopped at a traffic light on Prospect. That's when I realized he was in serious trouble. I asked if he was scared when he saw him and he said, "Why would I be scared of Isaac?" I told Nandita that Terence needed help, and she immediately said he could sleep on the sofa till he figured out his next move.

GARRET

I was patrolling the campus late on a cold afternoon, and it was so quiet I thought the university was on a break. Then I realized we'd been back for a week. I never got called anymore to break up frat parties or bust kids skinny dipping or stop a protest or a bar fight. Students stayed inside and studied now.

And they weren't allowed to gather in groups of more than eight.

I trudged over to the security office, punched out, and all at once it hit me hard. What the hell had happened to my life? I had to sit on a bench till my heart stopped pounding. I couldn't go home to that empty house. I thought about the Hampton Inn, then called my daughter.

ELLA

I open the door, and there's my dad trying to smile, a sad, middle-aged guy with a little stuffed kangaroo for Louise.

TERENCE

When Ella told me Dad was coming over, I said I'd leave. She told me I had to stay for the sake of the family, which got me riled. The family? Seriously? The doorbell rings, Ella gets it, and I'm shaking. Nandita came up behind me, put her hands on the back of my neck, and I felt this warmth all over my body. It was like she had some kind of mystery healing thing going on. She whispered, "Terence, if you think your father's a dick, you should meet mine."

So when my dad comes in with this kangaroo, I'm smiling and feeling like I can get through this. I said, "Thanks, Dad, how did you know I like kangaroos?" He hesitated, like I might be serious or, more likely, seriously nuts, and then he laughed and we were good. Well, as good as we ever were, which wasn't good. Then Louise came tearing into the room yelling for my dad, who scooped her up.

He had a hard time not crying.

ELLA

After dinner, when Terence was reading to Louise and Chandi in the other room, I told my dad I'd hit on the idea of getting a service dog for Terence. He was all over the idea. He'd have been all over anything I suggested at that point.

PAUL

The Great Leader loved everything about campaigning: the blazing spotlight that followed him everywhere, the vicious attacks on his opponent, the raving psychotic madness of his rallies, the triumphant display of his racism, misogyny, ignorance, and rage, which was guaranteed to inflame the opposition and fire up his weary base.

But the election of 2028 was different. With the Opposition Party in disarray, the liberal candidates were too easy to humiliate. The press had been beaten into submission, leaving only the soggy, ceaseless fawning from Fox, which had grown stale even to the Great Leader. The rest of the world kept a wary distance from the all-powerful, untrustworthy man-baby watching television in the Oval Office, who could make a promise and break it in the same incoherent sentence.

The Great Leader went to bed early on election night. The excitement of past elections was gone. The next morning, he surveyed his kingdom. He had won, again and again and again, and with no enemies worth attacking, he was bored and unhappy. During a commercial break, he wearily called his favorite toady at the US Fish and Wildlife Service to get the latest casualty count in the War on Endangered Species. Good news! He was tired of winning, but he still had a job to do.

19. spring/summer 2029

DAVID

My med school graduation took place on the hottest May 12th in recorded history, a pleasing 118 degrees. They rushed through the ceremony, but people were fainting before we finished the Bs. For eager young doctors, it was good practice reviving our fallen parents. I was surprised that both of mine showed up. I'd given up trying to figure out the shifting currents of their relationship, but they seemed comfortable together. Mom said Anjelica had wanted to come, but it was more risky than ever for people without papers since the Great Leader was hell bent on arresting and jailing every noncitizen. His latest executive order was a national population goal called "One Hundred Percent Pure" (OHPP), which was, for him, a more noble mission than ending war, poverty, and hunger combined.

After the graduation, the four of us—my parents, Sophie, and I—ended up at the Lion's Head Tavern, drinking beer. After the first pitcher, my mom asked when I'd be coming back home. I asked if she was assuming I'd be moving back into my bedroom at 117 Poplar with the *Star Wars* wallpaper, and my dad said, "You got that right, David."

My mom was always at least a year behind where I was in my life. When I was a kid, she always bought clothes for the smaller person I used to be.

PAUL

David had always been in a hurry. He couldn't wait to get out of high school, so he graduated in three years. Then he worked

179

right through the summers to get out of college in three years. And here he was getting out of med school in record time. Like anyone paying attention, he knew he had a limited amount of time to get things done.

RUTH

I worried about David staying in New York City, but he and Sophie had big plans, which they wouldn't tell us. Growing up, David was the most normal of our children, but now he was a mystery, which was why I kept asking him questions.

Paul accused me of nagging, but I looked at it as healthy parental interference—I mean interest.

DAVID

I learned long ago not to tell my parents much that mattered. They'd get too excited by remote possibilities and too upset by small disappointments, then I'd have to help them through their massive overreactions instead of just dealing with it myself. Plus, my siblings provided them with all the family drama they could handle. I didn't even tell them about Sophie until she and I were on solid ground, and when she got sick, I didn't say a word.

It was a year before we graduated, and she was having these stabbing stomach pains, and no doctor could help. This went on and on, and she finally went to see a woman, Bryce, who was involved in Eastern medicine, herbs, energy fields—everything our fellow med students found laughable. The day Sophie realized her pain was gone, she took a deep dive into alternative medicine.

One night we hit on the idea of a storefront clinic. According to the Great Leader, "If we give everyone health insurance, they'll just want to get sick," so there were many people whose medical plan consisted of hoping for the best. Our notion was to provide face-to-face, walk-in, pay-what-you-can, Eastern-Western health care. We spent a whole lot of time trying to decide what we'd call it. We finally settled on a small blue neon sign that said, "Heal."

PAUL

During sweeps week, NBC rolled out five straight nights of *The Reckoning*, a fictional trial of the Great Leader. It was thrilling to see his criminality openly debated on TV, and it got enormous numbers because actual news was under tight control from the FCC. But this was fiction, which allowed it to be true, and every night we watched the Great Leader finally being called to account for what he'd done to the country. On the last night, when record numbers of viewers assembled to learn the verdict, NBC was suddenly taken off the air for treason, leaving a breathless nation watching an ominously blank screen. The FCC had allowed *The Reckoning* to build a massive audience so that yanking the license would get maximum attention. In short order, ABC and CBS were suspended for their coverage of NBC. Years of dedicated presidential ass licking proved a shrewd investment for the simpering sycophants at Fox News, which by default became the government news source, Fox State News.

The chill was immediate. Cable stations were put on notice, and jokes about the Great Leader became toothless and affectionate. He was now our beloved uncle, a bit eccentric and vulgar, who had—like most cowards—an unquenchable thirst for violence. His sociopathy was repurposed as lovable character quirks for the home audience. With honest political reporting off the menu, the networks gloried in bold and hard-hitting takes on pop culture. The Kardashianization of America was complete. The average citizen might be uncertain of the identity of the attorney general (*acting* attorney general, for swift and humiliating dismissal) but had up-to-the-moment knowledge of which pantyless celebutante had been busted for doing a headstand on top of her pink Bentley after being denied entry to her ex-girlfriend's memorial service, following her tragic death during an after-party game of Russian roulette with the most recent cast of *Survivor: Syria Edition*.

Celebrities, and people who went to high school with celebrities, and neighbors of celebrities, and people who had sued celebrities, and celebrity look-alikes, and people who had *dated* celebrity look-alikes all sold the rights to their lives, and cameras would follow them everywhere so people who tragically had no connection to celebrities could sit home watching their favorite celebrities or near celebrities or future celebrities sleep or eat or watch other celebrities on TV, who might be watching other celebrities on TV, who might be watching other celebrities on TV.

Every night, Americans washed down their antianxiety medication with a brimming tumbler of Fireball and settled in to watch each other, hoping to find someone whose life was still worth living.

TERENCE

All the service dogs were super trained and knew a hundred commands, and the longer I was there the more I couldn't make up my mind about which one I wanted—which triggered massive self-doubt. I couldn't even do *this* right? Then Jarvis caught my eye. A black lab. Calm like I wish I was. A fucking beauty. We took a walk and that was it. Ella asked why I chose him, and I said, "The dude gets me."

After a week with Jarvis, I got more sleep than I'd gotten since Afghanistan. He did my job, checking the perimeter, making sure everyone was safe, and when I was upset or scared or having a nightmare, he was there. I told my dad I made the right choice with Jarvis, and he said it looked like Jarvis had chosen me. Either way, I had to take my game up a notch to be worthy of him.

ELLA

After dinner one night, Terence is on the sofa in the screened-in porch with Jarvis, listening to the Brewers game. I always loved sitting out there after the rain, but Terence had gotten there first, and I was careful not to be alone with him. I start upstairs and then I think: *Stop! I am so done being a victim. That is the single lousiest thing I could pass on to my daughter.* So, I grab an Old Milwaukee and go to the porch. We listen to the end of the fourth inning, more nothing from the Brewers, and during the break he thanks me for Jarvis. I tell him it wasn't easy, and he launches into a riff about the endless, spirit-crushing, bullshit paperwork dealing with the VA, and I say, "I'm not talking about the VA, Terence—it wasn't easy for me to help you because of what you've done." He starts to explain about his PTSD, and I take a monster slug of my beer, and after all those years make myself say it: "Terence, I'm talking about what happened long before you deployed. When we were children, you and me."

We sit there in silence. The fifth inning is starting, and he's struggling, and I think, fuck you, Terence, I'm not going to help you out, deal with what you've done. But he can't. He sits there, cold, angry, shut down. I see the enraged little boy in his eyes and I think he's going to hit me. And maybe he would have, except Jarvis starts gently rubbing his snout against Terence's leg. Terence's face starts to relax and then his whole body sags. He finally turns to me and says in this small, broken voice, "I can't forgive myself for that."

I take his hand and say, "Well you fucking better find a way, Terence, because I'm not going to lose another brother."

TERENCE

Everything got better once Jarvis came along, but he couldn't help me figure out what to do with my life. One night, I ask Ella what she thinks our mom would want me to do, and she says, "Get an education, which you could do for free on the GI Bill." So, I checked it out and found out I had to take a remedial writing class. I said fuck that, but Ella begged me to do it for Mom. I figured I'd try this one class, and when it sucked I'd bail.

The first day, I'm there with all these goofball kids who don't know dick but are smarter than me, and the teacher comes in, this black guy, Daniel, who makes us go around the class and introduce ourselves. I hate that shit. Then he says we're going to do a writing exercise.

I walked out. I can barely get through a sentence talking, and now I'm supposed to write some kind of school bullshit in front of everyone? Fuck it. Freedom.

Daniel follows me out and asks where I'm going. I tell him it's nothing personal, I can't do this shit. He says writing is just thoughts you write down and I can think, can't I? I tell him, not so much with the PTSD. He says, "Man, do we ever need your voice in there." He tells me to do the writing exercises, and I don't have to read them to the class.

Between Ella and my dead mom and this Daniel guy, they had me surrounded, so I go back in and try to write. But I know I'm a fraud since I never even read.

ELLA

Nandita suggested she take Louise on her free days, so I could get a part-time job. It sounded good, until I considered my lack of skills, experience, and education, coupled with my laziness, bad attitude, and limited availability. If I were in a position to hire myself, I'd say, "I'm sorry, but we don't have anything for you at the moment." I could only imagine what people who weren't me would say.

But I knew if I didn't get in the game, I was doomed to finish life at home, a bitter old sow with barely any sexy memories to get lost in. The best I came up with job-wise was appointments at several temp agencies, which made for a complicated day, but things were so much better with Terence, he offered to pick up Louise and make lunch for her so I could do the interviews. It was a criminally hot day—yet another record breaker, but we'd stopped caring about such things—and I was sweating and nervous and tried too hard, but I gradually calmed down and found, to my surprise, I was having a good time. If nothing else, I was talking to adults I wasn't related to. By the last interview, I was making fun of my own hilariously thin resume, and the frosty, middle-aged woman interviewing me started laughing, and then we just talked to each other like friends. She told me I'd do fine out there, and she could probably get me a job at the agency if I wanted. I floated out of there feeling like I should maybe turn in my lifetime, all-inclusive pass to the Festival of Self-Loathing.

I got home and there's Terence in the kitchen carefully making this amazing-looking sandwich for Louise. I told him about my triumphant day, making myself sound funnier and more confident than I actually was, and he told me about picking up Louise as if it's some kind of dangerous, top-secret mission. Then

185

I asked where Jarvis was. He looked like he got slapped and yelled "Jarvis!" and we went running outside. The heat slammed into us, and we're scared shitless of what we'll find when we open the car door. But Jarvis wasn't there, so Terence ran down the street to look.

I went charging back inside, and Louise jumped out from behind the door shouting, "My fellow Americans!" She was wearing a big, rubbery Richard Nixon mask. I nearly collapsed from fright and screamed, "What the hell are you doing, Louise?" and she started to cry. I ripped off Richard Nixon's face (fulfilling a national fantasy) and tried to comfort her, and she said, "Uncle Terence was showing me old Halloween costumes." Dear god.

I went racing up the stairs to the second floor, up the stairs to the attic, threw open the door, and the heat nearly knocked me down. I had to blink through my sweat to see anything, and as I staggered around the attic like a drunk, I tripped over Jarvis, who wasn't moving. Fuck! I picked him up, all ninety pounds, and went stumbling down the stairs, barely keeping my balance. I could hear Terence coming in from outside screaming, "He's gone! I can't find him!"

I ducked into the bathroom on the second floor and put Jarvis in the tub and started running water on him. "Terence!" I yelled, and he bounded up the stairs. One look and he took charge, telling me to get a bowl of water.

He was talking softly to Jarvis when I got back, and he had a damp towel, gently cooling him down. I heard Louise crying, so I went running for the stairs, tripped on the rug, and took an epic tumble, crashing and rolling all the way down, landing on my back, stunned. When I opened my eyes, Louise was standing over me. "You shouldn't run on the stairs, Mommy, that's what you always tell me." I pulled her down on top of me. She said she'll never be Richard Nixon again, and I told her nothing was her fault.

If Jarvis is okay, we'll all be okay. If he isn't, we won't be.

GARRET

I came home, and the house was quiet. Usually, I'd find Louise and Ella disco dancing or baking cookies or roughhousing with Terence. I went out to the porch, and Terence was just sitting there. I asked if he was okay and he couldn't talk. I thought he might have had a stroke or something. He finally said, "My days are over, Daddy."

Then Jarvis came padding in, barely moving, and looked at Terence sitting there in pain. He tried three times before he was able to jump up on the sofa.

ELLA

Any other dog would have died, but Jarvis knew our little family couldn't have gone on without him. Accidentally locking Jarvis in the steaming hot attic was one more thing Terence couldn't forgive himself for. Hearing him mumbling about how he didn't deserve to live got me stirred up about our childhood.

Terence had been a lonely, troubled kid who took out his aggressions on me. Our parents let it happen. I was unprotected, but so was Terence. We were children. One night, I asked my dad why he didn't ever come up to rescue me. He said, "I didn't want to know what I'd find at the top of the stairs." Really, Dad? He started talking about what he and Uncle Paul faced growing up. Because of mental illness, their mother wasn't there most of the time, and the General's philosophy was to let the two boys work everything out themselves. Friends of my parents had told me they were afraid my dad and Uncle Paul would literally kill each other.

"I get it," I said. "Dog-eat-dog is a family tradition."

TERENCE

Ella wanted to know how the writing class was going. I stupidly let it slip that Daniel was okay with me not reading my stuff out loud. Then she asked why I was such a pussy, and I knew I had to go to the next class, read my story, and get it over with. How bad could it be?

It was about the cousins when we were high school seniors. We'd make this speech at Sunday dinner about what we were going to do next. And how each of us got treated different. Me the most when I said I was enlisting instead of going off to a big-deal college like Mickey and Kate. When I was writing it down, it hit me that the story was about me and my dad.

I got to class feeling like I'm going to throw up, but I can't have my little sister think I'm a pussy. This nervous white lady comes in and says she's the new teacher. I asked if Daniel's coming back, and she said no, Daniel isn't at the university anymore.

I packed up my story and walked out. Fuck it.

part four

20. fall 2030

ELLA
(age twenty-five in 2030)

One night, Louise was running around with the crown I got for being Winter Queen. She was doing these crazy poses and we were all laughing our asses off. About the only time Terence laughed was with Louise. Seeing the two of them together made me think about Bobby. If I hadn't been so stoked to go to the Snowflake Ball and get that crown, I'd have been with him that night when he needed me instead of on a dumb date with a boy who meant nothing to me, and he wouldn't have disappeared.

Louise would have a dad. I'd have a husband. And Terence would have a best friend. My selfishness had wrecked our lives. And there was poor Terence, lost in his head and hurting, and he didn't even know the truth.

After Louise was in bed, Terence and I had a beer on the porch. Hard conversations with us always seemed to involve the porch and beer. I finally told him the thing that had haunted me since high school—how what happened to Bobby was my fault, and I couldn't forgive myself.

Terence sat there for a long time in silence. I was just about to say, "Okay, now you know the truth, I'm going inside," when he said, "Ella, all these years I've been blaming myself. I was his best friend, and I didn't have a fucking clue what was happening with him."

So there we were, finally admitting our guilt.

Then Terence said that when he was getting therapy through the VA, he talked about what happened with Bobby. The shrink got him to see that Bobby was dealing with stuff that was much bigger than Terence and me. We couldn't have stopped it no matter what we did. Bobby was one more casualty of war, even though his thing happened here. I don't know if that's true, but it made me feel better. What really made me feel better was talking to Terence about it. We were closer than we'd ever been, which isn't saying much, but it was a start.

As it turned out, that conversation made Terence feel better too. Something lifted. Instead of lying around on the sofa all day with his phone, he started to help out. I was making dinner every night, and he'd pitch in.

The kitchen had been enemy territory for Terence, but now he was an occupying force. We'd plan dinner, make a list, go out and shop, and I could see he was starting to like the structure. Anyone who can read a recipe can learn to cook—except my dad—but Terence was on a mission.

We hit on this ridiculously ambitious cooking project and gradually moved page by page through Mom's cookbooks, a different recipe every night. He studied what I did and started to get the hang of it. As a cook, I was strictly Double-A ball, but I was good enough to show Terence the basics. There came a point when he started to take over. Our mom used to play old Broadway cast albums, which got lodged in our heads, so I'd find Terence in the kitchen, this big galumph, shirtless in an apron with a Brewers cap on backwards singing "On the Street Where You Live" or "The Hills Are Alive" as he's slicing and dicing.

With most things—work or girls or making friends—Terence usually tried too hard and got in his own way, but cooking was different. The more he cooked, the deeper he got in the zone, relaxed and focused. One night, I told him he was way past me as

191

a chef. He started blinking hard and said, "Ella, my whole life, this is the first thing I've ever been good at."

Once his confidence kicked in, he was unstoppable. He'd read cookbooks and watch cooking shows and challenge himself to get to the next level. Something inside him had been unleashed. He told me he dreamed about food more than sex and started telling me a dream. I said, "If it's a food dream I'll listen, but otherwise you're welcome to shut the fuck up."

RUTH
(age fifty-nine in 2030)

Paul and I had bought 117 Poplar years ago through university housing. Once he lost his job and moved out, I was forced to think about our precarious financial situation. With no money coming in, the mortgage was an issue, and the university wanted to buy the house back. I'd always assumed we'd roll out of there on twin gurneys but, like most assumptions, it was ultimately pretty laughable.

After all those years, we had to get out.

ELLA

Terence had decided to scale the dizzying heights of turducken—a chicken cooked inside a duck cooked inside a turkey. Whoever invented turducken, I'd like to know how much they had to drink before that brainstorm hit. We had a few minor setbacks in the R&D phase but once we took our game up a notch, he suggested we invite Nandita and Chandi over.

Louise and I got seriously into the presentation: candles, best china, Coltrane's *Ballads*, and when Terence triumphantly presented his glorious turducken, everyone cheered, and he just smiled like he knew he was kicking ass. Nandita said, "Terence, this is a turducken's turducken." I thought he was going to kiss her.

Later, when he emerged from the kitchen with a flaming baked Alaska, my dad said, "What did I do to deserve this?" I think he meant to say it funny about the meal, but it came out serious, like after Mom died he was finally appreciating what he still had.

PAUL
(age sixty-one in 2030)

We were at our usual haunt, the Franklin Cafe, and everyone else was getting served and we didn't even have menus. Finally, the waiter came with our food. Ruth, who can be a bit rough on the human race, waiters in particular, pointed out that we hadn't ordered. The waiter said, "Compliments of the chef," and left ribs for me and grilled swordfish for Ruth. "They must be pushing a new menu," I said. It just happened to be our favorite food, and it was amazing.

That's when Terence came out of the kitchen wearing an apron and a big puffy chef's hat and a huge smile.

RUTH

When he tried to brush off our compliments, Paul said, "Knock off the false modesty, Terence, you're brilliant." Terence laughed, which I hadn't seen since he was about nine years old. Paul and I had gotten together that day to deal with money problems, but we left Terence a giant tip. He gave me hope the rest of us could somehow make it through the storm.

KATE
(age twenty-eight in 2030)

I turned out to be a uniquely gifted dope fiend. I had a kind of genius for knowing who was carrying quality product and where the finest nearly new cuisine could be found. One night, I went back to the Franklin Cafe and, to my surprise, the throwaway food was neatly placed in takeout bags in the back of the restaurant for those who found themselves between homes. I grabbed a bag and was stunned at the quality. I was a pretty picky eater for someone living on the street, but this sure beat the hell out of the boring-ass dinners my mom had put in front of us growing up.

I made return visits to the Franklin, and as word spread, I suggested we homeless folks should make reservations for the takeout bags, which didn't appear until the restaurant closed at ten. One night, waiting for my dinner, the back door opened, I made my way over and there was my cousin Terence with takeout bags. Terence, the misfit, the black sheep, the loser, was giving handouts to me, the undisputed star of the family, who, at the moment, happened to be an emaciated addict with a rapidly diminishing life expectancy.

I said, "Thank you, Terence," grabbed a bag, and hightailed it out of there. He called to me, but we both knew there really wasn't anything to say.

ELLA

Terence told us about Kate appearing like a ghost and grabbing the throwaway food and rushing off into the night. My dad blamed Kate for what happened to Isaac, so we never mentioned her name, but this was so disturbing Terence had to tell us. The other side of the family was blown to pieces with Uncle Paul and

Aunt Ruth split up, Mickey gone, and Kate a drug addict. David was the only one doing okay, and he had to escape to New York to have a chance. My dad said, "What can you expect from left-wing radicals who never disciplined their kids?" But we were all thinking about Kate out there trying to survive the night.

RUTH

You're supposed to make your kids take what they want out of the house when you sell it. But Mickey and Kate were gone, and David said we should throw out all his stuff. It was pretty emotional going through Mickey's old sports trophies and clippings, and Kate's room was like an archeological dig of her ever-changing passions. We found the Yamaha guitar we got her at age fourteen, which she'd left in a closet when she bought a fancy new one. Paul insisted on holding on to it, and we kept all their high school yearbooks and a few random things we didn't have the heart to throw out. In David's room, we found the football Terence gave him and the old video of his miracle touchdown at the Thanksgiving football game. I asked him if he wanted it, and he said he'd rather remember it than see how lame it probably was.

Paul and I took a break and watched the video. It was still awesome. There we all were before the storm hit, the General and Hadley and Isaac and Ella and Kate and Mickey and Terence and Paul and me and little David catching the pass and jumping up and down in pure joy.

ELLA

My dad would take off after dinner, and we never knew where he went. Terence thought he had a girlfriend. That was the thing about our dad, if you asked what was going on, he'd give some cryptic bullshit response so you knew less than you did before. I didn't give him the satisfaction of asking him what he was up to.

KATE

I was persona non grata at all the shelters in town, which takes some doing, so I found myself living in Tent City, a bunch of re-cycled disaster tents the city put up in a vacant lot so we'd die slower. It was a ragged, writhing mass of twitching human corpses in those tents, blank, emaciated creatures who were already dead but hadn't been told. I was one of them, but somehow I managed to hold onto my snobbish, judgmental nature. That will be my last faculty to go, long after my sanity.

One freezing night, I couldn't score no matter where I went. It was too cold even for the dealers; Plans B, C, and D didn't pan out; and a final Hail Mary for smack nearly got me killed in a middle-aged Satanist's creeped-out basement. I tottered back to Tent City, cold, dope-sick and desperate, pulled back the flap of a tent and was overcome by a piercing memory of camping with my dad and Mickey in Colorado when I was six years old, waking up to the intoxicating smell of bacon over a campfire and looking out to see Mickey in his pajamas crouched next to my dad, still sleepy, holding his hands out to the fire for warmth, and my dad seeing me poke my head out of the tent, smiling and saying, "Rise and shine, kiddo, today we're climbing the mountain." Gone for-ever, all of whatever was.

I slithered into the stinking, snoring tent, voices from the dark croaking, vague threats and ominous seductions, hard to tell one from the other, and huddled for warmth against another per-son, maybe a man, maybe a woman, maybe neither, maybe both; the distinctions had become irrelevant. I had my first coherent thought in days, that this is where I would die. Which gave me great relief, as there's a limit to how many mornings I could wake up in this ghastly living morgue.

That's when the flap opened and a harsh light probed the tent and I heard a voice: "Katie?"

PAUL

Terence was manager of the Franklin, and we were rooting for him to succeed, but we had second thoughts when it meant waiting for a table. One torrentially rainy day as we waited for our lunch, Sandy, the young, redheaded, too-nice-to-be real waitress, was dealing with seven college kids who kept changing their orders, knowing that Sandy prided herself on never writing anything down and always getting it right. There was an endless line of restless bare-fanged *sapiens* aching for a table and here was this cluster of time-wasting teenage goofballs rolling out their cutting-edge sophomore wit. When one smirking humorist slowly changed his order from fried to poached to scrambled, she instructed them all to simultaneously fuck themselves, grabbed her coat and umbrella, and announced to the entire dining room that if she wanted this kind of abuse she'd visit her family in Eau Claire, where her brother Dougie could get drunk and smash up the station wagon and bang his girlfriend in the family room and puke in church and that was all well and good, but if *she* came home one minute after eleven o'clock on a Friday night—she with a 3.8 GPA in organic chemistry!—her parents acted like she must be a worthless, two-bit crack whore, and she was grounded for weeks and had to do idiot chores like wash the drapes while Dougie's popping Jell-O shots in the middle of the day, and she has frankly fucking had it with everyone, including her stupid, lame-dick boyfriend Vince, who will find out tonight that he will never ever see her naked again and he knows why! Then she left. We had a clear view of Sandy opening her umbrella, and the wind promptly turning it inside out. She tossed the umbrella just as a bus hurtled by, splashing her, and as she turned to protect herself, she stepped into a puddle as deep as Lake Michigan and fell down into it, emitting what was, for us, a prolonged, silent scream at the unfairness of it all.

But it was worse inside, as disconsolate diners realized that lunch was now as uncertain as all their other plans for the future. Ruth and I were about to leave when Terence came out of the kitchen, observed the escalating chaos, and I thought, this is what success is, buddy, nothing but stomach-churning stress that will gallantly escort you to an early grave. Terence was trying to decide whether he should make a sweep through the dining room to get things under control or keep cooking. I said, "Terence, how about I help you out, take orders, bring food?"

He said, "Do you have any relevant experience, Uncle Paul?" I told him I'd been a waiter at a vegan joint in college for several hours before exiting over creative differences. He said, "You're hired. And would it kill Aunt Ruth to pitch in?" The old Terence would have been a puddle of misery, but this Terence was smiling, like he knew it would work itself out.

RUTH

We divided up the tables and took orders and brought food, and I told those college kids if they pulled their sophomoric shit on me I'd toss their dumb asses on the griddle and turn up the heat, and they all got polite in a mommy's-mad-let's-not-make-it-worse kind of way, and when we'd emerge from the kitchen with some-one's order, the whole place would cheer. As it turned out, Paul and I were both pretty good waiters except for him. He'd get in conversations with the customers, which slowed things down, but I'd forgotten how much fun it was doing stuff with him. He saw everything through his own gleefully distorted lens and couldn't help commenting. I was headed back into the kitchen at one point and he pinched my ass, which made me squeal and got a big laugh from the lunchtime crowd. It meant something different to me.

KATE

I managed to extricate myself from the writhing scrum in the di-saster tent and move toward the light, which was shining right in my eyes. I had no idea who was removing me from the epicenter of hell and it didn't matter. I was out of the tent. That's when I saw who my savior was: Uncle Garret.

The wind was whipping through the vacant lot, rippling the tents, and I was shivering uncontrollably as he guided me to his car, which was safe and warm—half-forgotten sensations from my childhood. When my teeth stopped chattering, I asked how he had found me, and he said, "I just kept looking."

ELLA

The temping was working out okay, but it was hard always being the new person: who do I report to, where's the ladies room, nice working with you, goodbye forever. So, I was all ears when Aunt Ruth told me Terence could use some help at the Franklin. Naturally, he'd never mentioned it.

RUTH

Paul put up a sign in the kitchen of the Franklin Cafe that said, "Under new mismanagement." Whenever Terence gave him a hard time, he'd point to it.

TERENCE
(age twenty-nine in 2030)

One afternoon, I could tell Uncle Paul had had a few beers, so I pulled him aside and said, "This doesn't work if you're drinking." He started to deny it, and I said, "You sound like you're fifteen. I'm telling you this because I don't want to lose my fourth—no, fifth—best waiter."

He said, "When did you turn into such an asshole, Terence?"

I said, "I've always been one, you just haven't been paying attention." We never had a problem after that.

PAUL

Jarvis was always calm, except for the first day Terence brought him to the Franklin. We were prepping for lunch, and he went padding into the kitchen, and with the food and the smells and the people, he suddenly started rushing around as excited as a writer at an open bar.

ELLA

We couldn't have a dog in the kitchen, so Jarvis would sit in the doorway watching us. The waiters had to step over him—a challenge with a tray—but we only had a few accidents, which was a small price to pay for keeping Terence on an even keel.

TERENCE

My friend Ronnie came wheeling into the Franklin one day. He asked if I was still at the U, and I told him my writing teacher had left so I quit. Turned out, he knew about a writing workshop for vets in a church basement run by a black dude named Daniel. I figured, what the hell do I have to lose, other than my self-respect? Writing was hard, but I kind of missed Daniel.

ELLA

Terence, Louise, and I were watching this TV show that put a laugh track on the news, which was weirdly appropriate. You'd see the Great Leader standing in front of Marine One, answering every question with an obvious lie. Raucous studio laughter was the best response.

That's when my dad came in with Kate, who was thin, pale and drawn. She'd always been so beautiful and confident I used to worship her, but now the light was gone from her eyes. We just stared, but Louise ran right into her arms yelling, "Kate!" Louise was always way ahead of me in knowing what to do.

Terence and I hugged her and Dad said, "Let's get Kate set up in the guest room." After she'd gone to bed, Dad said Kate made him promise not to tell her parents where she was. I asked why he'd worked so hard to find her since he'd vowed never to see her again. He shrugged like he hadn't even considered it.

For a smart guy, my dad never had words for the big things in his life, like forgiveness.

KATE

Waking up in that sunny bedroom was a dream. I couldn't quite believe I was really there. There was a knock, and Louise came charging in with a book, eight years old and ablaze with possibilities. She hopped up next to me in bed, and I read to her and got a tiny glimpse of what life could be.

That first day, everyone was so gentle. Ella made me lunch and told me about Terence and the Franklin Cafe. He'd started as chef, and then they'd made him manager, and now the owner had health issues and was selling him the place, giving Terence amazingly generous terms. Terence's unlikely success had given everyone hope, even me.

Except, by late afternoon, I could hear the ominous drumbeat of need, ever louder, and then the sick craving announced itself with a vengeance. Fuck me, I needed to score. I told Ella I was going to take a walk, and I almost made it to the street before Garret pulled into the driveway. I cheerfully announced I was off for a bit of exercise, and he told me to get in the car. Talking back was useless. "Where are we going?" I asked. He just stared at the road ahead.

For a savior, he was being a major dick.

TERENCE

Daniel played it cool when I showed up for his workshop in the church basement, but I could tell he was glad to see me. I listened to the other people read their stories. Daniel handled things, so even stuff that was flat-out bad seemed like it mattered.

Near the end, Daniel said, "Anyone else feel like sharing?" I raised my hand, pulled it down fast, but Daniel had seen it. No way out. My voice was shaking, but at the end they all cheered. That made me feel pretty good, until I remembered they'd clapped for everything, even the random shit that made no sense.

But Daniel made a point of telling me I should keep writing about my family.

KATE

We're driving and driving, and it gets dark and Uncle Garret's got Fox State News on the radio, self-important smugsters wallowing in a clean sweep for the Ruling Party in whatever election had just happened.

I ask him again where we're going, and he doesn't say a word, just suddenly pulls over to the side of the road and stops. He turns and he's looking at me in this intense way, and I think, *Oh, fuck, is he going to kiss me?* I kind of pull back, and he gets closer and closer and tells me he's taking me someplace I sure as hell don't want to go. And there's only one way out. If I tell him what he needs to know, he'll drive me back to the house. I say sure, whatever, Uncle Garret, what do you want to know? His voice gets scary low, so I have to lean in to hear him. He says, "Katie, you and Mickey have always been close. You need to tell me where he is. I want to help him." I tell him I have no idea, I haven't talked to him since before the bombing. He just smiles this creepy smile like he knows I'm lying and off we go.

And I'm thinking, the only reason he saved me was to lean on me to get to Mickey. I don't know what the diagnosis is of a sick fuck but he sure fits.

Somehow I fall asleep. I'm having this jagged dream of running away from a vicious gang of business leaders in bespoke suits with machetes, but my feet keep sticking to the pavement, and the men are getting closer and closer, laughing like entitled hyenas, and the pavement makes a sucking sound, and I can't move my feet and one of the businessmen whips his machete at my neck

203

and I start to scream but can't make a sound because my head is bouncing down the street, still screaming. I'm thinking, *Man, dinner is going to be a challenge,* and then I have a sadder thought: *I'll never kiss anyone ever again unless I can find my head, which is rolling out of sight.*

That's when my door is yanked open and hands are pulling me out of the car and the real nightmare begins. I start screaming—thankful, in my groggy state, to discover that my head is still safely attached—as two towering, take-no-shit dudes drag me into a building, and Uncle Garret drives away. I'm fighting for my life, but one of them hits me up with a shot of something consequential and the night is done.

I wake up another day in another place, a small cell, bed, sink, toilet. There's a button labeled "press for assistance," so I do. A woman in a red jumpsuit opens the door and says she'll take me to the cafeteria. I ask her where I am, but she's on a headset dealing with issues relating to parking passes, which are far more important than my existence.

It looks like I just made it for the end of dinner. The cafeteria is practically empty. I go through the line, and there's only one choice—is that even a choice?—an unfathomable stew. I sit at one of the long tables and call to a frumpy, frightened, fiftyish woman—although she's probably a hope-deprived thirty-year-old—sitting alone. "Excuse me? Where am I?" She puts her teeth back in and smiles. "That's up to you."

What the fuck? I'm talking location, GPS, latitude/longitude, maps, not Eastern philosophy. Did I get ditched at some kind of spiritual retreat? I'm finishing my mystery stew when the woman says, "You'll feel better now. They put it in the food to level us out." She struggles to her feet and wanders out, and I realize I'm the last one there, so I leave, not feeling so bad. Maybe there really was something in the stew.

I'm walking down an endless hall, lost in a shivering paranoid dreamscape of surveillance cameras and institutional lighting, and there's an announcement over the PA: "Lights out in five minutes." I walk faster, which only makes sense if you're headed in the right direction, which hasn't been the case since middle school. I see a red-jumpsuited woman locking one door after another. She growls, "You have two minutes to be in your room." I tell her I don't know where it is. She gets on the headset, talks to someone, then tells me, "Room 205. You're not even close." She gives me directions slowly, as if telling a drunk four-year-old how to get to preschool, and it's a relief to return to my heartbreakingly empty room.

It has to be home because I have no other.

21. spring 2032

RUTH

We moved out of 117 Poplar with no place to go because I couldn't face the harsh truth that after all these years I'd no longer be living there. It was my old book club friend Pam Rayner who bailed us out. She invited me and Anjelica and Gabriel to move into her guest house, so there we were in a luxurious gated community with all the amenities, like tennis courts and a pool and a beautiful garden for cocktails at the end of the day. After a couple of martinis, we'd make dinner, everyone pitching in. There was no question that Gabriel was expected to cook and clean and pull his weight, which Paul and I never demanded of our precious children. Maybe that's why they pursued careers as criminals and addicts.

KATE

We were on a tight schedule at the RJ Manning Rehabilitation Center. That's where they'd placed me in an act of inspired perversity. Fifteen minutes for breakfast, then off to my job in the laundry, which meant raw and blistered hands, then a small group meeting followed by a large group meeting. Whatever medication they were feeding us seemed to work; the raging fire of need was down to a few smoldering embers. By lights out at 9 p.m., I was exhausted. There was no personal time, just the relentless process of breaking us down and rebuilding us. We were a neighborhood of teardowns.

Drifting off to sleep one night, it hit me that the regimen at RJ Manning seemed pretty close to the way Mickey described his brief time in the psych center.

RUTH

I asked Pam if it would be an issue having us in the guest house when her husband came home. She said I shouldn't worry, as Bill had gone off to Greenville, South Carolina, to be with his mother during her final days. That was seven years ago. His mother had seemed to be on firm ground, so Bill came back home, which is when she went into cardiac arrest. He went rushing back and she promptly rallied.

Since her life appeared to be in Bill's hands, he rented a little apartment next to her retirement home. After a few years when he was old enough to qualify, he got a room right next to hers, as he'd made friends there and was involved in a long-running bridge tournament. It was a comfortable life for Bill, having dinner with his centenarian mommy every night in the midst of an ever-changing community. He and Pam talked on the phone before dinner and he'd describe in paralyzing detail the twists and turns of the bridge tournament, during which she leaned hard into her second martini. Except for the bridge reports, it seemed like a happy marriage. Pam liked having company, and we settled into an easy rhythm.

Here in paradise, with my lover and her child and my old friend, I was happier than I'd been in ages, which meant that it couldn't last.

TERENCE

I changed up the menu, and the Franklin Cafe took off. Carl, the owner, was my biggest fan. He'd say, "Terence, you're like the son I never had." When I pointed out that he had two sons, he said, "I'm eighty-one years old, I can't be expected to remember *everything*."

He put me on track to be the owner in three years. His wife had passed, and he said he wanted to visit Florida while it was still there. I told him he'd better hurry.

RUTH

One sunny morning, we were scrambling to get Gabriel ready for school running late as usual. He and I were waiting by the door, all set to go, when I heard Anjelica on the phone. She sounded dead serious, but I couldn't make out what she was saying. I knew better than to push her to tell me what it was all about. She did things on her own time.

She didn't tell me until we'd dropped off Gabriel at school and were headed back home. She'd gotten word that her husband, Dr. Morales, had, after years of detention, made it over the border to Canada.

We walked in silence back to our spectacular home on that perfect spring day.

TERENCE

I got worried that the popularity of the Franklin was getting to be a problem. I'd see people give up on our line and go across the street to the diner whose business was booming with our castoffs. A Yelp review of the Franklin had a Yogi Berra quote: "Nobody goes there anymore because it's too crowded."

I wanted to make Carl proud of me, so I started scouting around to open a sister restaurant. I got it down to two locations but couldn't decide which. I asked Nandita, since she had strong opinions about everything. She chose the one on Livingston, and then I asked if she'd manage the place. She said she didn't have any experience, but I told her I knew she could do it, and I needed someone I could trust.

When the deal went through, there was a story in the Sunday paper with a picture of me with a smile that was way too big for my face. I hadn't looked that uncool since my class photo in sixth grade. Still, it was a pretty heady time for me.

RUTH

Late one afternoon, Pam and Anjelica and I were out back of Pam's house having cocktails and watching Gabriel play soccer with other kids from the gated community. A girl scored a goal and the laughter and yelling and teasing felt timeless, children playing as the sun goes down, a lovely glimpse of Americana that we once thought would go on forever. I said, "It's good to be reminded what innocence looks like." Pam pointed out that this brutal era will pass, and if we're patient and hopeful and stay involved, we'll get our country back.

We sat in silence until Anjelica said, "You are wrong, Pam. It's too late. While we sit here with our drinks, people are locked up and broken and dying, and their lives will never be the same, and the people who love them will never be the same, so life will never be normal again." She didn't raise her voice but it came from the depths of her soul. She got up and walked back to the guest house.

Anjelica and I were still sleeping together, but I was already missing her.

KATE

When I got a tap on the shoulder from a guard at RJ Manning, I was ready to confess, but I couldn't think of a single thing I'd

209

done wrong. I was sent to security and they directed me to an office down the hall. The door was open so I went in, and this guy was staring at me. It wasn't till he smiled that I recognized him.

PAUL

That summer we started experiencing the truth about climate change, which, like just about everything else, was far worse than anticipated. In a rambling, three-hour, Mussolini-tinged press conference, the Great Leader had a good laugh about global warming. He remembered much hotter summers when he was a typical orange-cheeked, racist child millionaire coming of age in Queens. How hard his tiny underused brain had to work to not understand what was happening all around him. His closest advisors were required to not understand the same things he didn't understand, so as to preserve a solid core of ignorance at the top. Discussing the weather had become a political act. The way to show your patriotism was to deny science, common sense, and that your Mini Cooper was melting into a puddle in your driveway.

I'd hear people at the Franklin talking about where to move to escape the heat. I couldn't imagine leaving town, but staying here was starting to seem foolhardy.

KATE

The man smiling at me was Neil, Isaac's old friend. "Hello, Kate," he said, "what are you doing here?"

"I'm a drug addict," I proudly announced. "What are *you* doing here?"

He told me that after Isaac was killed, he'd done time for the kidnapping of the senator's daughter then bounced around in a hopeless funk and finally got a gig as a social worker.

I stopped him. "How did you get away with spending so little time in jail?" Neil looked sheepish. Turns out he was a trust fund baby. His father, who'd made a killing in some dark unknowable corner of the financial swamp, stepped up with a sizeable contribution to the Great Leader's perpetual reelection campaign. In America 2031, you got all the justice money could buy. Your pardon was your receipt.

The Great Leader was privatizing everything he could think of—we were saved only by the barrenness of his imagination—and the company Neil worked for got the contract to handle rehab for the government. It wasn't until later that I found out Neil's company was a wholly owned subsidiary of Pearl Pharma, which had created an inspired self-sustaining business model of bribing doctors to prescribe their drugs, which got people hooked, then lobbying the government to pay Pearl for handling rehabilitation, so the addicts they'd birthed could become productive members of society before Pearl once again leaned on doctors to prescribe their drugs, causing them to fall back into the bottomless pit of addiction and then recover through Pearl-run rehab. It was brilliantly sociopathic and endlessly lucrative, a merry-go-round of creating and curing addicts, and with their enormous contributions to the Ruling Party, Pearl never had to worry about government oversight.

As for Neil, he was clearly a pawn in a bigger game—like the rest of us—but I couldn't help holding him responsible for what happened to Isaac. Even so, it was nice to know I had someone on the inside, as I'd observed that people disappeared from this place without warning, and it wasn't necessarily through the heart-stirring miracle of recovery.

A week later, I got an assignment outside the facility because of my impressive progress. This was a big step. Working on the outside meant you could expect to get released if you didn't fuck things up, which was historically a high bar for me.

TERENCE

Carl came up to me at the grand opening of the Livingston Café, when diners were cheering, and told me I had the magic touch. He was off to Florida on vacation, I was in charge of two hot restaurants, and my only problem was the limited number of hours in the day. He said he had connections and would get the mayor to temporarily expand each day to twenty-eight hours, so I had the time I needed.

Nandita was learning the ropes managing the Livingston, so I got called over there a lot. I'd see things that weren't quite right, but business was so good I didn't want to rock the boat. One day, I got a call that the air conditioning was down at the Livingston, and when I got there, the lunch crowd had left. All of them. You didn't stay anywhere without AC. We got the cool air going, but the next day we weren't quite as full.

Over the next few weeks, we built our business back up and then the AC started going out over and over. No one could figure it out. It was like a monster trying to kill us, and it did. The word on the street was that the AC was shaky, and the lighting too bright, and the bar too cramped, and the Livingston wasn't up to the standard of the Franklin. We were getting smacked down because of our own success.

Nandita felt like it was all her fault, and I spent too much time boosting her up. I'd talk to our accountant, Ed, Carl's guy, who'd walk me through the numbers. We were overextended. This was not sustainable.

It was the hottest summer ever and what people wanted more than good food was dependable AC. The best people we brought in couldn't figure out why it kept breaking down.

KATE

I was on a team charged with cleaning a small office building. With the immigration freeze, there was no one left to do such work, and there were many jobs Americans wouldn't do anymore, from cleaning to harvesting to defending the Constitution. Time to call the addicts! So, we rode in like the cavalry with our cleaning products to make America sparkle again. It was pretty exciting to be out in the world, even though they kept a close watch on us, and our team leader, Raelene, was a tough drill sergeant who'd write us up for the tiniest infraction.

ELLA

Snow days are the closest I've ever come to believing in a higher power. An out-of-nowhere announcement first thing on a wintry morning and then a stolen day to do whatever you want, a divine gift from above.

It was different for Louise. We'd start the day by checking the heat index and air quality and gauge whether it was safe to go to the park. She was smitten with roller blading and absolutely fearless, and we'd go flying along the bike paths dodging in and out of bikers and boarders and skaters and runners, and had a ton of close calls, but we were just so happy to be out there. Everyone was. You couldn't take mornings like that for granted anymore. Everyone went to the park early; by the afternoon, it was too hot to do anything but hunker down someplace with AC. People would take siestas through the long, sweltering afternoon and then go out at night when it was cooler. It's like we woke up and found ourselves living in Barcelona.

One morning, as the heat kicked in, we got juice from the truck and sat on a bench taking off our blades when Louise said, "Mom, why are there so many mosquitos?" One more thing I sensed but couldn't allow myself to know. Mosquitos had always been something to complain about in the tent at summer camp, but now they were everywhere. Uncle Paul said they were on a mission to kill off the species that was destroying the earth. I used to think Uncle Paul was joking about stuff like that.

We hurried to the car, slapping them away, but for every one you killed fifty more were on the attack. For the first time, I saw fear on Louise's face. *This is the world we're leaving her,* I thought. Great job, everyone, thanks for caring!

KATE

One night, I was cleaning an office when I noticed a family photo on the desk. It was a jolt to see who the dad was: my old boyfriend from the university, Glenn. I left a note on his desk saying he looked even better than he did in college, and I was glad he'd found happiness, unless that was just a random family he'd rented for the photo. I didn't sign it. The next night, there was a super-serious letter telling me he'd always felt guilty about how our relationship ended, and he thought about me all the time. Whoa! I flashed on Glenn on a warm spring night, the two of us sailing on quaaludes and an uncharacteristically fine bottle of Côtes du Rhône we'd lifted from an upscale faculty meet and greet, and in the first blush of sunrise, tightrope walking between drugs and alcohol, I asked him if he loved me and he whispered, "Baby, I love you so much, I'd like to clone you and have a threesome."

That was Glenn, a Perfect Master of wild sex and getting high and doing stupid, crazy shit. The two of us would get so convulsed with laughter we faced death from hilarity.

This person in the letter sounded ominously mature, like the fun had been surgically removed. He tried to explain what had happened in college when he checked into the psych center as a volunteer lab rat. There was a whole medicated truth-telling side of what they did, which made him believe his true destiny was going back home to take care of his family business, but he'd since come to the conclusion they'd broken his spirit at the psych center and what he thought was the truth was in fact surrender. This was a heavy trip for a cleaning lady to process. I wrote him a breezy note wishing him happiness and a good life, and in his next note, he said he needed to see me. This shit was getting real. Did I want to have a potentially hot meet-up looking like what I was: a dope addict just trying to survive another day?

That night I sat at his desk trying to figure out what to do. The fates had conspired to make our lives intersect after all this time, and of course I wondered why our relationship had ended so abruptly. On the other hand, I was in recovery, and he was married, and nothing good could come from our getting together. On the other hand, I've never been an "on the other hand" kind of person. I wrote him a sexy note, telling him if he was in his office at eleven o'clock the next night, we could catch up and see what happens. I put the note in his desk drawer and had leaned back in his chair to reflect on how cataclysmically horrific this decision was when I saw on top of a bookcase a red hat. *Glenn is a Red Hat?*

Just then Raelene materialized in the doorway, glaring at me. "What the fuck are you doing, girl? Sitting on your scrawny ass like a motherfucking CEO?" I bounced up from the chair, pleading

215

with her not to write me up, when she started laughing. "Look at this shit I found in some VP of Dick Licking's office." She had a high-end trove of executive snacks and we started chowing down, laughing like the criminally insane we almost were. I asked her if we'd get busted, and she said no, this was the last night we'd be in the building.

It wasn't until we were in the van headed back to RJ Manning that I remembered I'd set up a romantic interlude with Glenn that was never going to happen. Fuck it. Fuck all the Red Hats. But don't fuck 'em.

PAUL

The last human on earth will die when a blood-engorged mosquito returns for one last bite. Then they'll have the planet all to themselves.

TERENCE

I'd overslept and was running late and Jarvis was taking his sweet time, so I literally pulled him out the door. We were in the car driving to the Livingston, and I was so in my head I didn't notice Jarvis coughing softly, over and over. I headed straight to the vet, and I told Ella and Nandita they were in charge.

ELLA

Terence had been doing so well that we stopped worrying about him. I blame myself more than anyone else because, well, that's my thing. I should have known PTSD doesn't just go away. When he told me about Jarvis, I heard the old Terence, lost and scared. I told him he had nothing to worry about with the restaurants, we were on it.

Nandita and I were an excellent team, and we planned how we were going to break it to Terence that he worked for us now. I think we were kidding. But we had no idea how bad the situation was with the restaurants because Terence didn't tell anyone. The only one who knew was Jarvis.

TERENCE

When the vet told me Jarvis had heartworm, I started to cry even though I didn't know what it meant. Turned out he'd gotten it from the mosquitos, and he'd supposedly survive with injections I could give him at home. Jarvis had saved me, and now I was going to save him.

Ella and Nandita would fill me in on the restaurants, but the issues were either too big to deal with or not important compared to Jarvis. Either way, I was spending most of my time at home with my dog.

RUTH

Terence had expanded at the exact wrong time. How could he have known that the heat would be so savage people would start leaving? Those who could afford it went to their summer homes in the Upper Peninsula, others moved in with friends and relatives in parts of the country that weren't hit so hard. The people left behind kept saying, "Why us?" and I would think, "Why *not* us?"

22. fall 2032

PAUL

Elections had become as ritualized as in any authoritarian state, a kabuki dance of dominance. The Great Leader would toy with the Opposition candidate like a cat playing with a half-dead mouse, batting it around for sport then carrying it in his teeth for approval from his roaring, bloodthirsty base. During the debates, he accused the Opposition Party candidate of treason, wallowing in the cruelty of dismembering his opponent with baseless accusations. The parade celebrating his victory featured tanks and generals and an orgy of military might to make his cowardly, draft-dodging heart swell. It culminated with the arrest of his defeated opponent. As the man languished in prison, his brilliant, accomplished wife spoke eloquently on his behalf.

The Great Leader invited her to lunch at the White House and afterwards announced that not only was she very much his type, she had won him over, and he promised her husband a pardon. Sadly, she died forty-eight hours later of a massive stroke at the Great Leader's Washington hotel. He spoke movingly at her memorial about his extraordinary electoral victory in 2016, the greatest in history. Coincidentally, that same day her husband was sentenced to death, the mandated punishment for treason, which, the Great Leader made clear, was out of his hands. We must live by the rule of law.

Enthusiasm to be the next Opposition candidate was muted.

KATE

We were cut off from the news because rehab wasn't possible if we tried to shoulder the weight of a collapsing world on top of our own struggles. But Neil told me about the storm that hit Florida. Hurricane Ronan destroyed everything it touched. There weren't even points of comparison anymore, the storms got worse and worse, and once again, the fate of the nation was up to prisoners and addicts and the indigent and anyone else who didn't have a voice worth listening to, which was a rapidly growing percentage of the population.

Neil showed me footage of Florida, which looked like the end of the world, and I flashed on myself in the middle of the death and devastation and got a wink from my old friends Fear and Chaos, who'd led me down such dangerous paths but had also given me great joy. I asked Neil if I could volunteer, and he said, "You already did."

TERENCE

Once Jarvis recovered, I went back to work. I'd wake up every morning with a knot in my stomach and spend the day trying to make sense of what was happening. We were underwater. Finally, I dropped by Ed the accountant's office. He said, "Terence, I talked to someone who might be of interest to you."

GARRET
(age sixty-five in 2032)

Terence told us he got approached by a company that wanted to buy both restaurants. He said the deal was no better than okay, and anyway he couldn't do it without Carl, who was the legal owner for the next three years. Carl was still in Florida and unreachable because of the hurricane. If Terence took the deal, he'd feel like he failed. If he didn't take it, he was headed for bankruptcy. Ella told him he'd had an amazing run, and now it was time to get out. She'd take charge of tracking down Carl, so the restaurants could be sold.

Here's my son, admitting he failed, and my daughter, stepping up to help him. I wish Hadley could have seen that I was doing an okay job as a dad.

ELLA

Dad said, "Someone did a damn good job raising you two," and Terence blurted out, "Yeah, I miss Mom." It could have gone either way, but Dad laughed and said, "I do, too, Terence."

That's when the weather events were piling up on top of each other: wildfires, hurricanes, droughts, tornados. The world was spinning out of control. I was watching the Weather Channel every night to see if Florida was still on the map. I had to find Carl, so Terence could sell the restaurants. I made a bunch of calls. I kept running into dead ends until I reached his son Jimmy in San Diego, who told me his parents used to stay at the Sagamore in Miami.

KATE

The relief work in Florida was an excellent test of whether I could stay off drugs. The pastel Florida dream was a desolate battlefield where both sides lost and the wounded were dying. We worked all day searching for survivors and at dusk vanned back to disaster shelters where I'd have nightmares about the waterlogged horror until we woke up and went back to picking through Miami hotels demolished by raging water and unimaginable wind, and there was no life remaining.

Except one day in the Sagamore. I found myself squishing down a soggy hallway, and there was a man walking ahead of me I didn't recognize from our crew, so I called out, but he kept going, and when I tried to catch up he picked up his pace. Just before he went around a corner, he looked back and smiled. It was Isaac.

I screamed and ran after him, and when he darted into a room, I followed. He wasn't there. I yelled, "Isaac!" Nothing. Then a gurgling sound from underneath a transcendently ugly sofa emblazoned with winking mermaids that had been hurled across the room by the wind. Neil came rushing in, and we managed to move the sofa, revealing an old man barely breathing. Neil and I stuck around until the EMS people showed up. Weirdly enough, the old guy turned out to be from my hometown.

ELLA

Terence gave me credit for finding Carl, but I had nothing to do with it. By the time I found out he was alive, he was on his way home.

TERENCE

The night before the closing, me and Carl decided to say goodbye to the Franklin. Everything had been cleared out, so I brought food and started cooking, and we called up Ella and Nandita and Aunt Ruth and Uncle Paul and had a monster of a last supper. The regulars showed up with cases of beer and wine, and it turned into just about the best night we ever had there.

PAUL

Carl made a speech about how the single best thing that ever happened to him was meeting Terence, except for marrying his wife

221

and having two kids and the Brewers winning the series and the first time he ate lobster and buying a Harley when he was eighteen and finding his dad's *Playboy* collection when he was eleven, and he went on for maybe five minutes about all the things that were better than meeting Terence.

We watched Terence smiling at the old man. When he finished, Terence stood up and said, "I can't top that. I love this man, and I thank God or whoever else is responsible for saving him."

RUTH

I saw a couple of the regulars waiting on Paul, and then Sandy, the excitable waitress, came in with her ex-and-now-current boyfriend Vince, and it hit me why the Franklin had been such a sensation. This little community had a life of its own, and people could feel it when they walked in, and word spread and, yes, Terence's ribs were legendary but what made it special was a bunch of people caring about each other and having a good time.

Boy, did we ever miss it when it was gone.

23. summer/fall 2033

KATE

We left Florida when we got orders to head to California, where the wildfires were out of control. There used to be a season for these things, the Santa Ana winds and the wildfires and the rain, but now the only thing predictable was chaos, but you couldn't always count on that, either.

Neil had worked things so he and I were driving the van cross country, and the others got some kind of roll-the-dice Spirit Airlines flight where there was a 40 percent chance the plane wouldn't fall out of the sky but you couldn't beat the price. We split the driving, and there'd be long silent stretches, but then the words would come in a rush. Neil asked if I was scared when I saw Isaac in the Sagamore, and I said, "Why would I be scared of Isaac?" I knew Isaac and Neil had been close, and finally I asked him if they had been lovers. Neil said, "It wasn't anything like that. I was a disciple."

Driving through the night, we both started to feel that Isaac had brought us together. It made me look at Neil differently. Maybe he was just as innocent and just as guilty as the rest of us.

RUTH

I was about to leave the General's room at Blue Hill when Ella and Louise burst in. Of course, the General and I wanted a full report on everyone. Ella gave us an update on Garret and Terence and her friend Nandita, and then Louise said, "Mom, you forgot about Kate." Ella froze. That's when I found out they all knew about Kate. Except for Paul and me.

PAUL

It was still called the Franklin Café, but it wasn't the same. Ruth and I went back out of habit, but the menu was down to a single disappointing page, and the waiters were recent graduates of Disobedience School. I probably would have remained a regular, because I don't notice things like lousy food and rude waiters, but Ruth has standards. She broke the Franklin habit by inviting me over to Pam Rayner's for lunch.

Ruth whipped up a salad that tried hard to be interesting, and we ate out by the pool. That's when she told me Kate had been found and was in rehab. For a few moments, I couldn't speak, an affliction I (and the world) don't normally have to endure, thank God. I asked who was responsible for this hopeful turn, and she said, "Your brother Garret."

KATE

It was starting to get dark, we were both exhausted, and driving all night was not an option. Neil said, "Keep your eyes out for a motel, Kate."

Here we go. A motel. There was absolutely no way I would sleep with him. We were two lonely souls on a cross-country trek between coastal disasters, and I could feel how much he wanted me, so I'd have to be strong. I saw a Days Inn up ahead but didn't say anything. He stopped anyway. We went inside, and there was a pasty-faced cipher with a name tag that said "Dick" at the reception desk. If he'd been any more bored, he'd have tipped over. Behind him was a plaque with a photo of Monica, Employee of the Month, round, Guernica-style haircut, and a smile that couldn't quite mask her suicidal tendencies. It made me wonder about the runners-up.

I was waiting to pounce just as soon as Neil tried to book us in the same room. This was my moment to clarify things once and for all. The only reason I was going through this rehab ordeal was to get my life on track, and sleeping with my sponsor would be a giant step backwards into the abyss. Would I have the strength to even attempt recovery again? For him to put me in that situation was immoral. Then I heard him say, "You got two singles, Dick?"

What the fuck? He didn't think I was interesting enough or attractive enough to make even a token pass? Fine. At least I knew where I stood. He handed me my room key, and I headed for the elevator without a word. He asked what was wrong, and I snarled, "Figure it out," before letting the elevator doors close in his face.

PAUL

The General seemed to have the inside track on what was happening in the family, so I went over to Blue Hill before confronting my brother. It was always a tricky dance with my dad, trying to avoid the gaping sinkhole of politics. He'd stayed on board with the Great Leader until basic human decency caused him to jump ship. Now it was hard to tell where he stood. He'd spent his life in the military and had fierce conservative views, but the Ruling Party had long since abandoned conservatism in their cowardly embrace of the Great Leader, whose ideology didn't go much past what made him feel good from one moment to the next, whether it was ripping infants from mama's breast or wiping out the pygmy raccoon or sucking reflectively on his second scoop of ice cream while you had to settle for one.

I asked if he'd seen Kate, and he said no, she was still at the rehab facility Garret found, but Ella and Terence and Louise had seen her before she went in. For a moment, everything went black. All those sleepless nights haunted by my lost daughter when the rest of the family knew exactly where she was.

It's the thoughtlessness that counts.

DAVID
(age twenty-eight in 2033)

My dad called to find out what I knew about Kate. When I told him she'd cut off all communications, he launched into a paranoid rap about how everyone knew what was going on except him, and he wouldn't stand for it. Once I talked him down, I realized how hurt he was. He couldn't understand why Kate wouldn't have anything to do with him. My dad didn't call much, so I packed in as much as I could about Sophie and me. "Heal," our clinic for uninsured people in the Village, was actually happening. We were so consumed by it, we were able to ignore the citywide panic over the rising water. We knew we'd have to leave sometime, but we couldn't tear ourselves away from our patients who'd been shut out of the health-care system. We were the last line of defense, a couple of twenty-something docs naïve and/or grandiose enough to think they could make things better.

In the bleakest times, we'd tell each other our work was a shared psychiatric disorder, a folie à deux, in which one person is delusional and convinces the other the delusions are real. We'd go back and forth as to who the crazy one was. I was a pretty consistent winner. We had concocted a sisyphean enterprise that was doomed from the start, the clock was ticking on how long Manhattan would be above water, and it was easily the happiest time in my life.

If you ever want to truly appreciate each day, set up shop in a dying city.

ELLA

We were just sitting down to dinner when Uncle Paul showed up, which never happened. My dad said, "Perfect timing, Paul, pull up a chair." He looked raggedy and exhausted, like he could use a good dinner and a few laughs, but he was too agitated. He said, "Everyone knows where Kate is except me. That's not acceptable." My dad said Kate needed time to herself, and Uncle Paul started to come at him, like, are you telling me you know what's best for my daughter? My dad jumped up and turned on Uncle Paul, who'd put up his fists, and we're thinking here it comes, they're going to beat the shit out of each other, when Louise said, "Why don't you just tell him, Grampa? He's her daddy." Dad was so surprised to get called out by a kid, he shrugged and said, "She's at the RJ Manning Rehabilitation Center. It's where she needs to be." Uncle Paul just nodded and left.

I followed him outside and apologized for the way he found out about Kate—Louise blurting it out to Ruth at Blue Hill. He said, "Ella, you raised your daughter to tell the truth. Most people don't do that." I went back inside, and there wasn't much to say.

Kate had made us promise not to tell her parents where she was, everyone had tried to do the right thing, and now we all felt bad. Typical family moment. At least in our family.

TERENCE

We'd worked our asses off at the Franklin, bitching and moaning and dreaming of a day off. Now that the place was gone, we missed it like crazy. The one I really missed was Nandita, so one day I went over to her apartment to make lunch. I tried to tell her how lost I felt not having a place to go every day and how seeing her always made me feel better, and—because she was so easy to talk to—I blurted out that I couldn't imagine my life without her.

I've never been any good at saying how I feel, so it came out weird and heavy like a borderline-psycho marriage proposal. I always say either too much or not enough, and that day was no different, like I'd crossed some invisible line everyone else knew about.

I went into the kitchen to make lunch. She followed me and just stood there, and it was like when you know bad shit is going down, but you don't know what it is. She finally said, "Terence, I have to leave." I said, "Because of me?" She said, "No, you idiot, they're repatriating me. To India. I can't even say 'back to India' because I've never been."

I couldn't understand it. She was born in the USA but because her parents weren't citizens she was now an "anchor baby," and they were cracking down. I started to say, "They can't do that," but of course they could do any fucking thing they want.

I hugged her, and we went to the living room and sat on the sofa and kissed for the first time. When we heard Chandi coming up the stairs, I said, "Nandita, I'm going to India with you." She shook her head like it would take too long to explain how ridiculous I was, then she kissed me again before Chandi got to the top of the stairs.

It was the best afternoon of my life and also the worst. Either God can't make up His mind or He has a really fucked-up sense of humor.

KATE

Finding all those bodies in Florida was a blight on our souls, and waiting for us in California were the fires of hell. Is it any wonder we took our time? Neil was driving and must have sensed I was yearning for home because he drove to town without a word and parked near Lakeview Lutheran Cemetery. It was a brisk fall day ripped from my childhood. We got to Isaac's gravestone and realized it was his birthday, so we sang him a silly "Happy Birthday."

I knew Neil wanted to talk to Isaac alone, so I went to Aunt Hadley's grave and told her how much I missed her. When we were leaving, I looked back and someone was standing where we'd been. Ella was visiting her brother on his birthday.

PAUL

My first thought on entering the RJ Manning Rehabilitation Center was that if you weren't on drugs when you got here, this place would make them mighty tempting. The combination of long halls to nowhere, institutional lighting, constant garbled announcements on the PA, and a robotic red-jumpsuited staff obliterated any hint of humanity. I had no doubt the only laughter was produced by residents exiting reality into full-blown insanity. These rehab people were clearly in the business of breaking spirits, so the addict could be repurposed as a dutiful, flag-saluting, God-fearing citizen whose vote could be counted on to continue the fine work of our irrepressible authoritarian state. I couldn't imagine they'd have much luck with Kate. Better a druggie than a drone.

I reached the reception booth, which was encased in bullet-proof glass, and it was oddly refreshing to be greeted without the gleaming reptilian smiles that customarily welcome one to an institution calibrated for despair. The receptionist, pale, lethal, her skin a size too small for her body, glared at me with pure menace. "Can I help you?" she said, the unmistakable subtext being that she'd quite enjoy stripping me naked, hanging me upside down in the adjacent torture chamber, and attaching electrodes to my genitals. I asked if I could visit Kate Weeks, which triggered a slight, fang-revealing smile. "Kate Weeks is on assignment."

"What does that mean? Where is she? What have you done to my daughter?"

The glass door slid soundlessly shut, and I was alone in hell.

KATE

It was a ten-minute walk from the cemetery to our house. These were the same streets where I'd gone trick-or-treating and learned to ride a bike and walked with Mickey to the bus stop on cold winter mornings. I saw the house where I first kissed a boy, Roger Sweeney. Before he ran off to hide from me in the basement, he said, "I'm not ready for this, Kate!" We were nine. My entire childhood had played out right here. But it felt different now, and it wasn't just the storm I'd been through. The houses were squalid and run down, and strangers on the street looked away when they saw me. Where had everyone gone?

I almost walked past our house, it looked so faded and forlorn. How could they have let it go? It had been such a long time since I'd communicated with my family, I had no idea if they'd even want to see me. I went up the walk and rang the bell and waited. A TV was blasting Fox State News. In my childhood home? I was about to leave when I heard footsteps, and the door opened. A skinny man in a threadbare Green Bay Packers sweatshirt was standing there, watery eyes, unshaven, ghostly. I knew I should know him, but the years of drugs had rattled my brain, and by the way he was staring at me, I could tell he was trying to place me too. I said, "I'm Kate Weeks, I used to live here." He said, "Oh, Kate, I'm Howard Groom. Your old guidance counselor."

I told him he didn't do such a bang-up job guiding me, and we both managed a laugh. I could tell he was trying to locate that confident, pretty, optimistic high school senior in the gray, shivering apparition standing at his door, while I was trying to find the genial, upstanding family man in the sad, shriveled creature staring at me.

"How long have you lived here, Mr. Groom?" I asked. He looked away and told me he'd been placed here after he got out of prison. "This is where they put us. They say we're sex offenders. Those of us who stood up to them."

There were no words. We just stood on the steps, two broken souls. Our university town had been such a glorious hotbed of activism, which is why they had to stamp it out.

RUTH

Anjelica decided they'd leave when Gabriel's school year ended. I couldn't bear to count the days, I just wanted to live in the time we had. Pam asked why we didn't *both* go to Canada. I told her that Anjelica's husband was waiting for her.

I was already the past.

KATE

We were sitting in the van in silence. I told Neil I wasn't going to California to fight wildfires. And I wasn't going back to RJ Manning. They were stealing my life. My so-called rehab—for three long years—was just state-mandated incarceration. They'd used me to clean up the messes they created. And there was no end in sight. Mr. Groom had given me guidance after all. That's what they did to good people who stood up to them. I wasn't going to be enslaved by them any longer, and I wasn't going to stick around and fight. I was going rogue, and Neil would have to decide for himself what to do.

He was quiet for a bit, and then he told me to get out of the car. In my paranoid state, I thought he was going to drive off and leave me to fend for myself. But he got out too and came around to my side of the car, dropped down on one knee, and asked me to marry him.

I couldn't breathe. My last marriage proposal had turned tragic. But seeing the way Neil was smiling at me, I felt this rush of hope and love and everything I'd been living without for so long.

RUTH

We had an end-of-summer party for Gabriel and his friends. They were swimming and playing, and I had to stop handing out chili dogs to go inside and cry. Anjelica joined me, and we watched out the window at all the fun. Then Pam came in and announced she was going to drive Anjelica and Gabriel to Canada. Even though they'd probably be fine on their own, this was a better way to go. She didn't have to spell it out. They'd be safer crossing the border in a Tesla with a rich American woman as perfectly turned out and charming as Pam Rayner.

Pam had always been the Queen of False Equivalencies, believing both sides had a point, but she'd never met anyone like Anjelica. Now she understood you were on one side or the other.

TERENCE

The last thing I wrote in Daniel's class was the news we'd heard about Kate getting married. He asked if I'd rewrite it with more detail. He was more excited about that one story than anything else I'd written.

RUTH

When the awful morning came, I was all cried out. I hugged Anjelica and Gabriel, and they got in the Tesla and off they went. I watched until they were out of sight, then went back to the guest house, which felt empty even with all my stuff still there. I tried to come up with one thing to look forward to.

Then I thought about Kate. Happiness was still possible.

part five

24. spring 2034

ELLA
(age twenty-nine in 2034)

Destination weddings: you're expected to burn through your hard-earned cash to jet off for a two-night-minimum at Hotel Rip-Off-by-the-Sea to be an extra in a super-choreographed home movie celebrating the eternal love of a desperately mismatched couple, which they watch adoringly while eating off the high-end china you went broke buying, until they run out of things to say, cheat with a fetching member of the wedding party, get divorced, and spend a nostalgic evening dividing up the spoils of their picture-book wedding, while you're working a second job to pay for all the fun you didn't have.

Am I bitter? No! This has nothing to do with being a single mom on a limited income, it's about narcissism that's truly clinical, as if we all should suddenly be as giddy and spendthrifty as the temporarily happy couple.

After the budget-busting blessed union of my old boyfriend Tyler Cole in Montecito (currently separated, dating a bridesmaid), I swore off destination weddings.

But I couldn't wait for this one, and Canada's not that far.

RUTH
(age sixty-three in 2034)

Sitting with Paul before the ceremony, I started to cry. He whispered, "When did you become such a mewling infant? You could at least wait for the bride."

236

I tried to explain that it wasn't just the wedding, it was seeing the family together. It brought back all those Sundays at the General's house, which I used to dread and now missed terribly. Here we all were.

Well, most of us.

ELLA

The hardest thing was telling my dad we were going to the wedding. He got that look that had been a surefire source of terror since childhood and left the room. I asked Terence if he was still planning to go, and he said, "Fuck yeah!" And I wouldn't have missed it, so there we were, squeezed into this tiny little church, which was a surprise because we figured they'd just go to a justice of the peace.

The doors in the back of the church opened, and Louise, the flower girl, came down the aisle, the most beautiful child who ever lived (speaking objectively as her mom), then I saw someone dart into the church as if he couldn't be seen.

RUTH

When Garret showed up, I lost it. We were all there. I buried my head against Paul, making a sniffling-snorting sound. He put his arm around me and whispered, "You're an embarrassment, Ruth. If we weren't separated, I'd leave you so fast."

ELLA

My dad never explained why he came to the wedding. After Mom died, his hard-ass thing didn't work anymore. He'd scare people away, and without her to smooth things over, he'd find himself alone in an empty house getting old.

Maybe that was too much for him, knowing all of us were here.

PAUL
(age sixty-five in 2034)

My lifelong goal (which I've largely achieved) is to be a spectator, safely removed from the action. Why do something if you can watch someone else do it?

So it was jarring to get grabbed by David just before the ceremony. "She changed her mind, she wants you to walk her down the aisle." I told him it wasn't fair, we hadn't practiced. David said, "You have to practice *walking*, Dad?"

KATE
(age thirty-two in 2034)

My dad had been acting like a normal dad, all nice and polite and appropriate, and I wasn't going to stand for it. So, I made him walk me down the aisle. By the time David managed to round him up, the wispy 107-year-old organist had launched into a deeply funereal "Here Comes the Bride" that had people looking for the coffin.

I offered Dad my arm, he took it and snarled, "This is bullshit."

I said, "That's my daddy!" and off we went, banging through the doors and down the aisle to where Neil was waiting.

PAUL

At the reception, they were all doing this weirdly precise line dance, young, old, drunk, sober, stoned, demented; they're smiling and happy, and where the hell did they learn it? Did they all sign up for a class and forget to tell me?

Garret asked why I wasn't out there with the rest of the family. "I might spill my drink," I said. "Why aren't you?"

"I might kill the groom," he said, moving on to the bar. I watched Kate dancing between Neil, whom my brother would like to kill, and David, who was as deeply focused as if he was landing a jumbo jet full of orphans in the middle of a tornado with one engine out. My money's on him every time, the orphans would live, but does he have to overthink *everything*? Or maybe that's why he's the most successful of my children, not that the competition is all that fierce.

At the end of the line, more graceful than all the others combined, was the one person who could have gotten me out on the dance floor. Ruth caught me lurking in the shadows, Knob Creek in hand, and gave me an encouraging little nod of her head, eloquently communicating: "Christ, Paul, would it kill you to have some fun for a change?"

I responded with a smile that said, "If we love each other then why are we apart?"

We do better without words. If we didn't talk, we'd still be married.

ELLA

Louise and I had been a team for so long I didn't even think about meeting guys anymore, but Neil's ever-smiling cousin Will kept asking me to dance, and it was fun to feel like I wasn't just somebody's mom and that a male of the species who wasn't a relative wanted to spend time with me. Plus, Louise was twelve years old, dancing wild with other kids and didn't need me.

RUTH

The band went on a break, and Neil got up on the bandstand, and the room got quiet. He knew that some of us blamed him for what happened to Isaac, and here he was becoming a member of our family. He said he wanted to make a toast, so the waiters handed out champagne, and he plunged right in, saying the only reason Kate was with us today was because Garret had saved her life, a debt he could never repay.

Then he talked about how Isaac was the one who brought him and Kate together, and he could feel that Isaac was with us in that moment. He paused, and in the silence three notes came from the piano on the bandstand, one after the other. No one was near the thing. I got this chill—I think we all did—and Neil smiled as if he was plugged into a different frequency. He said, "I wasn't able to do what Garret did—save a life—and the only way I can live with that is by loving Kate."

I sneaked a look at Garret, who was staring hard at Neil, not giving anything away.

PAUL

When Kate jumped up on the bandstand, things got quiet again but not a good quiet. She had this secret smile, which, ever since she was a baby, means she's going to do something she shouldn't. It's the look she had just before she jumped off the garage roof when she was seven and broke her collarbone, her life since that moment confirming she learned nothing from the experience.

Then she sang a cappella, which was terrifying. When she was twenty, she sounded like Joan Baez, pure and beautiful, but now her voice was shot, ghastly reportage from some war zone only she had ever seen, and there was no looking away. She was an upside-down school bus on the median about to burst into flames. This wasn't Joan Baez, it was Marianne Faithfull's *Broken English*, a cadaverous tour guide for your favorite circle of hell.

240

Nobody could breathe; we were willing her through the song, which finally revealed itself to be "Both Sides Now." At the end, there was silence, then we all started madly cheering because she beat it, this was her fuck you to the universe that tried to kill her, she was with us for another day, and that was enough.

That's when I felt a hand on my shoulder belonging to a beady-eyed, crew-cut hydrant, ripped, flushed, high-end suit, diamond earring, wired for communication. "Excuse me, sir, Mr. Flynt from the main office. Could you come with me?"

I asked if there was a problem, and he said something about a deposit for the facility. I told him I'd taken care of it, but he squeezed my arm so hard I gasped. Everyone was crowding around Kate, so they didn't see me follow Mr. Flynt down the stairs.

He stopped at an exit door, and I asked to see the manager. He said, "This way." I've known too many people who disappeared over the past fifteen years. This is how it happens. You're in your life and then you're not. Mr. Flynt pushed open the exit door, and I followed him into the parking lot. Through a dense fog, I could barely make out the soft red glow of taillights.

It had come to this, as I knew it would. My turn to disappear. "Let me say goodbye. Everyone I love is inside."

"Not everyone," he said. "Get in the fucking car, man." We crossed the parking lot, Mr. Flynt opened the door, grabbed my shoulder and spun me into the back seat. I sat in the dark, just me and the driver.

At least that's what I thought, until I heard a voice right next to me.

GARRET
(age sixty-seven in 2034)

I got my beer and turned around and saw this goon take Paul downstairs, while everyone else is watching Katie fighting it out with a folk song. By the time I made it through the crowd, Paul and the goon were gone. I ran to the window in time to see Paul get slammed into the back seat of a station wagon.

It was tough to see the license plate in the fog, but I was pretty sure I got it.

RUTH

By the time the party ended, I was exhausted from dancing, fired up by the excitement of the night, drunker than I'd been in years, and ready to throw myself at Paul as if it was prom night. Our separation had been a dismal failure, and now, in the exuberance of our daughter surviving her addiction and getting married, we would find each other again. Nobody would ever know me or love me or make me laugh or annoy me or excite me like Paul. Where the hell was he? I tried calling, but he had a tense, unresolved relationship with his phone, and I had to leave a message.

We were all staying at the Kewadin Hotel, and I just made it onto the last van going back. I went to Paul's room and knocked. Nothing. I had this awful knot in my stomach, but nobody else seemed worried, which made it worse. I told David how panicked I was, and we got the hotel clerk to let us into the room. There was Paul's jilted phone on the nightstand, burdened by all my agitated messages. I wanted to call the police, but David said he'd actually been missing for only an hour and was probably off in a lounge someplace explaining gerrymandering to a defenseless bartender aching for last call.

I didn't sleep, and early the next morning, I banged on Paul's door again, but he hadn't come back.

TERENCE
(age thirty-three in 2034)

Our party was straggling into the breakfast room, happy and hungover. Me and Jarvis had our own table, which suited me fine. There'd been enough chatter the night before to last me for months. We'd made it through two days with no news, which was another reason we were feeling pretty good.

But they had the TV on, and there it all was.

ELLA

Staying glued to the news gave you time to normalize the insanity before the next incoming attack knocked you on your ass. If you got it all at once, it was overwhelming, which is what happened that morning.

News broke about the mass migration at the southern border, which made the "caravans" the Great Leader used to bleat about look like what they were: impoverished families hoping for a better life. These people were not after freedom and opportunity because those days were gone.

They were starving, and if they got shot by troops at the border, well, it was better than quietly dying because there was nothing to eat.

TERENCE

You'd look up from your omelet at the TV to see families walking straight into the bullets that would kill them, and the waiter's asking if you want more OJ.

DAVID
(age twenty-nine in 2034)

The Great Leader's numbers always jumped when the shooting started. USA! USA! USA!

ELLA

I was sitting with David and Sophie when she gasped and grabbed his arm. Coverage had switched to the breakwater in lower Manhattan, which was swamped by the storm, and the city was gradually disappearing. Their life was going under.

TERENCE

When Aunt Ruth came into the breakfast room, she looked so freaked I figured she'd been watching all this fucked-up news. I heard her say, "David, I can't find your father."

That's when my dad called me.

RUTH

Poor David was trying to deal with Sophie and what was happening in New York, and he had to drive me to the police station. I kept making calls, and he finally said, "Who are you calling?" I had to admit I was calling Paul. He said, "You know his phone is in his hotel room, right? And he's not there?"

I didn't know what else to do.

PAUL

In the darkness of the back seat, I heard Mickey say, "Hey, Dad," as if he'd been away for the weekend instead of thirteen years. I grabbed him and we hugged. I asked him what the hell was happening, and he said there were too many wild cards if he'd gone to Kate's reception, which he very nearly did. Instead, he had Mr. Flynt, aka Bill Truby, his "associate," get me into the car. I asked where we were going, and he just said, "It's good to see you, Dad."

All that time apart and he wouldn't talk.

DAVID

We got to the police station and told Detective Pettigrew the situation. He asked why Kate had gotten married in Canada, and Mom said, "Have you kept up with what's happening in the US? The good times are over, sir." She forgot to mention that Kate and Neil had bolted on a government-mandated rehab program and were fugitives.

He said, "So your family has no connection with Canada?"

We told him about the cottage where we used to spend summers. It had belonged to the General, but he passed it on to my dad and Uncle Garret. Their family never took to it, so it was pretty much ours growing up. We hadn't been there for years.

TERENCE

When my dad said he needed me, it pissed me off how grateful I was. It looked like I was doomed to spend my entire life trying to win his approval, headed for middle age like a needy five-year-old. He'd fired me, undermined me at every turn, and that morning when he called me away from the breakfast room, I was still trying like hell to measure up to whatever he expected of me. Then he started asking my advice.

I couldn't even count on him to not trust me.

PAUL

e off the highway, bouncing down a twisty road in the woods. I couldn't get a fix on anything until we lurched to a stop. Mickey got out, so I did too, and followed him into our old cottage. We were in the kitchen when he turned on the lights, and I saw him for the first time. Full beard, hair to his shoulders with a slash of gray, and he'd lost weight. It was hard to see the football star in this gaunt, serious man, but the eyes gave him away. "You look good," I lied.

He smiled. "You look old." He asked if I still drank, and I told him I'd stopped last night but was ready to pick it up again. He got a couple of Molsons from the refrigerator, and we sat in the living room.

I asked if he was living there and he said, "I can't tell you what I've been doing; there are too many people involved. I hope you understand."

I said, "I don't see you for thirteen years, you kidnap me from your sister's wedding reception, you won't answer a single question, and you hope I understand? I haven't understood one thing since November 8, 2016."

He told me he was trying to save the family. We'd lost our jobs and careers and our relationships, and we were dealing with addiction and jail and the endless soul-crushing trauma of life in the Great Leader's America, and there was no way we'd survive because it was only going to get worse. I'd almost forgotten what Mickey was like when he got wound up. Exhaustion set in—it had been the longest day of my life—and I fell asleep while he was still talking.

I woke up the next day and he was gone. There I was in our beloved old cottage for an entire day, so out of it I felt like I'd been drugged. That night he came back, didn't even tell me where he'd been. Everything was a mystery. He cooked dinner, we drank beer, and I tried to find out what the hell had happened to my son.

DAVID

Even at night, the road was awesomely familiar. My earliest memories are driving on this road with Mom, Dad, Mickey, and Kate in a frenzy of excitement. The summer never really began until we got to the cottage.

I'm driving too fast, the car's skidding, my mom is telling me to take it easy, we're scared we won't find Dad and maybe a little scared that we will. It was her idea that somehow he might have gone there. She was saying how sorry she was that Garret and Terence had gone back home. This is the kind of situation where they shine. Then, from the end of the long driveway, we see a strange car next to the cottage. My mom said, "I think we should stop, David. Nobody comes here except in the summer. Something's not right."

I'd left Sophie on the phone trying to pick up the pieces of our lives, which were disappearing underwater in Manhattan. Our future was gone, and for once, I didn't feel like playing it safe.

PAUL

When Mickey talked about Ruth and me splitting up, it was pretty clear he was plugged into what we'd all been doing for years. "Who have you been talking to?" I asked. He said, "Whatever was going down, we never missed *The Whiskey Hour with Dr. Paul Weeks*. Where exactly did you get your PhD, Dad?"

I asked who "we" was, and he just smiled.

I didn't even know what to ask him. He was a fugitive, wanted for murder; new territory for me. I said, "So you can't talk about what you've been doing, and you know everything *we've* been doing. All these years apart, and there's nothing to say?"

He laughed and said, "Jesus, Dad, I've missed you so much."

That's when we heard a car outside. Well, Mickey heard it. What I saw was his face turn cold and a pistol materialize in his hand. This wasn't the son I remembered.

RUTH

It was so dark, and what was this car doing at our cottage? I said, "David, don't get out of the car." But of course he got out. Maybe if Paul and I had disciplined our children even once, they might occasionally do what we suggest.

David was making his way to the other car when a man came out of the cottage with a gun. He stared at us and said, "We're drinking Molsons if you'd care to join us."

PAUL

I couldn't see Ruth's face, I just saw her moving toward Mickey like she was in a trance. She threw her arms around him, and they both just held each other.

It was way beyond words.

TERENCE

Me and my dad were checked into this crappy little motel outside Sault Ste Marie. My cheapskate daddy sprung for one room, twin beds, too much togetherness for me. He explained why he ended up coming to the wedding and what we were doing here. He called it a "mission." I called it a lousy place to spend the night. Course, I didn't say that out loud.

PAUL

David said he'd be fine sleeping on a futon in the living room, and Mickey went off to his room, and Ruth and I went to the room with the double. We never said a word, just fell into bed together as we had for years and years before the world blew up.

I said, "This is the first night we've known where all our children are in thirteen years."

She said, "Are we terrible parents?"

I said, "No, but I don't think we're going to win any awards." She punched me, and it was as sweet as a punch can be.

RUTH

When we got up, Mickey was gone. Everyone was in various stages of rising and preparing to shine, and it was just like when Paul disappeared. I was the one in a panic. Paul suggested I "calm down." If I ever commit homicide—and I have no specific plans to do so at this time—it will come on the heels of those two words. I started laying out all the reasons we should be worried, when Mickey came in with groceries.

DAVID

Mickey and I whipped up breakfast, and it took me back to how much fun it was when we were kids, doing random stuff with my big brother. I thought, man, he hasn't changed a bit, he's still a total goofball. But when a car pulled up outside, he was in another head, calculating fight or flight. Then he saw Ella and just melted. Then Louise and Sophie. He made Sophie feel welcome right away, and with Louise it was love at first sight.

We managed to keep things light during breakfast. Then these strange people started showing up. My dad was checking them out, so he could pick them out of a lineup.

RUTH

Mickey's friends weren't top-notch in the hygiene department, and they'd obviously been thinking about something else when their parents had tried to teach them manners. Mickey introduced them as they wandered in, and they gave us this semihostile stare like you'd get from chimps in their cages when din-din is late, then they got coffee and said they were off to work. They had this spooky Manson Family look.

I said to Mickey, "I like your friends," as if he'd brought his Little League team home for hot dogs and root beer.

He said, "That's my mom!"

Louise asked the question for all of us: "Who *are* these people, Mickey?" It's easier to do that when you're twelve.

Mickey said, "Oh, they work for me." From the time he'd learned to talk, we could never get anything out of Mickey until he was ready to give it up.

PAUL

Ruth, Mickey, and I took a walk on what used to be the beach but was now choked with bushes and battered by storms. There were no summer folks around, but there was activity in the other cottages, which seemed to be under construction. We didn't recognize a soul, but they all knew Mickey.

He told us the summer people had stopped coming after a flood eight years ago. There had been huge damage, the beach was ruined, and they let the property go, so Mickey managed to buy up the cottages for back taxes.

KATE
(age thirty-two in 2034)

Neil and I were sharing a fruit bowl in bed at the hotel and discussing what we were going to do that day, which for us was long-range planning. That's when Sophie called and told me they found my dad, which wasn't that big a deal, since I didn't know he was missing. She said he was out at the cottage with Mickey.

When I dropped my phone, it went straight into the fruit bowl.

ELLA

Mickey and Louise and I were pulling the old Sunfish out of the shed when Kate and Neil showed up. She got out of the car and came over to us, all Kate cool, and said, "Hey, Mickey, what's happening?"

He said, "Going sailing, you want to come?"

She said, "Maybe later, dude."

Then she choked up and he came over to her. I heard her say, "I thought you were dead."

And he said, "You too." She pushed him away, and then she hugged him.

PAUL

For days, we were jammed into the cottage together. We'd be outside all day doing whatever we wanted, which, for me, meant staying inside. Then it started raining, and there was no escape, no solitude, just the people you love most at close quarters, which is its own special corner of hell.

The third day of rain felt like a perverse social experiment by some obscure midcareer faculty member whose bid for tenure was charting each person's breaking point. We'd each creep off to our own secret place to be alone, and someone else would have gotten there first.

RUTH

One morning when the rain finally ended and the sun burst through, Paul and I were sitting on the porch drinking coffee. We watched as Mickey was sitting in the old rowboat we'd had for centuries, trying to decide if it was worth it to fix the leak. David came out on the dock, untied the rowboat, and gave it a hard push, so Mickey was floating away in a leaky rowboat. It was exactly the kind of thing they'd do to each other when they were kids. It was beautiful.

Paul asked me how long this could go on. I told him I didn't know. It was so hard to think about ending this magical interlude with our three children.

One morning we heard hammering from Howell House, the biggest on the beach, three stories, old, dark, funky. Mickey's people were renovating it, starting with the roof, which had only leaked for the last thirty years. Mickey said some of us could move in when the work got done, so we all pitched in.

PAUL

Mickey would get up early every morning to tend to the garden. He was always up there alone for about an hour before others would straggle in to help. David and Neil and I would go off to work on Howell House. Mickey's strange people turned out to be hackers who'd drift off with big mugs of coffee to start their hacking in one of the other cottages. That's what our days were like.

TERENCE

We parked under the trees at the end of the drive. 6 a.m., there's Mickey working in the garden by himself. My dad was all about preparation. We'd scouted out the situation, and we knew what to do. We just had to do it.

GARRET

(age sixty-seven in 2034)

Me and Terence never had problems working together. He was the kid who'd always volunteer. Even if he was clumsy, he'd keep working till the job was done. His whole life, he never found any shortcuts. That's a good thing in this line of work.

TERENCE

Mickey was in his own world, as usual. It wasn't that hard for me and my dad to sneak around the edge of the garden. Our plan was to come at him, so if he ran, he'd be running away from the cottage and into the woods. That's pretty much what happened. Except he was bent over planting something and he straightened up, and that's when he saw us.

GARRET

Everything was written on his face, plain as day. He recognized us, started to smile, then clocked what was going down. You don't survive as a fugitive for thirteen years by trusting a soul.

TERENCE

He ran toward the woods, just like we planned. I had a flash of, "That's Mickey, that's my cousin!" But my dad had drilled it into me about Mickey being a terrorist, family or not, and we had a job to do. Without the rule of law, we've got nothing. And Mickey needed to be brought to justice.

GARRET

He was in good shape, running a damn sight faster than me and Terence. We could see him moving like a freakin' gazelle, and the one thing we didn't figure on was that he knew these woods like the back of his hand. We're huffing and puffing and tripping over rocks, and the son of a bitch is getting away. You disappear into those woods and if you know what you're doing, you're gone for good.

I look at Mickey headed for daylight, and what I see is that my one chance to redeem my life is ending.

TERENCE

My dad yells, "Take him down!"

GARRET

I knew I couldn't catch him. But Terence was military, he was always working out. He should have been able to keep up with Mickey, so I yelled, "Run him down!" Heat of the moment, Terence heard it wrong.

TERENCE

This was my dad's mission. He was my commanding officer. I had to obey his orders. I had a clear shot at Mickey, maybe my only one before he was gone in the woods. I stopped, pulled out my pistol, aimed, and fired.

GARRET

Mickey went down hard.

TERENCE

I froze up. What the fuck had I done?

GARRET

I never ever planned it to go down like that. It was supposed to be about justice, not a cold-blooded killing. It was my fault. Terence was just trying to carry out an order.

TERENCE

He's lying still on the ground, and all I could see was Mickey as a little kid. Back then, him and me were close, he'd always watched out for me and yeah, we'd drifted apart like people do. But he was a big part of my life when we were young. And I shot him in the back. What had happened in my head that I could do that? I wanted to fucking die myself.

GARRET

Me and Terence can't move. We're staring at Mickey and then we see him trying to get up. I say, "Come on, Terence," and we go running up to him. All three of us are breathing hard. He hadn't been hit by the bullet, he'd tried to dodge it, landed on a rock wrong, and taken a nasty fall that knocked the wind out of him. Terence took one arm, I took the other, and we walked him back to our rental car.

TERENCE

Once we got in the car and caught our breath, Mickey was pretty calm, considering his uncle and cousin had shot at him and grabbed him out of a garden early in the morning and piled him into a car and were driving him off to someplace unknown. My dad had told me to keep my gun on Mickey just in case. Mickey says, "Terence, can you put that thing away? It's really annoying."

He thinks having a gun aimed at him is annoying? After I tried to shoot him?

GARRET

We're driving through the Sault when Mickey asks what the plan is. But he asks it, like, where are we going to have breakfast? IHOP? It wasn't until we made the turn to go through customs that he understood what the plan was. He says, "Back to the USA, huh? You really think that's a good plan, Uncle Garret?"

I said, "Mickey, we live by the rule of law. You broke the law. You killed someone. I should have stopped it, but I didn't. It's not too late for me to do the right thing."

TERENCE

We're getting closer to the place where you can't turn back. My heart is pounding, like, this is it. But Mickey stayed cool. He says, "Uncle Garret, I agree with you. What I did, I'll regret for the rest of my life. Every day, I try to find ways to make up for it, which I can never do." Then he says, "What do you think will happen to me once we're back in the US?"

GARRET

I told him he would finally face justice for what he'd done. And his fate would be up to the legal system.

MICKEY

I told him he was living in the past. The rule of law doesn't exist in the United States anymore. They're executing people, and I would be one of them because I have no money and no connections, and I oppose the Great Leader and the Ruling Party. I said, "Uncle Garret, you're not taking me to the country we both used to know. That country died a long time ago."

GARRET

If Mickey had been yelling or pleading, I wouldn't have heard him. But he was just talking to me, man to man.

MICKEY

I told him that what I did was wrong. It had come out of a misguided attempt to stop what was being done to the country we both loved. And it wasn't so different from what Isaac did, trying to shake people awake so children would stop being killed at school.

TERENCE

We never mentioned Isaac. Ever. It hurt too much. And it stirred up stuff we never wanted to think about. That's the way our family was. My dad would probably say we honored him with our silence. I don't believe that. I think we never knew how to deal with it and move on.

When Mickey brought Isaac up, I saw my dad flinch like he'd been hit. I knew Mickey was playing the last card. It would go one way or the other. That's what Mickey figured too.

GARRET

I didn't *plan* to turn the car around. Few feet further it would have been too late.

TERENCE

Once we turned around, my dad just kept driving, staring straight ahead. Everything he'd worked for and believed in his whole life was gone in America. Justice, the rule of law. He probably knew it before, but when Mickey said it, well, it was just fucking true. It was all over. I was in the front seat, so I could see the tears. Mickey was in the back seat, I don't know if he could.

My dad said, "You and Isaac . . ." He couldn't finish.

MICKEY

It's like he was making this connection for the first time. And once he did, he couldn't drive me over the border. It'd be like he was doing it to Isaac.

We drove back to the beach in silence. There was too much to say to make talking possible.

TERENCE

We got in sight of the garden. It seemed like years ago we'd hustled Mickey into the back seat. My dad stopped the car. Mickey said, "Some morning, huh?"

My dad said, "Yeah. You take care, Mickey."

MICKEY

As soon as I opened the door, I saw Ella and Louise in the garden. They were always the first ones to join me in the morning. Louise yells, "There you are! We didn't know where you went!" She came running up to the car. That's when she saw Terence and Uncle Garret. She squealed with joy. Who the hell can resist that?

TERENCE

I get out of the car to give Louise a hug and then my dad gets out, and he's a goner. He's trying so hard not to cry and then, fuck it, he rushes over and sweeps Louise up in his arms and holds her like he's never going to put her down.

MICKEY

Louise says, "I'm really good at croquet."

Uncle Garret says, "Well, you're gonna have to prove it to me, kid," and we all go trooping back down the long driveway to the cottage.

RUTH

Paul and I moved up to Howell House and took the master bedroom on the third floor. Every morning, we'd sit by the window and watch the sunrise. We have a long history of analyzing everything into submission, but we didn't even ask each other what we were doing or how long we'd be staying. It was all so fragile, our relationship and this stolen time with our family. And the last years at home had been so hard.

PAUL

Mickey's people were weirdly shy and giggly around me. I asked Mickey about it, and he said, "Dad, you're a celebrity thanks to *The Whiskey Hour with Dr. Paul Weeks*. They think you should do more." I had a bit of free time—all day every day, actually—so at dusk on the porch in preprandial overdrive, Mickey set me up with Holly, a spirited wizard of technology, pierced and tatted with a dazzling smile, and I did my first podcast:

For years, the Great Leader had deprived himself of what he wanted most: to wear a military uniform like the demagogues he'd come to adore through the tiny fragments of history he'd encountered without opening a book. And now the time had come, he'd earned this moment, and there he was in all his fraudulent glory, a rank, blistered orange sausage with saggy, flapping arms encased in a mauve uniform and high boots, strutting toward a podium in the Rose Garden where he stood with an otherworldly smile. He knew he'd won. He'd made the entire country as empty, weak, and frightened as he'd been, since the sky blackened on the day of his birth, a sorry, unloved pet never housebroken by his emotionally incontinent parents. He was no longer alone in the endless void, he had 300 million fellow sufferers who'd quietly succumbed to the creeping contagion of his existential vacancy. He had an announcement to make. The staggering problems of social media had at last been solved. Personal security, foreign interference, and the bullying, trolling, hatred and shame that made every day a trial were relics of the past. The government was taking over the amoral-leftist-corporate-social-media monsters that had spiritually savaged the nation. The Great Leader would henceforth maintain the internet as the Founding Fathers had envisioned it, with respect for all white citizens with proper papers, a love of country whose actions can only be understood by those at the top, and mandatory Christian values starting in utero. Abortion would be stopped once and for all by arming fetuses (pending background checks in a nod to the liberals). Finally, someone with the courage to clean up the pluralistic slop the country had been marinating in for far too long. If we do what we're told, we are free! His clownish sycophants—who, defying both physics and biology, maintained a vertical posture with no backbone—matched his ghoulish smile. They knew when they joined the Great Leader's team of dunces, they'd prebooked a one-way, all-expenses-paid trip on a cramped coach seat to hell. These shivery moments in the hot glare of fame made it all worthwhile, even knowing their trousers would soon be yanked to their ankles and they'd be publicly flogged by their demented master, drunk on humiliation and rage, who wouldn't stop spanking until their cabinet-level buttocks were a rosy pink, perfect hi-def viewing for the audience at home washing down their Fatburgers with growlers of PBR, cheering on the Great Leader and his retinue: a gleaming, machine-tooled wife; a pair of blank, empty-headed sons with the charisma of cheese; a porcelain daughter with her uncomfortably fey husband, a gaggle of aging porn-star ambassadors to small African nations, and several mirthless harridans authorized to translate his psychopathic babble into official, state-sanctioned lies. Some would note, squinting through their stupor, that the Great Leader had stuffed the crotch of his too-tight uniform in one more failed attempt to impersonate a man.

GARRET

When me and Terence and Mickey went into the cottage that first morning, Mickey said, "Look who I found!" Everybody made a big deal about us, and we all had pancakes together. We didn't say what had happened that day, with me and Terence busting Mickey and shooting at him. Every family has to work shit out its own way, and we all got through it alive. Maybe he told 'em later, I never knew.

I just know the family took us in, no questions asked.

RUTH

One night, I said to Paul, "Do you think we'll ever get back to where we were?"

He said, "No, that's gone forever. We're headed someplace new, Ruth."

Falling back in love with Paul was even better than the first time.

ELLA

We were on top of each other in the cottage, so Louise and I moved up to Howell House with Paul and Ruth. They had a going-away party for us at the cottage, even though we were only moving fifty yards away. A week later, David and Sophie joined us, and it was such a relief to have all that room to spread out.

GARRET

I'm not like my brother. He can waste a whole goddamn day sitting on his ass with a book. I have to be getting stuff done. And there was plenty to do. The cottages needed to be rebuilt and winterized and generally taken up a notch. It turned out to be the kind of work I like. End of the day, you can see what you accomplished. You earned that beer.

TERENCE

Everyone slipped into some role—like my dad doing carpentry and Uncle Paul with his podcasts—but there I was, on my own, like usual. Me and Jarvis would take monster walks, disappear for hours, my dumb old life coming back, like I'd never been a big-deal chef and run two restaurants.

Ella picked up on where I was at—as usual—and told me we were going to team up and cook. I told her I wasn't interested, as if that mattered to her. So I moved up to Howell House, and Ella and Louise and I would make a daily run into town for supplies, and then we'd start cooking.

There was a big living room, and everyone would squeeze in for dinner, sitting wherever they found a spot, and our goal was to blow their fucking minds.

ELLA

Mickey's people would join us for dinner, and one night I found myself talking to a big-bearded, puffy guy named Perry, one of the computer geeks. I thought we really connected until later when Kate asked a bunch of questions about him that I couldn't answer, and that's when I realized I'd done all the talking.

No wonder it was such a good conversation.

KATE

Like the hardest of the hard-core socialists I've known, Mickey and his crowd had a gift for making money. When my dad's podcast started to catch on, they came up with a series of brilliantly annoying ads for adult diapers and breast pumps and anal wart removal. Ella's new friend Perry had a slight speech impediment, and he was the designated product spokesperson. They slowed down his voice, exaggerating his stutter, and played polka music in the background. You couldn't listen to these ads without wanting to kill yourself and/or a loved one.

So they offered a commercial-free version of *The Whiskey Hour* for ten bucks a month. People loved the podcast, hated the ads, and subscriptions poured in as Mickey and his weird-ass pals predicted. I found them cackling as they counted the cash. Socialists indeed. My dad with his fake doctorate and twisted worldview was a star, and the bitcoins were rolling in.

PAUL

I'd been there for the golden years of the USA, but now that our country was circling the drain, I'd jumped ship for Canada. It felt wrong. Maybe if I had a bit more character, I'd have gone back home and fought the power instead of sipping bourbon on the porch and making podcasts, safely hiding out in a commune. But it sure was fun.

DAVID

My mom told me she'd heard from Anjelica. There had been some kind of mix-up. She and Gabriel made it over the border to Canada but couldn't find Dr. Morales.

PAUL

There was a tiny group of concerned citizens who'd march in front of the White House every day. It made the Great Leader seem magnanimous to allow a protest that could so easily be stopped. He called them the Sad Losers, so that's what they became on Fox State News. Tour groups would be shown the Sad Losers for photo ops and easy laughs. A few dozen people registering their polite opposition to the Great Leader's autocratic USA, that's all that was left of the resistance.

Another quaint vestige of democracy was the oversight role of Congress. The Opposition Party kept holding hearings to call the Great Leader to account, knowing that whatever they found would be batted down by the majority leader, an ancient toad-faced toady, barely living proof that the good die young. It was an exercise in futility used by the Ruling Party to prove, over and over, that the Great Leader had done nothing wrong and the Opposition Party was bent on revenge because they couldn't win an election.

TERENCE

Ella hadn't had a real boyfriend in years, and now she was hooking up with this computer dude named Perry, and Paul and Ruth seemed to be back together, and Kate was happier with Neil than I'd ever seen her. You couldn't spit without hitting someone in love, and yeah, how great, everyone's so friggin' happy. What it mainly did was turn up that voice in my head telling me I never fit in.

I had to make a move, even if it was a dumb one.

DAVID

I got chosen to drive my mom to pick up Anjelica and Gabriel. She was as giddy as a sophomore on a first date. I kept thinking, *This will end badly.* Either Anjelica will have moved on, and my mom will be devastated, or they'll rekindle their thing and my dad will be devastated. One way or the other, devastation was waiting. I asked what she wanted, and she said, "Whatever happens, happens."

I said, "Mom, this *que será, será* bullshit won't fly. What are you going to do?"

We got to the bus station and there they were. My mom took a deep breath and said, "Wish me luck."

RUTH

Driving back to the beach with Anjelica and Gabriel was so comfortable we picked up right where we'd left off. Of course, there was the question of what would happen when we got back to the cottage.

DAVID

My dad was gracious, and we all survived dinner. Ella had moved in with Perry so her room was free, and that's where Anjelica stayed, right next to my mom and dad's room.

Everyone acted like this was the most natural thing in the world, and maybe it was.

PAUL

I was mesmerized by the congressional hearings of the Opposition Party. There was something deeply moving about these much-maligned people continuing to do their jobs day after day, pursuing democracy when it didn't exist anymore.

When they started looking into the connection between the Ruling Party and We the People, I called Mickey.

MICKEY

We the People was from a previous life, the activist organization I'd joined back at the university. Now we're hearing that it had been created by the Ruling Party to infiltrate the left. Starting in 2021, they began recruiting subjects for what they claimed were studies on educational approaches to benefit the underclass, but were really techniques for breaking down an individual's belief system in the interests of extreme propaganda.

One of the early breakthroughs happened at the psych center, where important tests to ultimately benefit the Ruling Party were conducted before it was bombed by radicals.

PAUL

I looked at Mickey, and tears were rolling down his cheeks. All those years ago he was right. He'd been on to their evil game, tried to fight it, and it had wrecked his life. But there was no easy vindication, because Cal was dead and the bastards' work had continued.

MICKEY

They refined the disinformation virus and were able to target individuals anywhere in the country to change their beliefs. Using the personal information that people gave up so readily on social media had, of course, been a big factor in the Great Leader's power grab in 2016.

Now it was surgical. A whistleblower revealed an early beta test that targeted fifty couples with the goal of ending their relationships through personalized online contact. After three months, forty-six of the fifty couples separated, including four suicides, three homicides, and one murder-suicide, in which the shooter got the order wrong and performed the suicide first. Of the four couples who stayed together, one had gone on safari with no online contact, one had a member with a psychotic break who was institutionalized, and two had been kidnapped in unrelated incidents in Tucson.

In short, the test was a rousing success. The most intimate relationships could be destroyed online by the state, which encouraged them to roll out a person-to-person targeted online campaign to secure a permanent landslide for the Ruling Party.

Democracy, which had long been on life support, was flat-lining. Time to call the morgue.

TERENCE

It was a stunning drive down through the Upper Peninsula, but after all the wild passion of the beach community, our university town seemed dull and dreary. The Great Leader's America was a place where you were expected to shut the fuck up and do what you're told.

I got to Nandita's apartment, and there was no one home. I sat on her steps and waited through the afternoon and into the night. That gave me plenty of time to think about how I was going to feel when she showed up with her new boyfriend. One more ridiculous plan in a life jam-packed with them. Why didn't I tell her I was coming and avoid the pain?

I finally saw her trudging down the street alone, exhausted. When I stood up, she started running as fast as she could on those tired legs and threw herself into my arms. "It's you," she said, "It's really you."

That poor-dumb-me voice in my head had not one thing to say.

DAVID

We put solar panels on all the cottages and got wind power going and built a breakwater with sandbags on the beach. Then we went after the big abandoned barn in the middle of the field. It was a huge project insulating it and solarizing it and plumbing it, but we all pitched in and got it done. Uncle Garret was a total workhorse. He never said much—he never had—but it seemed like he was glad to be there.

MICKEY

I'd lie awake nights trying to figure out what we had to get done by winter. There were so many people to take care of, and I felt responsible for every one of them. One night, with my mind NASCAR-ing around an endless track littered with smoking wrecks and crumpled bodies, I popped an Ambien and finally drifted off to sleep, blissed out to be in a warm bed with the wind rattling the windows.

My dad woke me up to tell me the water was rising. I went out into a savage rain with the water getting higher and our people piling sandbags as fast as they could to save Howell House. There was this black guy I'd never seen working next to David. He didn't stop till the job was finished.

TERENCE

Aunt Ruth wanted me to pick up stuff from her friend Pam Rayner, so I drove over with Nandita and Chandi. The three of us went trooping into the gated community, which was a museum of How Rich People Used to Live, like we took a wrong turn and walked into 1980.

Pam was super nice and had all Ruth's things packed up and wanted to know how she was. I said, "Oh, fine," but Pam was worried. I mean, Ruth goes off to a wedding in Canada and never comes back. I told her about the community we're building in Ontario and how Nandita and Chandi are being forced to leave the country.

Pam wanted to hear everything. She ended up giving us lunch—soup and salad, but still—and kind of boasting about how she was pretty good at getting people over the border. I told her we'd be okay, and then she said so quietly we could barely hear her, "I haven't talked to anyone for weeks . . ."

MICKEY

The next night, dinner at Howell House, the room was full, people scrunched up wherever they could find a spot. I happened to look across the room where the black guy from last night on the beach was sitting, and he smiled at me. Man, I got so shaky I tried to eat but couldn't taste my food, so I went down to the beach to check out the water situation, and he's suddenly next to me. Didn't say a word, just hugged me. My whole life, there's only one person who's ever hugged me like that. Dee. He whispers, "It's me, Mickey, it's me." I push him away, so strangled I can hardly say the words. "Who are you?"

He comes closer, and I look in his eyes, and I know who it is. He starts to put his arms around me, and this time I push him so hard he stumbles and drops down hard on the beach. I'm half-crying, "This isn't happening. This isn't what it is. I dreamed about this for fifteen years but I didn't dream it like this." He gets up and says softly:

"This is what the fucking dream is, Mickey. This is who I am, it's who I've always been."

I can't breathe, can't think, can't stay a moment longer, the world's too small, I have to get away from this thing that's exploding my brain, so I get in my truck and back all the way out the long drive at fifty miles an hour, speed through town like I'm seventeen, end up in the bar at Swallows Inn, bang down a murderers' row of tequila shots and see this sad-eyed woman, thirty-six, divorced, school teacher, or maybe she's twenty-four, single, client rep, or maybe she's forty-two, escaped con, ice-picked her spouse. It doesn't matter, she's the only woman there and what I need like never before is a woman, so I sit next to her, get a nibble with a smile, reel her in with a drink, twenty minutes later we're out in my pickup, clothes in a tangle at our feet and she says, "He's in prison, and he isn't getting out, but I can't do this."

We put our clothes back on, and I drive her home. We sit in the truck, and I try to tell her what happened to me down by the water when my past came roaring back at warp speed with a different face and a different body. Just then a light goes on in a dark house, and a little girl is staring out at us. I'm overcome by love for this woman I just met, tell her we can save each other, we can love each other till the end of time, this is our moment and it will never come around again. I kiss her gently on the lips, and she says, "You'll be okay, just give it time," and goes into the dark house where the little girl is waiting up.

RUTH

As a teenager, Mickey went through a phase when he'd sulk in his room and only come out for school and football. Now there was no school and no football, and he won't come out of his room, so I asked Kate to talk to him. She has a gift for making things either much better or much worse, so I kept my fingers crossed.

KATE

I've always gotten a lot of pleasure from disappointing my mother, but Mickey had been holed up for days and everyone was concerned, so I did what she said, knocked on his door, and heard a grunt instead of a selection from, say, the English language. It was the middle of the day, the room was dark, and

271

he was lying in bed with a book. I asked what he was reading, and he had to look at the cover to find out. I'd never seen my brother like this, depressed, suicidal, whatever. I told him I loved him—which I had never done before—and he winced at the word "love."

I got David to talk to him, figuring this was a job better suited to a doctor than a folk singer. Afterwards, I asked what his diagnosis was, and he said, "Mickey's really fucked up." I suggested he put it in layman's terms. Mickey was such a giant oxygen-sucking personality, and now he's Major Tom, quietly drifting off into deep space forever.

We were all freaked out, Mom the most. She was already coming apart, shacked up with my dad while her ex-or-maybe-current lover's in the next room, but Mickey's meltdown was the straw that fucked up the camel's back.

DAVID

Mickey accused me of "playing doctor." That pissed me off. My family doesn't think I'm an actual doctor—apparently because I'm still nine years old—so I got up to leave and he asked about the black guy who worked so hard on the breakwater. I told him his name was Daniel, he was Terence's writing teacher at the U, and he left when he found out Terence wasn't here. Mickey said, "Terence is coming back, isn't he? How is he supposed to get in touch with this Daniel person?" I told him I'd find out if he left contact info for Terence.

It struck me as a bit curious that Mickey was suddenly so concerned about Terence getting together with his old writing teacher, but Mickey was never easy to figure.

RUTH

The next morning, Mickey's truck was gone. There was so much work to do, it was hard to believe he'd just abandon us.

MICKEY

Parking at the Omni Hotel was stupidly expensive so I circled the block and found a space just before this prick in a beat-up old Honda Civic could steal it. I rammed my nose in first and started to execute an award-winning parallel parking job, except my truck was three inches too long and I had to cut bait. As I drove past the bastard-in-waiting, I flipped him off, but then I see it's an ancient fossilized woman with enormous glasses and a neck brace, and she smiled and waved to me with such kindness I double-parked, hopped out, and got old guiding the slowest driver in North America into my space. My major psychological development over the past thirty years is recognizing when I'm being an asshole, which doesn't prevent the behavior, just diagnoses it.

I was in a mad rush to get to the hotel, but now I'm delaying with this altruistic, we-are-the-world parking assistance, which means I must be scared shitless of what's going to happen. To prevent the possibility of chickening out, I ditch the truck in valet parking, pony up the kind of dollars I used to pay for rent at my classiest apartment back at the U, and head for the hotel. I'm standing in the lobby debating my next move when I feel a familiar gravitational pull to the hotel bar, where so many great life decisions are made.

Middle of the afternoon, a few married guys are slumped at the bar, staring vacantly into their vodka tonics, wondering why they'd been so excited about this brief, joyless escape from home, and there in back by the window Daniel is staring straight at me, and the son of a bitch doesn't even have the decency to look surprised.

I sit down at his table and a Labatt's Blue is waiting for me. How did he know I was coming? He nods to the window, and I look out to see the old lady glacially emerging from her Honda. Babies are born faster. "Nice job parking," he says. That's instead of hello. I asked how he found me in Ontario, and he said Terence had written about the cottage and Kate's wedding in his writing class, and he figured it out from that. He asked how I found him at the hotel, and I told him I knew the bread crumbs he left for Terence were meant for me.

Then the two of us started drinking beer for real and spiraling back through the years to when we were at the university together, working at the library, and falling in love.

ELLA

Louise and I were walking back from the garden late in the afternoon when a car comes rumbling down the dusty drive to the cottages. It stopped next to us, and there's Terence with the biggest smile I've ever seen on a human face. He says, "Get in!" So, Louise and I pile into the back seat next to Jarvis, and there's Nandita and Chandi and Pam Rayner, and we all started squealing.

We squealed all the way to the cottage. Jarvis looked concerned.

MICKEY

Of course it ended for us back at the university after the bombing, when I went underground. But Daniel claimed the change happened before that, when we both volunteered as research subjects at the psych center. For me, it was a mission. The government was brewing a dark cauldron of evil, and I was gathering intel behind enemy lines.

Daniel had been coming from a different place. There were flyers for the research study around campus that said, "Do you have the courage to face the real you?" He had been struggling with that question his whole life and was desperate to finally deal with it in a safe situation, which this wasn't. It was about mind control. At the beginning of the weekend, everyone had to write an essay on "What I believe." What followed were seventy-two hours of psychological warfare to change our belief system and get the most useful version of the "truth," involving brainwashing and psychotropic drugs and harsh, fucked-up interrogation that a civilized country would call torture but our government considered a friendly interview.

For the smart, brave, vulnerable young African American woman Daniel had been back then, the relentless psychic assault resulted in what the flyer promised, *facing the real you*, who was now sitting across from me in the hotel bar, drinking beer.

PAUL

Ruth was flirting with Anjelica, while Terence and Nandita were all over each other, and Ella and Perry were laughing at a private joke, and Kate and Neil and David and Sophie were engaged in a riotous philosophical conversation, and Pam Rayner was circulating in her gracious, well-brought-up way. There was no time to let things take their natural course. If we wanted something, anything, we had to make it happen now. Small talk was one more endangered species, and I was rooting for total extinction.

Later, Ruth apologized for lavishing so much attention on Anjelica, and I said there isn't enough happiness in the world, so she should grab it wherever she finds it. She said, "That's very noble, Paul, but could you be just a little bit jealous?" I said I'd work on it.

MICKEY

Back at the university, I'd been involved in nonviolent protests through We the People, but after that weekend at the psych center, I got swept up in a subterranean radical cell and what felt like an inevitable march toward the bombing. Just as the psychological assault in the research study ultimately served to reveal Daniel's true nature, maybe the violence I embraced was also triggered by what happened that weekend.

The only other person I knew who'd volunteered for the study was Kate's old boyfriend Glenn. After that weekend, he abandoned progressive politics and went back home to run his family's furniture business.

RUTH

I was kissing Anjelica and then kissing Paul, and then Paul was kissing Anjelica, and I said, "Even if Mickey never comes back, look what he's created." The room was crackling with life and love and laughter and sex, and what else do we need?

Paul said, "I think we need more wine."

MICKEY

The hotel bar was buzzing with the nighttime hook-up crowd, and I was debating yet another round when Daniel said, "Let's go to my room." The moment had arrived. This is where I'd tell him that, while I'd always love him, I could go no further. I'd banged up against the edge of my comfort zone, same-sex drinking. The tragedy was that we couldn't change who we were. From a passionate young couple in those heady revolutionary days at the university, we'd morphed into a pair of random dudes slamming down pints in a hotel bar in Ottawa. And that was the end of our story.

Except we'd been talking for hours, and it was like when he was Dee and we'd talk all night. I didn't want it to end. It was her mind and her heart and her spirit I'd fallen in love with, and here it all was again except deeper and freer and funnier and tougher, and I was terrified of losing it and even more terrified of pursuing it. Fuck! It was an impossible situation, and I needed more beer, but my glass was empty and my mouth was dry, and there was something I wanted to say but I couldn't find the words, so, like the newly crowned Sultan of Lame, I heard myself say, "This is a huge adjustment for me."

Daniel stared soulfully into my eyes and said, "For both of us. You think I like that beard?"

TERENCE

I got back from a food run and looked out on the porch of Howell House, and slumped together on this ancient sofa were Mickey and Daniel. What was weird was how unweird it was, like they'd always been together, which I guess they kind of had.

Daniel gave me a hug, and I said, "Now I know why you wanted me to write about my family."

He laughed, and Mickey said, "Hey, Terence," but it sounded friendlier than anything he'd ever said to me.

25. fall 2034

RUTH

I kept thinking about the General. Since we'd never actually decided to stay in Canada, we didn't think of bringing him up to join us. I'd call him every Sunday, and he was getting worse and worse at hiding how lonely he was. I said to Paul, "It's all well and good for us to not make any plans, but we really have to do something for the General." He said he'd talk to Garret.

GARRET

Everyone was so busy, they never even thought about the General. I finally said to Paul, let's fly him up here. So we did.

PAUL

Garret picked him up at the airport. It seemed like he'd be most comfortable in Howell House, so we switched rooms around, and he moved right in. Everyone made a big fuss about him, which is all he ever wanted from the human race.

GARRET

I was struggling with the situation. I couldn't in good conscience be a part of this group. My politics weren't their politics. I didn't want to argue with them, and I didn't want to pretend I lined up with them, either. I was feeling like a damn hypocrite. I had to get out of there, go back home, make the best of it.

My plan was to leave Sunday morning when everyone gathered in the barn to sing hymns and spirituals and semireligious whatnot and I could slip away unnoticed. I finished packing my car when Mickey came out of the cottage and said, "No goodbye, Uncle Garret?" I told him this was best for everyone. When he asked why, I said, "Bottom line, my beliefs are different from everyone else's." And he said that's exactly why I should stay. One of the problems I have with Mickey is I disagree with everything he says and does, but I can't help liking him. Even when I was about to drive him back to the USA to turn him in.

He suggested we get coffee and sit on the porch, and I said it had to be quick because I want to be gone before church lets out. So, I went point by point how I disagreed with him. He said, "Uncle Garret, sitting here on a porch in Canada, we can go head to head on politics, but that's not possible anymore in the USA. If you don't line up with the Great Leader, you're a traitor." He was right, but I didn't want to get into it with him.

He said the country was going to change real soon. I asked how, and he said, "What do you think we're doing here, Uncle Garret?"

MICKEY

Like any true conservative, Uncle Garret was appalled by the Ruling Party, but he sure wasn't on our side either. We talked long enough to realize there were a few things we agreed on, like how the world was becoming unlivable for the human race. Sometimes, all it takes is the looming extinction of one's species to open up the conversation.

It was the longest one on one I'd had with him since he convinced me to play football at the U.

GARRET

Mickey heard Daniel in the kitchen and went inside, and I realized, damn, I stayed too long. Everyone's coming back from the barn. I sat there checking out the beach, trying to remember what it had looked like when we were kids. Different time, different world, different view from the porch.

I was just about to get up when Pam Rayner appeared in the doorway saying, "Oh, I'm sorry, you probably don't want company." I told her it was fine, since I was leaving anyway, so she sat down with her book and said, "I never was much of a group person, but I've spent so much time alone it's a comfort to be around people." I told her I'd been spending a lot of time alone but still wasn't sold on the human race. She laughed and said it was nice to know at her age she's still capable of changing, and I said the way the world's spinning, we have no choice.

What stood out about Pam was that she wasn't afraid of silence. Some people—and by "people" I mean my family—are like deejays afraid of dead air; they have to fill it even if they have nothing to say. Pam listened. She asked where I was going—I'd already forgot I told her I was leaving—and I said, "Inside to get lunch. Can I bring you something?"

DAVID

One of the new units we built in the field was designated as the Clinic. Sophie and I set up shop there, and people would come in if they got the flu or rolled an ankle or were involved in some fluky nail gun accident. With all the construction projects, there was always action of some kind, but our patient hours were mainly devoted to a single individual. The General suffered from a range of legitimate health issues, but on top of that he was a world class hypochondriac.

One afternoon, Sophie was wheeling him back to Howell House so he could recover from not having a heart attack when I saw someone making the long walk down the dusty road to the cottages. He had the unhurried pace of a man who's traveled the world on foot and wouldn't accept a ride. I went rushing out and yelled, "Dr. Morales!"

He came strolling over and said, "David?" It was the first I'd seen of him since our long-ago Thanksgiving chess match. I walked him down to the cottages, where he met his son for the first time.

PAUL

I spent my online time telling people to get offline. Stop being data points they can use to manipulate your beliefs. Our only defense against the madness is to live in the world.

DAVID

Dr. Morales joined me and Sophie at the Clinic. He fit right in but was still on the gruff side, just as I remembered.

MICKEY

My dad was old school, but he had a totally unconscious gift for marketing. The more he told people to get offline, the more followers he gained. What sold his rap was that he meant it.

Then they started to show up in person.

DAVID

Sophie and Dr. Morales and I were in the Clinic and heard laughter. We looked out, and several twentyish wanderers were ambling down the drive toward the cottages. I asked where they were headed, and they said they wanted to meet Dr. Paul Weeks.

KATE

They kept coming, survivors who'd managed to crawl out of the quicksand of America 2035, a parade of psychedelic explorers, ambitious dropouts, bankrupt millionaires, snowless ski bums, divorced women in search of authenticity, divorced men in search of divorced women, the bicurious, the bicommitted, the bipuzzled, the unjustly accused, and the secretly guilty, all parched for what they couldn't find in the United States: camaraderie and informant-free fun and a chance to cavort nude in the sunshine without surveillance tapes to be used against them at a later date. They knew us from *The Whiskey Hour* and were up for anything, yearning to create wild transgressive tales they could someday recount to their grandchildren or alien captors.

MICKEY

I was taking a break with my dad when a few backpackers came up on the porch and said, "How does this place work?"

My dad said, "Feed the community, and the community feeds you."

They mumbled, "Heavy shit." My dad had become a master of the oblique non sequitur that left people in respectful confusion.

They camped in the field, and most found a way to fit in. Some left pretty quickly when they realized this was a working community, not some hedonistic orgy of drugs, sex, partying, and all-around bad behavior.

We saved that for the weekend.

TERENCE

The community was catching on in a big way. To me and my dad, who didn't buy the politics, that meant trouble. We'd served and sacrificed for our country, and we were uncomfortable being part of a group working against it, even though the United States had turned into something we could hardly recognize.

Uncle Paul and Mickey and Daniel were great at stirring things up, but we started to wonder if they had any idea where all this was headed.

GARRET

Pam Rayner helped me translate the family's radical politics into something that almost made sense. It helped that I cared so much for her, which opened up a part of my life I thought had died with Hadley. There were times I worried I was compromising my ideals, but I was happier than I'd been in years.

So I moved in with Pam and kept a steady watch on what was happening.

TERENCE

I overheard Mickey and Daniel strategizing about all the people showing up from the States. Mickey said, "The problem is we're full. We can't take any more."

I said, "Dude, you sound just like the Great Leader."

He flared up until Daniel started laughing, and then Mickey said, "Fuck you, Terence," but he might as well have been saying, "I love you."

Daniel was the best thing that ever happened to Mickey.

GARRET

Terence and I were the only ones who saw the potential danger of a bunch of doped-up, unvetted, peace-and-love migrants moving in. Paul loved being the center of attention, but he was clueless about the way the world actually worked.

TERENCE

My dad and I handled security and started checking out the folks showing up. Nothing obvious, just casual conversation. You can find out a lot if you know what you're doing.

PAUL

Oddly enough, it was Garret who found out Mickey's plan. He mentioned it like I already knew. Being senselessly competitive with my brother since the beginning of time, I acted as if I did. But all I knew was what Garret told me.

RUTH

When Paul said Mickey was planning to "reboot America," I didn't understand what it meant. Shut it down and start over? Isn't it too late for that?

Paul said, "It's been too late for a long time, but that's no reason not to do it."

ELLA

I asked Mickey about this "reboot" business, and he just smiled, so I asked Perry, and he said it means exactly what it says. Which was pretty annoying, considering I was sleeping with the guy.

GARRET

I found out that Paul would take long walks alone on the beach in the early morning. I told Terence and we filed that away, since Paul was the main reason people were showing up.

TERENCE

This new guy, Bruce Melvin, early twenties, was one of the mystery hangers-on. There was something about the guy I didn't like. Maybe that Nandita was super friendly to him. She asked if I was jealous, and I said no, but I'm pretty sure I was lying.

GARRET

One night, Terence said to me, "Dad, if you had to pick one person who's up to no good, who would you pick?"

I studied the folks hanging out after dinner and said, "Bruce Melvin." I don't know why.

TERENCE

The first morning tailing Paul on his early morning beach walk, I'm hiding in the bushes when a branch catches me in the eye, and I say, "Fuck!" Paul wheels around and sees me and asks why I'm following him. I tell him I wasn't, but we both know I was, so I apologize. He says he'd ask me to walk with him, but this is the time when he prepares to be awesome.

RUTH

Back at the U, we had taken our lives for granted, as entitled people tend to do. It broke Paul's heart when they didn't give him tenure, and he never found his footing after that. But once he started doing podcasts, people treated him like the brilliant professor he used to be.

He got his mojo back, and it was a wonder to see.

TERENCE

I didn't tell my dad that Uncle Paul busted me on the beach. I didn't want to see that look on his face. So, I just kept a bigger distance from Paul when I tailed him. Nandita told me Bruce's story: disowned by parents, no cash, trouble finding his place in the world—welcome to the club—but she was so sympathetic and so not interested in him romantically, I eased up on the paranoia. I told my dad Bruce was okay, and his response was silence.

Which, in the funhouse world of my dad, means he doesn't agree.

RUTH

There was always something going on at the barn, music or dances or lectures, and people from town would show up. The big fear of the parents was that their teenagers would run off and join our commune, but as it turned out, it was some of the parents who moved in with us. The cottages were full, so we started building these small, energy-efficient units all over the field.

One night, we were walking to the barn, which was already half-full for a performance by local bagpipers—which nearly kept Paul in his room—and I asked if we'd decided to stay here. He said, "Absolutely not, but I sure can't see leaving."

TERENCE

Nandita would tease me about tailing Paul. She said I did it because the early morning was my favorite time of day, and I loved being alone. She was right. Like usual. I got pretty casual about what I was actually supposed to be doing to protect him.

DAVID

When my parents emptied the house at 117 Poplar, I was sure I didn't want anything. But I was glad they'd saved some stuff, like the football Terence gave me after my miracle catch.

RUTH

Thanksgiving Day, Louise and I were in the kitchen making pies and listening to Paul's holiday podcast:

PAUL

Good and Decent People used to think the Great Leader would gracefully step aside when he lost an election. But dictators never leave of their own accord. He postponed the election because of a National Emergency: he was about to lose. Good and Decent People thought when the election finally rolled around, the Great Leader could be defeated, fair and square. But dictators don't do anything fair and square. The Ruling Party poll-taxed and deregistered and reverse-gerrymandered and conspired with foreign powers so he couldn't lose. The Great Leader used to joke about making himself President for Life and now he'd done it, changed the rules so he'd never have to leave. The lesson? When humorless people make a joke, it pays to listen. Good and Decent people said after the Great Leader dies we can take the country back to Camelot, when we were proud to be Americans. But dictators don't leave when they die. That porcine explosion of rancid, orange flesh babbling obscene threats in the Oval Office is an animatronic figure. The Great Leader died years ago doing what he did best: cheating at golf. He picked up his errant drive from a sand trap and tossed it onto the eighteenth green, where it rolled right up to the cup and dropped in at the exact moment a massive sinkhole opened up in the sand trap and swallowed the Great Leader, ensuring that his last words on earth would, fittingly, be a lie: "Hole in one!" But even in death, he continues to work his diabolical magic. Life expectancy has been dropping year by year because we have declared war on ourselves and we are winning. Our weapons are suicide, homicide, and unfathomable deaths by despair. How can we give in to despair when we have smart TVs and 4000 channels and phones with more capabilities than entire regions of the country and self-driving cars with the most technologically advanced cup holders in human history and appliances that talk us through our day and laugh at our tired jokes and surgery that makes us look the way we did at twenty-four when surprised by a burglar? Because that's not all we have. We also have mortiferous levels of stress, which build and build until our heart goes boom and we're flat on our back in the driveway staring up at the clouds, where we see the faces of everyone we ever loved, wondering in our final moments why we were so anxious. Was it the brutal hours at a soul-crushing job that made our throat constrict, so all we could manage in the sales meeting was a deathly whisper? Was it the marriage that tanked when the only jobs we could find were on different coasts and we thought that made sense? Was it the cold realization that we haven't had a best friend since seventh grade and our last meaningful exchange was in a lesbian chat room when the other lesbians were undoubtedly guys like us, slumped on Barcaloungers in the basement, EZ Fit jeans at our ankles, chomping McNuggets and swilling rum-and-Pepsi, vainly trying to summon an authentic human emotion? Was it our stepparents living in an aquarium in Florida whom we always forget to call, especially on holidays? Was it the realization that in nine years we've never talked to the neighbors, and at this moment, our only hope is that one of them will see us splayed out like a squashed bug by the breezeway of the house we can't afford and save us? Wait! We hear a voice—"Look at that fat fuck in the ugly pants lying in his driveway"—and our dying thought is, why didn't we ever talk to them? Why didn't we fire up the barbecue and cook hot dogs for the kiddies and flirt (respectfully) with the wives and drink Coors Lite with the guys and chat about the Final Four? What was it that consumed every hour of every day, so we can't remember a single moment of joy? Was it the free-floating smog of hopelessness hanging over the remnants of our civilization that we breathed into our lungs from the moment we opened our eyes on another unwelcome day? My friends, like opioids and binge drinking and erotic asphyxiation, the Great Leader is one more manifestation of death by despair. That we settled for him is no different than when we gobble handfuls of Oxy on Sunday night because the thought of fighting for putrid scraps one more time with a rabid pack of Monday morning rageaholics is worse than death. Our country is a compassion-free zone. We live in the killing fields of misery and stress, where there is no victory, no retreat, only surrender, but stress is not bound by the Geneva Convention, so when we finally have had enough and raise the white flag, stress will keep murdering us, one by one, just as long as we grimly accept our fatal solitude because we've given up on finding a sense of purpose or someone to love or a community where we truly belong. Happy Thanksgiving!

RUTH

When Paul finished his heartwarming holiday podcast, Louise looked outside where they were choosing up teams for football and said, "We have all that, family and purpose and community. We're going to live forever!" Then she went running outside to play.

I knew the General wouldn't want to miss the game, so I wheeled him onto the porch where we could watch together, just like old times.

DAVID

Late in the afternoon, there were snow flurries, but nobody wanted to stop playing. I was glad Mickey was on my team. He made some unbelievable catches, and they *had* to be because my passes were all over the field like drone strikes launched by a drunk. The best part of my game was trash talking. I ragged on Terence's team, dirty demeaning stuff that caught them off guard, me being a sensitive, caring doctor. My feeling was, fuck 'em, I want to win!

We'd been out there for hours when the General started bellowing, "Next touchdown wins!" Which made everyone mad because both teams knew for a fact they were way ahead. In the huddle, Mickey started taking charge, and I said, "I got this." We lined up with Ella as quarterback. She took the snap, I dropped back and she lateraled to me, I made a Hall of Fame fake to Mickey on the left, and then I turned and Louise was all alone in the end zone, and I couldn't lob it because Terence was racing over for the interception, so I fired the ball hard, and it slammed into her gut and knocked her down, but she held on to the ball.

I figured, hey, if she's hurt, she'll get excellent medical care.

RUTH

Louise came up on the porch holding on to the ball, which David gave her after the touchdown and described exactly what happened in fantastical detail, even though we'd all just seen it. Paul had joined us for the end of the game. It was getting cold, and everyone trooped inside to get ready for Thanksgiving dinner.

Mickey, Kate, and David were the last ones on the field. There were our children, laughing about something, and Kate stuck out her tongue to catch the snowflakes, and I turned to Paul and he answered the question I didn't ask. "Yeah, Ruth, we did okay."

ELLA

At Christmas, we each picked a name from Secret Santa and improvised. Kate wrote a song for Terence, I knitted one sleeve of a sweater for Neil. Uncle Paul's gift to my dad was a podcast that didn't mention the Great Leader.

PAUL

With the holidays approaching and the end of a long year in exile, it should be clear that we're on our own. Don't look to god or the government or Powerball or the hazy comfort of the afterlife for salvation. All we have is what's around us, this life, this day, this moment in all its raging beauty. There's nothing waiting for us at the end, no participation trophy for soldiering through, no final rebate from the home office for how unfair it all was, no apologies from the bullies who ruled first the playground and then the government (we were sure their cruelty would catch up to them, but of course it never did), no passing of the baton to the next one who will run our race. No, there's just the yawning abyss waiting to swallow us up in one final cosmic bite for all eternity. And then nothing. Nothing and more nothing until even the endless nothingness is nothing, which means if nothingness is nothing then there has to be something. And there is. But let's not bet on it or pull our punches or back off from the big risk; there's no reason to play it safe when we already know the end of the story. Turn the page, whisper the last sentence, the final chapter is done, close the book, turn out the light, say goodnight forever. Forever. Forever and ever, beyond our capacity to imagine. But wait! Don't forget to hang a stocking for Santa because you just never know. Merry Christmas!

KATE

My present from my mom and dad was my old Yamaha guitar, which Terence had brought up from Pam Rayner's house. After all these years, it was like reconnecting with a dear old friend who'd stayed exactly the same. I started practicing and found an ancient notebook my parents had saved from 117 Poplar, which had a bunch of song fragments from when Isaac and I were writing together. There was one called "When the World Was New" that we had worked on for years.

Without drugs, and back in the place I loved most, the world was talking to me again.

DAVID

I went back and forth on whether to ask Dr. Morales the big question, and finally I just blurted it out: "Do you want to play chess?" I'd been putting it off for a simple reason: I hadn't played for years, and I really wanted to win. In preparation, I had been paying Louise a dollar per game to play with me. She barely understood the rules, but I knew she'd pick it up fast and she had. She'd even beaten me a few times, because it's impossible to predict what a beginner will do, and some of her ridiculously bold attacks actually worked. I gradually got my head back into it, so when Dr. Morales agreed to play, I was ready.

There we were, locked in another epic battle. He wasn't as sharp as he used to be, and I almost took pity on him, but then I remembered how he never once let me win as a child, and I went in for the kill. I was two moves from checkmate, and my heart was pounding. It was shameful that beating this poor refugee who'd spent much of his adult life incarcerated was so important to me. Just when I'd embraced my own shallowness and could smell victory, I glimpsed that tiny smug smile I hadn't seen since I was a kid.

The smile that said he was going to win.

TERENCE

I'd gotten so used to following Paul on his quiet morning stroll, it made no sense when Bruce Melvin slipped out of the bushes. I rushed him from behind when I saw the pistol. I dived and knocked him down, but he got his shot off.

RUTH

That's what I woke up to, a gunshot. And somehow I knew.

GARRET

Terence and I were outside the Clinic, waiting to see if Paul was going to pull through, when Terence said, "Dad, I blew it, just like the bombing. I was too late."

TERENCE

My dad just looked at me and then looked away. Didn't say a word. Would have been nice to talk about what happened. Even a few words.

RUTH

Paul had been shot in the back. He survived, but when he returned to our room after five days he looked old. And weak. All of a sudden he'd stumbled into old age, and I felt like I wasn't far behind.

TERENCE

Nandita blamed herself for convincing me Bruce wasn't a threat, and I blamed myself for not sticking closer to Paul. Everyone felt bad, and we didn't know what to do with Bruce. We found out later that the Great Leader had called Dr. Paul Weeks an enemy of the state.

MICKEY

I had a huge argument with my mom about what we should do about Bruce Melvin. It got so heated, she told me to go to my room. Thirty-eight years old and mommy hits me with a time-out. She later said she was kidding, but she wasn't. Ask anyone.

KATE

We had a meeting in the barn to decide Bruce's fate, and we were all over the map. Turn him in to the cops? Send him back to the USA? He'd have gotten the Medal of Freedom from the Great Leader. Mickey said we should handle it ourselves, but how? Build a jail? Execute him? Everyone loved Paul, and there were some pretty brutal suggestions for Bruce's punishment from a bunch of peaceniks.

RUTH

It was Garret who said we should put Bruce on the work chart.

GARRET

The best thing Mickey and Daniel did was their chart. Everyone had a job, and everyone else was depending on it getting done. There'd be the usual complaints and poor-me bullshit because that's as much a part of being human as our kidneys. But having the rest of the tribe count on you for survival gives you a purpose every single day. That's what I miss about the military.

ELLA

My dad drives me nuts 98 percent of the time, but it's worth it for the 2 percent when he makes me proud, like when he spoke up in that meeting.

MICKEY

Garret got us to see Bruce as a lost kid who had bought the free-range hate the Great Leader was peddling and thought it was his patriotic duty to get a gun and come after Paul.

RUTH

I think what Garret went through with Isaac enabled him to have compassion for Bruce Melvin. In Garret's mind, Isaac got led astray by radicals, just like Bruce Melvin got led astray by the Great Leader.

Garret and I were never close, but I felt like after all these years we started to understand each other. We'd been through so much together. One afternoon, he asked if I'd take a walk with him. I thought he had something he wanted to discuss, but he hardly said a word. He just loved walking in the woods and wanted to share that with me.

KATE

We were wary of Bruce. He kept to himself and didn't say much. The one who reached out to him was Jarvis, who had the gift of making everyone better. Since Bruce wanted to be with Jarvis, it meant spending time with Terence, so the two dudes became friends in spite of everything. The three of them would go on walks, and you could see the change.

Day by day, Bruce depended on us and we depended on him because that's how the work chart was set up.

RUTH

One morning, I looked out at the beach and saw Terence pushing the General in his wheelchair and Jarvis and Bruce leading the way. Terence stopped, and the General stood up from his wheelchair and started walking briskly. They kept going like that until I couldn't see them anymore. I asked Terence about it later, and he said, "Oh, he does that sometimes." Our lives were getting slower and deeper, and things like the General walking the way he did twenty years ago would happen with no explanation.

It felt like some kind of great mystery was unfolding all around us.

MICKEY

Word had spread to the outside world that Dr. Paul Weeks had been shot by a Red Hat, and there was huge anticipation of what he would do in response.

RUTH

Paul spent lots of time on the porch reading and staring into space. For PT, he'd walk into the kitchen for another drink. I was shocked that he wanted to do more podcasts.

MICKEY

I thought it was a mistake. My dad seemed softer and more sensitive than he'd ever been, which was the opposite of his rants.

We had no idea what his followers would think of the kinder and gentler *Whiskey Hour.*

PAUL

We were all victims of the Great Leader, but we still felt bad for his wife. As a younger woman she endured the escort's nightmare—hooking up with a john who never left—which resulted in her becoming First Lady. She often had to excuse herself from state functions because the mere sight of her bovine life partner with his creepy, cold eyes cannibalizing her made her throw up in her mouth. She'd known for years he was a closet necrophiliac who could only love a woman who was as dead as he was. She longed for the heedless days of lucrative promiscuity when she wasn't required to have opinions or speak in complete sentences, but now she was chained for eternity to a terminal narcissist whose soul was a black hole that swallowed everything in its path and was too dense to allow any light to escape. One day, she wandered away from the White House and wasn't seen for months until BuzzFeed reported a brief sighting at the Iowa State Fair where she was observed eating deep fried cheese curds in the company of John F. Kennedy Jr. The Q Anon crowd went wild but it enraged the Great Leader, whose marital vows as he understood them allowed for the occasional nine-second romp with a fading porn star while in another zip code but certainly didn't permit his wife to consort with the dead. That was his department. When it became clear that she had come to her senses and would never return, the Great Leader turned plaintively to his daughter, the surgically triumphant Princess I. A baby was necessary, so the torch would not be passed to his dim, vacant sons who'd learned their ignorance and cruelty at the feet of the Great Leader himself. Princess I rose to the occasion and became First Lady-Daughter, so committed to her new role she miraculously gave birth to Baby Fred. When the subject of paternity arose, the Great Leader leered like an acne-ravaged freshman who'd gotten lucky Friday night with a sorority queen, slipping his tiny orange claw up the princess's royal skirt as her shiny lacquered face cracked in pained, grisly laughter and she stared at the Fake News reporters with the same wolf eyes as her father/husband/coparent, a regenerating lump of lies, hate, and toxic sputum. The happy couple displayed Baby Fred in public (pay per view: 750 dollars) and the heir apparent, apparently hairless except for a single telltale sprout of orange rising from his glistening empty dome, was wearing a tiny military uniform with an extra sleeve in back for the unfortunate third arm which a dewy-eyed Fox State News jezebel called a symbol of the First Couple's "awesome and enduring love." The vice president, who adored fetuses but hated babies, smiled obsequiously at the Great Leader and croaked, "It has your eye." When Princess I looked down into the single rheumy eye staring up at her with pure hate from the jiggling scoop of malignant inbred flesh she'd birthed, she too threw up in her mouth, which was one of the many demands on the First Lady. Clearly, the nation was in good hands.

MICKEY

As it turned out, we needn't have worried about my dad's level of bile. It was permanently full to the brim. That's when *The Whiskey Hour* really took off. The combination of getting shot and coming out swinging fired up his followers. Holly, the tech wizard who recorded the podcasts, told him he was a "thing," and he said it beat the hell out of being a person.

PAUL

Getting shot made me homesick for the USA. As wonderful as Canada was, it lacked the beloved traditions of my country, like Fourth of July fireworks, the World Series, and random gunfire.

MICKEY

Nobody knew what the reboot was, but everybody was talking about it. We decided the Great National Reboot would take place on May Day, when the Great Leader was going to announce that Lincoln's face on Mt. Rushmore would be rechiseled into the Great Leader's turgid snout. It had to be done because the Great Leader was the best-loved American who ever lived and no one talked about Lincoln anymore.

PAUL

Since I couldn't convince my followers to get offline, I tried to get them to take action. Go to Washington on May Day for the Great National Reboot. Join the Sad Losers. My understanding was that this reboot thing would be a symbolic event, like levitating the Pentagon.

Ella finally said, "Uncle Paul, what you need to know is the reboot is real."

27. spring/summer 2035

DAVID

April 30, the eve of the Great National Reboot, the partying in the field went on most of the night. I stayed in the Clinic just in case, but there weren't any injuries other than a guy and his parrot falling out of a tree onto a large bald woman's cello. Typical party stuff.

KATE

We hadn't had a lazy day in a whole year. Ella and I went skinny dipping first thing, then we made blueberry pancakes and sat out in the sunshine with our books. It was that kind of day. Delicious.

RUTH

That night after dinner, we all gathered around a bonfire on the beach.

DAVID

I saw Kate coming down the path with that old Yamaha that used to be attached to her. I remember going to her room when I was a kid and talking to her about the problems I was having at school with Isaac and the Stop Bullying Now crowd. She listened and gave me advice, and the whole time she kept playing that guitar.

PAUL

She didn't make a big thing of it, just started strumming, and the buzz of conversation around the bonfire faded away. Then she sang. Her voice was thin and frayed, and it took me a while to get that this was the song she used to play every night after dinner. The one that had only the beginning, which she'd play over and over. It used to drive us stark raving mad.

RUTH

The song was so familiar. I could see Paul tensing up.

KATE

I could see the recognition from my mom and dad. Here it is, the song that never got finished. I thought, "Just wait, I'm going to blow your fucking minds." But somehow, I couldn't get past the beginning of the song. How could I have stage fright in front of my own family?

PAUL

It was deeply unsettling for me, like PTSD. The beginning of that song flashed me back to a time in my life I wanted to forget. I was watching Kate, and she had this look, kind of panicked, like she couldn't stop and she couldn't go forward. My drink was empty. I thought, I can't take one more second of this without a drink. We are all trapped in the beginning of a song that is endlessly repeating itself, and it's beyond poor Kate to get out of it. I went inside. I was hurrying, not smart when alcohol is involved, and managed to knock my glass off the counter. I had to clean up the broken glass, so I was inside longer than I intended.

KATE

What freed me up was my dad going inside. I guess getting a drink was more important than hearing the song I'd been working on for twenty years. As soon as he was gone, I heard another voice singing with me. That's when I knew I hadn't finished writing "When the World Was New" alone.

ELLA

Everyone was knocked out by Kate, but I felt blessed that I was the only one who was able to hear *him*.

RUTH

I couldn't stop smiling when I heard him harmonizing with Kate. Those two voices singing together had been stuck in my brain all these years since Garret's birthday party. Now I was hearing them again, and it was, well . . . a moment I will never forget.

PAUL

By the time I'd cleaned up the glass on the kitchen floor and refilled my drink and come back to the group, Kate had finished the song. Everyone was standing there in silence.

RUTH

Applause would have cheapened the holiness of the moment. Finally Kate said, "What, you didn't like it?" and we all started laughing and cheering. I felt like in that moment Paul and I got our daughter back.

ELLA

The only possible encore was s'mores for the kids, so I went back up the little path to the house. That's when I saw him in the shadows. He had that mystical smile from childhood, like he knew things he couldn't tell you. By the time I came back from the house, he was gone. I told Louise, and she asked if I was afraid. I said, "Why would I be afraid of Isaac?"

KATE

For years I'd dreamed about finishing that song and singing it for Dad. And when I finally had the chance, he decided not to be there. I knew I'd hurt him for years and years in all kinds of ways, and I wanted to tell him that the absolute best thing in my life was having another chance with him. And that I loved him. After all the hell I put us through, I'd finally reached a point in my life where I could say those words, which do not come easily to me.

But the moment was gone.

PAUL

Everything was happening at once. Kate was headed my way, and I was about to hug her and tell her how much that song meant, but David was suddenly in my face showing me on his phone what was happening in DC. People were joining the Sad Losers. Not a lot, but more were showing up every minute. The movement had been so tiny for so long, this meant something was happening. David said, "This is you, Dad, you did it."

Then Mickey grabbed me and said it was time for the Great National Reboot, the folks up in the field who'd come all this way deserved to be a part of it, and I should be the one to tell them. I said, "Mickey, I don't know what the hell this reboot thing is." He explained stuff that made no sense, but I figured I was as ready as I'd ever be, which wasn't ready at all.

Then I looked for Kate, but she was gone.

KATE

I had to get out of there before I started crying.

PAUL

We went up to the field and I climbed on the back of Mickey's truck so they could see me. I didn't realize how many people were there until they gathered around. It was just like the huge crowd for the Great Leader's first inauguration. Except mine was bigger. Check the photos. I said, "Brothers and sisters, the New Day is here. It's time to turn off, tune out, and drop in . . ."

MICKEY

He thought it was some kind of whacked-out performance art, and he's up there riffing on Timothy Leary. I called to him, "Dad, ten seconds!" He got everyone to count down with him: five, four, three, two, one . . . then silence. Nobody knew what was supposed to happen.

I got up there next to my dad on the truck and said, "Listen, people, unfucking America will take everything we've got, and it's starting right now! People are marching in the streets of Washington, and we've hacked into the power grid and seized all the data so their fascist empire is shut down and the city is dark. We're rebooting America!"

DAVID

Mickey called the computer hackers up on the back of the truck to take a bow after all those endless days hacking. By then, folks were on their screens yelling that it was happening: DC had gone dark and more and more of the Sad Losers were surging through the city.

MICKEY

There was already talk of the ransom the Ruling Party stooges would pay to get their data back. Not bad for a college dropout, huh?

KATE

It was tough feeling so alone in the midst of all that joy. I stuck around to cheer for Neil when he got up on the truck, and then I went to my room. I didn't want to bring anyone down.

ELLA

People would always remember they were a part of this, whatever it turned out to be. It felt like we'd been thrashing around in deep water for so long, and now we could touch bottom and maybe make it back to shore. Maybe.

DAVID

The Ruling Party's tireless efforts had succeeded. They'd strangled the schools and kept out immigrants and cut people off from political engagement and trashed science and hoarded all the money and lied relentlessly every single day so the population was blank and beaten.

But we were waking them up.

KATE

For hours, I couldn't sleep. The wind was battering the cottage, and the rain came sideways in wild sheets that shook the windows. It was the end of everything.

MICKEY

The storm finally ended the jubilation, and we all went off to bed. Daniel and I fell asleep happy. I think we all did.

KATE

I got more and more upset, so I did what I never do, which is take one of my mom's sleeping pills. My head hit the pillow. It's a cold winter morning, Mickey and I are hurrying down Poplar to the school bus, late as usual. I'm carrying my science project, a clever approach to converting dirt into electricity, potentially world-changing and pretty ambitious for a nine-year-old, but it really slowed me down. The bus is about to leave, so Mickey rushes ahead and tries to hold it, but Mr. Ruddy yells, "You need to think of others for a change!" I yell back that I'm trying to save civilization—I probably didn't need to add "asshole"—but he closes the door. I see Mickey's anguished face in the window as the bus drives off, and I'm standing there alone shivering with my science project. Why didn't Mr. Ruddy wait? Why am I always left behind?

A gunshot woke me up. I looked outside. The big maple had been snapped by the wind. Or hit by lightning. Whatever was out there was coming closer and would get us in the end. Neil slept through it, which made me happy for him and sorry for myself. How did he get healthy enough to sleep through the night while the most I ever got was a couple of hours of restless churn?

I slipped on a robe and went down to the kitchen, and the cottage was creaking and moaning and praying. It would all blow down if the wind picked up. Ever since we'd moved into Howell House, I'd been checking everyone's drugs to know what to watch out for so I could steer clear.

That night I found out the truth. They were for me. All of them. From the beginning of time, I've had a monster living inside me. My parents thought I was spirited or anxious or hyperactive or chemically imbalanced or whatever label would reduce my condition to something knowable, but I was so smart and pretty and popular there couldn't be anything really wrong with me, so they never saw the monster. Nobody did except in crack houses or back-alley dope deals or turning tricks in the back of a regional sales manager's Grand Cherokee during my great decline. With music and rehab and Neil, I got the monster to calm down. He trudged off the field and let me play my game. But he was always on the sidelines, watching every move I made with his shiny, yellow eyes. Lately he'd started pacing, shuffling his feet, clenching his fists. He wanted to get back in the game, and here he was with his abundant offerings: my dad's pills for postsurgery pain, my mom's pills for sciatica, Ella's pills for her migraines, Terence's antidepressants, plus a glittering cornucopia of narcotics of all sizes and shapes for the entire household to treat the increasingly untenable condition of being human. We were Americans, we lived from one blessed pharmaceutical fix to the next. Except for me. I'd been a good girl for so long. Spinach salad and protein shakes and yoga and meditation and now, in the wee hours, my skin was slowly sliding off my body and there was the monster, scaly and smiling. One yellow eye winked. The weekend's here, baby, since when did fun become a crime?

I grabbed my dad's pint of Heaven Hill and slugged it down. Such a harsh assault after all these years, and so very, very good. You could build a rich and fulfilling life around Heaven Hill. Then I took the pills. One from this bottle, one from that, one from another, a salad bar of doctor-prescribed narcotics. The family that gets high together stays together. I put my daddy's Oxy bottle in my pocket and went outside.

The storm was over. It was dark and silent, and god was in hiding. I headed up to the field, still wet with rain, barefoot, and wandered through the world we'd built, tent-fulls of pilgrims sleeping and snoring and coughing and scratching and dreaming.

A couple was sitting outside their tent murmuring to each other, smoking a joint. One of them I'd known when I was someone else. The bald-headed cellist from Dean's apartment. She winked and offered me a hit, and it would have been rude to say no.

The world gently turned and came back around, soft and shimmering, and what I felt was warmth, the tender warmth you can't get from anything but this, the warmth that fills you up when nothing else will. All those young bodies intertwined, holding on to each other for comfort in the night. They'd left their lives and everything they knew to come here. Because of us. We'd made our family big enough so they could be a part of it. More and more and more would come, and they would be us and we would be them until the whole world was one and our family would span the globe, a species, like chipmunks or pandas or grouse, and when we'd used up this planet, we'd blast into the deep blue and find another, and we wouldn't fuck it up like this one. The very first morning on our new planet, we'd get up early to take out the recycling and report our neighbor for using pesticides. We'd live forever.

I walked through the field and into the woods and washed down more pills with the Labatt's I'd thoughtfully jammed in the pocket of my robe. What a good camper I was, always prepared. And how foolish to think I was past this. That I could rehab the darkness away. The monster had always been waiting. This was his moment. He had won. It was time to embrace his victory because I had done everything I was put on this good earth to do. I had loved and been loved. I had caused such pain and felt such pain. I had said yes to everything and missed nothing. Unlike the monster, I had never spent time on the sidelines. I had always been in the game.

I made my way through the electric woods, each leaf, each branch, each bush glowing with life extreme, pulsating with its own inspired frequency, the mad forest symphony lifting me higher. It was all happening in the woods. The dope had been treated with something new and exciting, and the pills were the old friend I'd loved too much, and the beer was a sweet kiss from adolescence.

I could see a clearing off the path, a mysterious break in the trees caused by subterranean forces of nature or some primal ritual from the deep, a celebration of the Sun God, a dance to the rites of spring. A massive oak tree, wizened patriarch of the forest, was watching me, his dreamy moss-encrusted trunk beckoning. A forgiving haunt where a tired girl could lay her head.

I emptied the pill bottle straight into my mouth and took a long delirious slug of the beer that zapped me straight back to the college parties I went to with Glenn when I was still in high school, a talented amateur just starting to compete with world-class miscreants. At one party, an annoyingly woke girl in earth-friendly shoes asked how old I was. When I said sixteen, she said I shouldn't be with this sick, exploitive college man who had one thing in mind, I was still a child and should be with people my own age. I listened patiently as she squinted at me through granny glasses, clutching her organic wine, and then I suggested she go fuck herself, since no one else ever would, which speed-bumped the party but nothing could stop me on nights like that. Everybody wanted me. I dressed for sex and talked about Nietzsche and drank like a frat boy, and who doesn't want that? I'd get hit on by girls and guys, wonky freshmen and mordant PhDs and shy hopeful TAs with pale lipstick, and Glenn would watch with the kind of amusement that's only possible if you know you're going home with the girl. Sixteen, and I knew everything.

Somehow, as the years passed, I knew less and less and then nothing at all except how to score smack when everyone else has given up the chase, and now I was alone in this divine particle of time, blessed with the perfect knowledge I used to have. My heart swelled. I whipped off my robe and stood gloriously nude in the middle of the woods, saluting myself with Labatt's for fulfilling my final mission.

I had found the perfect place to die.

RUTH

I was dimly aware of Paul getting up in the night. He'd always been held hostage by his mind. If he hit on something, he'd have to write it down. With *The Whiskey Hour* and his near death by shooting and his slowly fading memory, it was happening more and more.

I was half-asleep and thought nothing of it when he wandered from our bedroom.

KATE

As my eyes drifted shut, I had a simple, clear thought: This is the last time I will ever close my eyes. And then I thought: That was my last clear thought. And, since I was thinking about my last clear thought, *that* was my last clear thought. And since I was thinking about thinking about my last clear thought, *that* was my last clear thought. It was turning into a pretty irritating death, so I mantra-ed my way into blankness, my head resting on the trunk of the wise old oak. I would forever be a part of this magical world, and even though rain had fallen most of the night, and I was lying naked under a tree, I was warm.

After a long life of needing something—money or a job or a lover or a car or lyrics or respect or acceptance or dope or hope or rent—it was quietly exhilarating to need nothing. I was free.

Before I shut my eyes forever, I saw a ghost moving silently toward me. He came closer and closer, his face so vacant he couldn't be alive. He was the one who would spirit me off to the next world. Guess I was wrong about no afterlife. My bad. He leaned over and shook me, and then I saw who it was.

My father had sleepwalked from his bed to the middle of the woods to save me. He didn't wake up until I burst out of my stupor. We both screamed.

DAVID

I was alone in the Clinic that night. With the hordes descending, we decided someone should be there around the clock. I saw my dad half-dragging Kate out of the woods. I thought she was dead. I rushed out, and we got her into the Clinic.

Given the population on the beach, we were well prepared for ODs.

KATE

After David worked his doctor magic, he and my dad and I sat in the Clinic looking out at the water. Hours later, there was a hint of a reddish glow, and we watched the sun slowly rising on another day, the greatest show on earth, back by popular demand. Like all the important moments in my life, there was no explanation. How did my dad know I had left the house? How did he know I was dying? How did he find me when he was asleep?

Logic is overrated, I choose to embrace the mystery.

PAUL

I'd love to take credit for saving Kate, but it wasn't me. It was a greater force in the universe, the one people worship in all kinds of ways and I never have. But I know it's there.

KATE

My mom used to say, the trouble I've had with my dad is because we're so much alike. She also said, "The difference is you actually go out and *do* all these crazy things, while your father is content to have a good seat so he can write it all down." That night, somehow, he wandered unconscious into the fray and found me in time. We sat together in the Clinic until morning and never said a word. It was the kind of silence that words would only diminish.

Still, it was pretty hard for my dad and me to be quiet. It's not our thing.

28. summer 2035

RUTH

When Paul asked what I wanted for my birthday, I told him, "Another year with you."

He said, "Just one? What happens after that?" I told him if he acted right, it might go longer, but I wasn't promising anything.

On the actual day of my birthday, I wanted to have dinner with just my family; partners would have to fend for themselves. It was warm enough, so we set the table on the porch of Howell House, and Paul and I were enjoying the evening, which was blissfully quiet except for the piercing shriek of the smoke alarm and the arguing, bickering, and laughing from the kitchen as our three children cooked dinner. They were far too proud of their creation, which frankly wasn't that special.

We were just about to eat when I said, "What are we grateful for?"

Naturally, they started making fun of me for suggesting our predinner ritual from a previous lifetime, but Kate said, "Hey! It's Mom's birthday." She took Paul's hand and Mickey's hand, and we all held hands as if we were back at 117 Poplar fifteen years ago, and Kate started to say something but couldn't finish. None of us had seen her cry since she was a baby, and she wasn't about to start now. Her whole body was trembling, and when she finally spoke she sounded like she was five years old: "I'm glad my daddy found me."

She was squeezing so hard, Mickey said, "Kate, that's really starting to fucking hurt." She let go of his hand but kept holding her father's hand.

It was the best birthday of my life, easy.

MICKEY

There was a lot I didn't tell my dad. I never talked about the other guys who bombed the psych center with me and how it all went down. Daniel's the only one who ever got the full story.

But I made sure my dad had his moment of glory after the big power shutdown. So, I didn't tell him we weren't the only ones responsible for the march of the Sad Losers and the Great National Reboot. We were working with other resistance cells around the world to attack the power grid in Washington and seize the data. We were one of many. I didn't want him to know that.

PAUL

It mattered to Mickey that he be the mastermind behind the country starting to come to its collective senses. The more time I spent with him, the more I realized he had dedicated his life to atoning for Cal's death. But, honestly, I'm not sure how important we actually were. I think the movement was starting to happen anyway. Of course, I didn't tell Mickey that.

DAVID

We got pummeled by one storm after another, and the water kept rising right up to the porch of Howell House. My dad had my old rowboat from childhood tied to the railing. Mickey had finally fixed the leak. Kind of.

PAUL

Survival is what turned the tide. When it became clear that the only hope was working together, the Ruling Party had no cards to play. Dividing us was all they had.

RUTH

Mickey and Paul have such grand notions about all we accomplished. But even if we do take back the country—and I have serious doubts—there are wounds that will never heal. There's no normal to go back to. I try not to talk this way around the rest of the family.

Behind the bluster they're a delicate bunch.

ELLA

Late one afternoon, I couldn't find Louise. Or Uncle Paul. I was almost worried enough to get help when I happened to look out at the water, and there they were in David's little rowboat. The sun was setting and Uncle Paul was rowing—at least he was supposed to be—but the oars were still and the boat wasn't moving, and he was talking and talking, and Louise was listening so intently, and that's how I'll always think of them.

LOUISE

I'd always planned to give my great-uncle Paul the last word. He's kind of the reason I did this project. That afternoon, the whole time he was talking, I noticed the rowboat was slowly leaking, but I didn't want to interrupt him because he was so fascinated by what he was saying. I figured one way or the other, we'd probably make it back to shore.

PAUL

Was everyone else in the family as honest as I've been, Louise? I bet they were, or at least tried to be. You bring that out in people. I remember your dad as a kid, younger than you, after his father rode off on his motorcycle. Hadley took him in like he was family, and he and Terence were brothers.

There was one summer, back when we all used to be up here together, he came with Terence's family. He was always up for anything, just like you. The first time he water skied, it took him fifteen tries and he was barely staying up, but he started waving to us and trying to do all these nutty tricks like he was a pro.

He'd wander into my office sometimes and look at me with those big, brown eyes, just like yours, and ask me questions, and no matter how busy I was, I'd find myself telling him whatever he wanted to know. One afternoon, he asked me what caused the Civil War, and I said, "Bobby, there's no short answer."

He said, "So tell me the long answer."

Sounds like you, doesn't it? Ever since you were little, you've always listened louder than other people talk. Most of us don't feel heard, don't feel understood, so when someone comes along, like you or your dad, who actually listens, we finally get to tell our side of the story. Remember when you told me the idea for this project? I asked why you wanted to do it, and you said, "I want them to know what we did when we were here." I asked who you meant, and you said, "The ones who will come after we're gone. I want them to know that we did our best. I just don't think it's all going to end with us. Do you?" Back then, I dodged your question, which means now I have to tell you the truth.

For the last nineteen years, it's felt like the end. Greedy, mean, deceitful, bottom-feeding slugs who don't believe in science or truth have taken over the country at the exact moment the earth has reached the point of no return. We made it through the winter, but the water is rising and where will we go? There's no escape from the future, kid. So yes, it's the end, it's where we've been headed for decades since we denied the hard truth of what was happening all around us. Back then, what we did would have made a difference, but now we're living in a global hospice, subsisting on kale and whiskey and nostalgia as we await the end. You've lived your entire life in the afterglow of a great civilization. We'll totter through the lonely dwindling *sapien* years, outrunning floods and fires, until the last of us finally seizes up and collapses to the ground, spirit broken, and succumbs to the blight we've birthed and fed and nurtured until it was strong enough to kill us. Whoever comes after us will be from another planet or another species or created by us in Silicon Valley with our astonishing brilliance, which wasn't quite brilliant enough to save us.

That's what I thought. But lately, with buds blooming and birds chirping and bears and alcoholics emerging from hibernation and blinking in the sunshine and you working so hard, talking to everyone in the family trying to make sense of it all, I'm not so sure. You wanted to know if I was happy. I stopped worrying about happiness a long time ago, but now I wake up every morning next to the woman I love, surrounded by my children and my extended family, who perplex me and enrage me and make me laugh hysterically, and shed a tear every single day of my life, and I'm glad we're all still here. Or most of us—even the ones who aren't here really are.

Am I happy? I don't know, but telling my story has made me fear I'm afflicted with a terminal case of hope for which there is no cure. And it's all your fault, Louise. You listened to me, staring with those big, brown eyes that won't accept the end. How could I not believe we'll find the strength to keep crawling forward and mutate into some kind of creature that can survive the storm? But enough about me. Which is a sentence I'm saying for the very first time. Did you get everything you need to tell our story? Because there's work to be done. There's always work to be done. We need to go out and cultivate our garden.

And maybe someday, if we just keep doing what we do, day after day, we'll be able to go back home. It's what I dream about every night.

LOUISE

That's it. I did it. I wanted to start with Paul and end with Paul because he was kind of my inspiration. And the most encouraging. And he talked the most.

After I finished, he hugged me and got all choked up, and that was about the best way my project could have ended.

GARRET

Louise, I know you're all done, nice going, but there's something I need to tell you so you understand what happened between me and Paul. Do you have time for this? I don't know what you've picked up from the others, but our mother would go off the rails sometimes. The General couldn't handle it. He'd usually just shut down. Go into his office and close the door. So, it would be just me and Paul and our mother. Times like that she scared the hell out of us because we didn't know what she'd do one minute to the next. She'd be screaming about how we'd wrecked her life and then she'd be baking a birthday cake, even though it was nobody's birthday. Hold on, that's not accurate. She never said *we* wrecked her life. *I* wrecked her life. She always favored Paul.

This one day in the summer, she flipped out bad. She was screaming at the General. He got this tight look on his face and went off to his club. Our mother was crying about how her life had turned out. We were little, I was maybe five, which means Paul was three. What the hell do you do when you're that age and your mother is crying?

She suddenly asks Paul if he wants to go into Pinecroft and get ice cream. That was the big treat for us. It didn't happen very often. Paul was this open-hearted little kid, bad eyesight, goofy, trusted everyone, loved his mommy. Of course, she'd ask him to go. I asked if I could go too, and she said, "No, Garret, this trip is just for me and Paul." If I'd been the kind of kid who cried, that's what I would have done. But I never gave it up to her or anyone else. It was sort of a family joke how I never cried. Some joke, huh? So off they went, and I'm all alone.

I was going to watch TV until someone came home. I made myself a big bowl of cereal to make up for the ice cream Paul was getting. And then—I don't know how—I knew. I just knew.

I went out to the garage and they hadn't left. The car was running and the garage door was closed. I went over to Paul's side of the car and opened the door and he wasn't moving. I pulled him out and opened the garage door and dragged him outside. Then I got our mother out, which was a big job, and turned off the car. I called the General at his club and then I called 9-1-1. The ambulance came.

Our mother had had enough of this life. She was going to leave and take her favorite son with her. She never had much use for me. I guess I wasn't cuddly like Paul. I wasn't the kind of kid you wanted to pick up. I was always more like my father.

Nobody ever talked about it. Ever. Except that day, after our mother was in the hospital, my father said, "Good job, Garret. You knew just what to do." Like rescuing a suicidal parent and saving your little brother's life is something every five-year-old should know. Paul doesn't even remember. My job was protecting him. His job was getting protected. That's the way it's always been with us. Seems like me and Paul never got past what happened to us when we were little kids.

The truth is, everybody always loved Paul. He was the life of the party. I was the one outside, standing guard. Trying to keep everyone safe. And let's face it, nobody gives a damn about that guy. Until the bad thing happens.

I never had what Paul has. This was the best I could do.

afterword

A series of health problems made it seem like Paul's last days would be at Howell House. Besides his gunshot wound, he suffered from diabetes, a lower respiratory infection, chronic obstructive pulmonary disease, lung cancer, tuberculosis, cirrhosis, a major stroke, a heart attack, and a paper cut that became infected. Paul's health challenges exceeded even the hypochondriacal complaints of the General who, at a sprightly 106 years old, bemoans the fact that he doesn't have the energy he had at 103.

What kept Paul alive was a primal need to outlive the Great Leader, who finally took decisive action to make America great and died quietly at home with a prostitute and a cheeseburger by his side. Our entire family gathered to watch his funeral, which was a tribute to all he stood for—with random violence, mass arrests, gunfire, and a ten-thousand-dollar admission fee, ensuring that the common folks he'd exploited for so long would be turned away.

But the funeral cortege was for everyone. The streets of Washington were lined with wary citizens confirming that, ding dong, the sociopathic strongman's dead. They had to see him in the flesh to make sure this wasn't his ten millionth lie. They watched the presidential float roll by, festooned with flags and guns and golf clubs and porn stars and the Great Leader himself, propped up on a gold throne in all his sad glory, wearing only an adult diaper and a lurid grin, his tiny hands rigidly fixed in the "thumbs up" pose he favored for all photo ops, whether election victories or national tragedies or Tuesdays. Everything was a win for the Great Leader, even his long-awaited passing.

…at night, Paul and Ruth announced that with the Great
……r safely dead, they would return to the United States. We
had a going-away party featuring what the family did so well:
cocktails and music and sentimental toasts and stories we'd heard
hundreds of times but had to be told again.

Once back in town, my aunt and uncle discovered that 117
Poplar had been broken up into apartments for student housing.
Ruth enrolled in classes so she and Paul could move into their
old house as students. They've tried to get the rest of the family
to come back, but after all those years it didn't seem like home
to most of us. It's been a slow, painful transition from the harsh
years of the Great Leader. As much as Mickey tried to reboot the
country, we're still stuck in the tragic mess our long-time president left behind.

And, of course, the Red Hats never went away. I asked Paul
how they can cling to their hateful ideology when it's been so
discredited. Paul said they don't care how history judges them
because they think it all ends with them. And if there *is* history, no
one will read it. *They* never did.

When the time came for me to go to college, I upheld family
tradition and went to the U, and my mother wasn't far behind.
Ever since I can remember, she's talked about how much she re-
gretted missing college. I finally told her—nicely—to shut up and
go. I even arranged my schedule so we'd have a class together.
I was assigned the dorm where Kate once lived, and my mom
thought it would be fun to be roommates. I didn't.

The rest of the family is still in Canada. Mickey is a fugitive
and can't return. He and Daniel are married and proudly leading
the community that prides itself on having no leaders. They're so
happy, it gets annoying sometimes.

Kate and Neil broke the law by leaving their government-mandated rehab program and don't trust what would happen to them if they went back. Kate recorded *Songs for Isaac*, which got her airplay and a tour. But she battled stage fright and knew where the stress could take her, so now she's strictly a songwriter who can occasionally be persuaded to play for the family. She's entering year ten of planning to be a vegan.

Nandita still isn't able to legally return to the States, and Terence isn't about to go anywhere without her. They started a catering company, tapping into a circle of high-end folks in town with an extreme party life.

Garret and Pam Rayner eventually married. For all the difficulties they've had, Garret wouldn't consider leaving Terence, and even started working for him. He has a bit of an edge as a bartender, making you feel special because he sure as hell isn't making drinks for just anyone.

David and Sophie have spent years talking about relocating, but they are indispensable to the community. And they're living their dream. It just doesn't happen to be in New York City, since the city doesn't quite exist anymore. Their two children mark the beginning of the next generation on the beach.

After years of separation caused by the draconian immigration policies of the United States, Dr. Morales and Anjelica have no intention of going back. David finally beat Dr. Morales in chess after 932 consecutive losses over fourteen years. Then he couldn't stop winning. They claim to be playing "just for fun," but both keep secret records of total wins and losses going back to their earliest games at 117 Poplar.

The hardest part of my life—other than the ongoing struggle to repurpose the country for the people—is that the family is apart. It blew up along with the country in 2016, but we found each other in Ontario and then split up again. I love being near my mom and Paul and Ruth, but I miss the beach community where I came of age and where we worked so hard to keep hope alive.

Our political efforts have become family lore, more dramatic and historically significant with each passing year. I don't buy it. Paul and Mickey and all of us may have had an influence, but I think what started to change was the dawning realization that the only way to heal ourselves and our country is to take care of each other.

The family thought they were living at the edge of history, when human life itself was in the balance. And they weren't wrong. But from where I'm sitting on a clammy winter afternoon looking out through the smog at gray empty streets, theirs was an innocent time.

They could still go outside whenever they wanted and breathe the air and drink the water and live in the real world instead of the virtual world. Back then, they could still deny that the worst would come to pass.

Hadley Louise Weeks
117 Poplar Avenue
December 12, 2051

THE END

aknowledgments

I'd like to thank Tom Reale and everyone at Brown Books Publishing Group, including its indomitable founder, Milli Brown. Their professionalism and collaborative nature made the creation of this book a joy.

A special thanks to Andy Wolfendon, an extraordinarily gifted editor whose insights into *It Happened Here* were inspired and inspiring.

I am also indebted to a wildly talented group of fellow writers who whipped out their machetes, donned their pith helmets, and fought their way through the tangled earlier drafts of *It Happened Here*. They include Jay Tarses, Russ Woody, Lewis Black, Willie Reale, Joe Cacaci, Kevin O'Rourke, Steve Deitmer, Lisa Kline, Cynthia Carle, Patricia Randell, Fred Graver, Gabriele Urbonaite, Rebecca Dresser, and Sam Dresser. The honesty of their responses was deeply hurtful and invaluable.

Thanks also to my brothers, Tom and George, and my extended family, all of whom are an endless and exuberant source of love, support, cocktails, and conflicting stories. This book would not have been possible without them.

Finally, thanks to my wife, Rebecca, and my son, Sam, with me every step of the way.

about the author

Richard Dresser is an award-winning playwright, screenwriter, and television writer. His many plays, including *Below the Belt* and *Rounding Third,* have been produced throughout New York, Europe, and leading regional theaters. He is president and a founding member of the Writers Guild Initiative, which conducts writing workshops all over the country with the mission of giving a voice to populations who are not being heard. Dresser teaches screenwriting at the graduate film school of Columbia University and lives in Hastings-on-Hudson, New York, with his wife, Rebecca.